Sin Eater

Sin Eater

Amanda Denham

Sin Eater
Copyright © 2020 by Amanda Denham

Content Editor: Kira Kitchen
Copy Editor: Andie Smiley
Editor-in-Chief: Kristi King-Morgan
Formatting: Bailey Kearney
Cover Artist: Amanda Denham
Assistant Editor: Maddy Drake

This is a work of fiction. Names, characters, businesses, places, events and incidents are either the products of the author's imagination or used in a fictitious manner. Any resemblance to actual persons, living or dead, or actual events is purely coincidental.

Printed in the United States of America

ISBN- 978-1-947381-42-1

www.dreamingbigpublications.com

I dedicate this book to my family, friends, and my boyfriend Shan for always being there and believing in me. This is also dedicated to all the dreamers, all the writers and artists, all the creative minds. Your story is worth reading!

Before

The first time I knew something was wrong with me was when I was eighteen. All I was trying to do was help, but instead, I did the worst thing I could have possibly done. What's bad is that I didn't even mean to. I had no control over it. My best friend was upset, and it made me sad, too. I wanted her to feel better. I wanted her to forget.

I did succeed, in a way.

* * * * *

I made her forget the one that hurt her.

* * * * *

But in the process, she forgot her family, her school, her friends…

* * * * *

I even made her forget me

Now - Purpose

I step outside my motel and look up to admire the first star of the night, shining through a haze of grey clouds. A faint line of gold sits on the horizon as the rest of the daylight bleeds away. Nighttime gives me more shadows, more places to blend myself in as I make my way around the town. It isn't a big place by any means, but I'd rather be safe than sorry. Getting caught on the street means questions, and questions lead to prying and pushing. I would feel like I do in the sun: exposed and naked. Nowhere to hide.

I scan the streets carefully, and I take every shortcut that I can think of. I cut across a couple of people's backyards, and thankfully nobody sees me. The slight drizzle is hanging in the air like a cold curtain. There really isn't a way to shield myself since I didn't bring an umbrella. I don't even have a jacket.

Nobody would be out on a night like this…except for me. I have a job to take care of. Everyone has a job, a purpose, a calling. Mine just so happens to be a little different. Mine has to be done in secret. That is why I must stay hidden.

I used to live here in Palmsville two years ago, so I find the client's address easily. I came to this exact place for Tammy Gardner's birthday party years ago. My childhood home is only a street over, and I remember my mother walking me to her house since I was only eight at the time. My client is Tammy's father, David Gardner. He has left a key underneath his back door's floor mat, as promised. I slip into the house quickly, taking one last look around to make sure that I was not followed. The house is dark inside, but I can see a dim light coming from a room down the hall. This was also planned—one room, one light, one client, and one person on my side to supervise.

I step into the room without making a sound, but both of its inhabitants raise their heads simultaneously as I enter. Mr. Gardner stares at me with squinted eyes and his mouth open.

"You're the Sin Eater?" Mr. Gardner chokes out. He looks like he regrets the words as soon as they're out of his mouth. "You're…different than I expected you to be," he finishes, looking down at his hands.

"Nothing is ever what you expect," my boss, Jak, says.

Jak is my only partner for these cases, but he uses different disguises for every job. Since there are only two of us running this operation, it's dangerous to let people know our very low number. I am an incredibly valuable person because of my gift, Jak says, so I have to be as protected as possible. However, instead of hiring other people, he has created an illusion for our clients by looking as different as possible every time he is seen. This time, he has chosen a wig with shoulder-length, jet black hair and seems to have used make-up on his skin to cover up his freckles. His green eyes are now a vibrant purple thanks to contacts, and he's wearing a black suit, shoes, and tie.

Mr. Gardner swallows hard and nods. I'm grateful that I'm in a full disguise myself, since I'm sure he would instantly recognize me as little Jayde Holloway, the girl who dropped an entire popsicle on his floor and then slipped and fell on it.

"What do you want me to do for you?" I ask, trying to keep my voice steady. I already know what he wants. His wife died, and he wants to forget the circumstances surrounding her death. When Jak showed me his paperwork earlier today as he was making preparations, my stomach turned at the thought of Mrs. Gardner being gone. Tammy and I barely spoke after elementary school and made other friends, but it hurts to know this family that welcomed me into their home is suffering. Jak only tells me the basics, so usually whatever the client divulges to me is a surprise. But this is how things have to be. I have to hear them explain all the details myself.

"My wife…" Mr. Gardner begins. He shakes his head and sits up straighter in his chair. "My wife passed away a month ago. She was shot by a man who broke into our house."

"Go on," Jak says, crossing his arms.

Mr. Gardner's eyes widen. I can tell that he doesn't want me to know what exactly happened. The look on his face makes me want to turn and run away, to never look back. Honestly, I feel that way about every job that Jak makes me do, but I have to do this for Jenny, my best friend, even if she doesn't remember me.

"I…could have saved her, but I wasn't here."

My blood runs cold.

"And where were you?" By the way he is acting, I already know the answer.

"…With another woman. In a hotel. A woman from my office." He begins to cry then, huge sobs of pain. "Please," he chokes out as he cradles his face in his hands. "Please, let me forget! I can't sleep. I can't eat. I can't go back to work. It's all my fault, and I can't live with it! I can't!"

Jak hands me an ink pen and a notebook. I tear a page out of the notebook, and then I slide the paper and pen onto a small table standing next to Mr. Gardner's chair.

"Write out everything you want to forget. Be very careful. You will forget, but you have to be very specific. I can't even guarantee that you won't lose more of your memory than you want."

Mr. Gardner wipes his nose on his shirt sleeve. "I don't care. Anything is better than this."

He begins to hastily scribble his story onto the paper. I see a woman's name, *Caroline*. He rereads it just once and delicately hands it back to me.

"He requested fire," Jak chimes in suddenly, and it makes me jump. The room is so quiet except for the man's crying that his voice sounds almost too loud.

Jak hands me a match. I read the note once, then again and again. Jak narrows his eyes at me, so I breathe in deeply and finally light the match. I always get nervous, though I should be used to this by now. I hold the match closely to the paper until it begins to turn a smoky brown. Mr. Gardner closes his eyes and bows his head. As the fire burns, I close my eyes as well and concentrate on Mr. Gardner's words as much as I can:

Burglar. Mistress. Murder. Guilt. Regret.

Caroline.

The paper quickly turns to ash, and I open my eyes just as it's about to burn my fingers. Mr. Gardner's eyes are now glazed over, much more peaceful than they were mere seconds ago. Jak picks up his briefcase and disappears down the hall. That is his sign that the job is done.

The client has forgotten.

I take what is most precious to people: their memory. It's so simple. Give me your woes, and I can make you forget them. I could make you forget everything, if I really wanted to. I cure wounded people and give them a second chance.

However, their second chance means parts of their lives are completely missing, gone forever. They will never know that self again, nor will they remember those who were lost. They can continue on with their life in ignorant bliss, but I will always know. I will carry it for them within my own memory. Their troubles will stay with me for the rest of my life.

Yes, I will erase, I will cover, I will bury.

But I will always remember. I save and I hurt, all at once.

I exit the client's house quickly. I can't help but wonder why it always has to be fire. I could tear the paper up, I could cut it with scissors, I could do anything to destroy it. But no, it has to be fire. I guess people like the finality of it, how it all turns to ashes. I wonder if their memories turn to ashes as well.

Jak already left without a word; we made plans earlier to meet behind my motel after this appointment to discuss our schedule for the week. He has no interest in sticking around to see how much the person remembers. It's dangerous to stay any longer than necessary. Once the client is aware of your presence, they may ask questions. They want to know who you are and why you're there. It's interesting, actually, because this version of themselves might even be upset with the fact that their memories were just erased. I'm always in awe of how many selves we can have. Maybe the "past" you wanted the pain to go away because it was too much to bear, but this "other" you would want to know, would want to experience it. However, we're not supposed to make them regret their decision, so we leave as fast as possible.

We take separate paths back to my motel. Jak usually drives us to our jobs in a rental car, but I asked to walk tonight. Jak protested at first, but he miraculously caved when I told him that I wanted to see my old house. We don't talk much about the past, but he must know how much I miss this town and my parents since they moved away.

Jak sighed, frustrated with my begging.

"If you don't meet me at the motel by 9:30PM, I'll come looking for you."

I guess he thinks this is some big plan to ditch him. There's no way I would do that: he knows too many of my secrets, and we both need the money. I'd prefer if my parents continue to believe that I'm still working at the art supply store, still seeing my friends, and overall living a normal life. They don't need to know what I am and what I've done, and Jak would run straight to them and spill it all if I back out.

I stand at the end of my old street, Cedarbrook Road, and stare at my childhood home three houses down. The lights are on, so the current owners must be inside. I wonder if they'll teach their kids to ride their bikes on this street like my parents did, or if they'll wait with them where I am now to board the school bus. A garage door on the house next to mine comes to life, and a car begins to back out of the driveway. I scramble to hide myself behind a tree in the yard next to me before it passes by. My phone chimes with the first alarm I set myself so that I wouldn't linger too long. There's just enough time to get to the motel by 9:30PM if I don't make any more stops.

To save time, I cut through an alley behind a cluster of buildings once I get out of the residential area. There are two restaurants, a small bookstore called the Book Nook, three clothing stores, and the Brew House. I used to love coming to this area. One of the restaurants, Anita's Kitchen, is still my favorite, even though I've traveled and tried all kinds of places. It serves a mix of Latin and American food, and sometimes on the weekends there would be live music on a tiny stage in the back corner. Back in high school, our get-togethers would usually begin at Anita's Kitchen, move on to browse for something to read at the bookstore, and then we'd end up at the Brew House for coffee. I didn't really like coffee, but I would sip on Jenny's.

As soon as I think of her name, I push the memory away. I can't think of Jenny King, my oldest friend, my best friend. She certainly isn't thinking of me. I accidentally made sure of that when I burned her memories away almost two years ago.

Fire…as soon as I lit the match at Mr. Gardner's house, I saw her face. I always see Jenny's face when the client requests fire. A part of me deep inside starts screaming, and I have to swallow hard and push it down.

I'm walking faster now, thinking that maybe if I push my body, my mind will stop thinking as hard. Before I can compose myself, I crash into some garbage cans sitting outside one of the building's doors, and they fall down on the ground along with me. I let out a pained noise as I land on one of my knees. Just when I think it can't get any worse, the back door of the building opens hastily, and a man pops out with a curious look on his face. I rush to stand, despite the stinging in my knee. The man's curious face turns into one of worry.

"Hey, are you okay?" he asks.

"I'm fine."

"You don't look fine," he remarks. "Did you just come from a party or something?"

"That's none of your business." I sound extremely rude, even to myself. To be fair, I do look strange in my disguises. Over time, I have collected a substantial amount of random accessories from thrift stores and clothing shops. Nothing ever really matches, but that's the whole point. I want to look completely outlandish, absolutely different from my normal self.

The man runs his fingers through his hair. "I'm sorry. You're right. I was just wondering. You do need to wash that off though," he says with a nod towards my knee. "Looks like a really bad scrape. I think we might have a first-aid kit somewhere around here."

"I told you that I'm fine." I just want to get out of here.

He keeps talking anyway. "Maybe you should take those goggles off when you're walking around at night. No wonder you got hurt."

"Thanks for the lecture."

"Thanks for the attitude," he says.

I glare at him, but then I realize he can't even tell through the goggles. I don't know how it happens, but I begin to laugh about the absurdity of it all. We're two complete strangers arguing in an alley with trash cans all around us, and I just tried to glare at him through goggles. I always think of the disguising function of the outfits, but I'd never thought of how ridiculous I must look in real life, outside of my jobs. My sudden laughter surprises the man, and he takes a couple of steps backward toward the door.

"I'm sorry," I choke through my giggles, "I just...realized how stupid I must look."

"No, no, it's fine," he says, relaxing a little. "You don't look stupid. Just...different. Like you're in costume. That's why I asked if you were at a party or something."

I open my mouth to answer, but I can't decide what to say. For some reason, I don't want to lie to him, but I can't exactly tell him the truth. When he sees that I'm hesitant, he holds up his hand to silence me.

"Nope, what you said was right. It's none of my business, even though you scared me half to death. Not to mention, you're destroying my trash cans!" He picks up one of the cans near him and begins to pet it, like it's a dog. "But no worries, they're strong little things, always willing to hold my trash. They're good friends."

"Are you trying to guilt trip me? Because it's not working. If anything, I could sue you and use all the money I get to buy a new knee."

"Ha! You can try. I'm a poor waiter who lives on tips. The best thing you'll get out of me is this fancy apron," he says, gesturing to his outfit.

My phone buzzes in my pocket with a text message, and I realize that I need to go. Why am I standing around talking to this guy? I have to meet Jak. That's probably him, wondering where I am. What if he asks? What would I say? "Oh, you know, just chatting with this waiter guy." That wouldn't go over well.

"Sorry for all the trash cans. I took them out here to spray them down a little, a couple of them got really gross tod-"

"I have to go!" I interrupt, a little too loudly.

"Well, okay. If you say so," he says. "Be safe going home."

I nod and try to turn around and walk as casually as possible. After I get a few feet away, I hear his footsteps catch up with me.

"Hey! Wait. I'm sorry. I don't mean to bother you again," he apologizes.

I slowly turn back towards him. More light is shining from the street here, and I see that he actually looks pretty young, probably in his early twenties.

"I know this might sound weird, but hear me out. You're wandering around in back alleys in the middle of the night. It makes me worry. Now don't get me wrong, you look like you can handle yourself. But if you get in trouble…I'm usually in that restaurant. Knock on that door, okay? Whenever." He pats me on the shoulder and adds, "Oh, and ask for me. Aiden."

Before I can respond, he takes a step back and turns to go. I do the same. I keep my head ducked down, and I don't allow myself to look back. This man saw me. Really saw me. Like I was just a person…nothing more, nothing less. He made me laugh. I don't think I've laughed in months. The worst part is that I enjoyed it. Desire is dangerous. I shouldn't desire anything.

But I do.

I desire for someone to look at me like he did, to not see me as a way out. For someone to actually offer *me* help for once.

When I get to the motel, I tell Jak that I tripped over some garbage cans and scraped my knee. I tell him that since it hurt, I sat in the alley for a few minutes to get the stinging to go away. He rolls his eyes at me, but he believes the story. Not that he has any reason to doubt me. I do exactly what he wants, and I even have the knee injury to prove it.

I don't feel bad about lying, since all I left out was the guy. No, not "the guy." Aiden. Ask for Aiden. It sounds almost musical to me. I shake my head of the thought.

This isn't supposed to happen.

I'm supposed to be a vision, an anonymous, a person that nobody will ever remember.

Now - Hidden

Hidden. That is me at all times nowadays. The next day after my little garbage can fiasco, I wake up determined to get some time outside in the sun. I skulk around way too much in the dark. Since I used to live around here, I decide to enjoy the things that I used to. A visit to Anita's Kitchen? Maybe I'll even buy a book, then go next door to grab some kind of sugary, caffeinated monstrosity from the Brew House. Today is the first off day in a series of off days until Sunday. I may as well make the most of it. Maybe facing some of the anxiety of being here and the never-ending parade of memories that keep popping up will help. My unfailing optimism...well, I'm good at faking optimism, anyway.

I roll out of bed with true Olympic gymnast-style grace. My feet hit the floor with a satisfying thump. Ten out of ten for Jayde, from Jayde. The cheap motel room that Jak chose for me isn't so bad. It isn't what you'd call fancy, but it has a warm, homey feel to it. The sun is peeking in through the floral curtains that match the floral bed sheets. In fact, this whole room is obsessed with flowers. Flowers in vases, a couple of flower paintings hanging on the wall, even the doorknobs are shaped like flowers. I glance over at the (thankfully) not flowery alarm clock, and its angry red numbers read that it's 11:27AM.

I'm usually an earlier riser, but anxiety kept me up last night, thinking about how I'd stood around talking to that guy in the alley. Why did I even talk to him? Why didn't I just walk away? But then I'd breathe and remind myself that I had on a very elaborate disguise: bright blonde wig, goggles, red lipstick, huge boots, poofy skirt, random scarf, the works. There was no way he'd be able to recognize me anywhere looking like my normal self. But then my brain would launch into its what if's, and then I'd remind myself to be logical again, lather, rinse, repeat. Same cycle over and over until I exhausted myself.

I pull on a black tank top and a pair of jeans that honestly should have fallen apart a long time ago. They have huge holes in the knees and frays everywhere. I like that they're a little ragged. They have seen life, some fun times. I almost put another wig on but decide against it due to how hot it is outside. Looking like myself for once would be nice, but I'm scared of being recognized. To be safe, I go heavy with my makeup and wear huge, blue sunglasses that cover half of my face when I leave my room.

The motel receptionist barely acknowledges me as I walk past her. One good thing about many motels: their employees pay no attention at all. Their main concerns fall into the categories of if you need more towels and crossing their fingers that you aren't trashing the place. Otherwise, you barely get eye contact. Who even cares that some random chick from room 301 is heading out? Not them, that's who. I could probably walk by in a fluffy yellow duck costume while trying to hula-hoop and the receptionist would just keep flipping through her magazine, like "Ho-hum, wonder what celebrity is pregnant or divorced today." I step outside to a day so bright that my eyes water a little. Thank God I decided to wear my sunglasses.

I head off in the direction of the very same restaurants that I was wandering around last night. I tried to convince myself not to, but I'd really like to eat at Anita's Kitchen again, and, as I comforted myself over and over, I'm unrecognizable. Even in broad daylight, I'm hidden. The walk is a little under a mile, but because of the sun, I'm already regretting the black tank top. Coupled with my long, black hair, I can feel the heat bearing down on me. I mentally pat myself on the back for my stupidity: Good job, me. You're a genius. As sweat begins to form on my forehead, I see the end of my journey. There are some empty tables in the shade in front of Anita's Kitchen, just like I knew there would be. I heave a huge sigh as I plop myself down in the first chair that I happen upon. Even though I lived here for practically my whole life, I still can't get used to southern heat in the middle of August.

As I'm fanning myself dramatically, I close my eyes and lean back.

"Yeah, it's a hot one today," a voice says nearby.

My eyes shoot open as I jump from surprise. And who do I open my eyes and see, which brings a whole new heart attack?

Aiden. The waiter guy that I spoke to the night before. Aiden starts laughing.

"You're a jumpy thing, ain'tcha?" he says, exaggerating a southern drawl.

"No!…Yeah. You scared me," I babble, trying to regain my composure. He's wearing the waiter's uniform that he was in the night before. I could have sworn he worked at the restaurant beside this one, but maybe I didn't remember correctly. It was dark, and their back door might be farther away, closer to the next building.

"Sorry. Didn't mean to. Menu? Maybe I can recommend some melty ice cream before you yourself melt into a puddle?"

He talks so quickly and my head is still reeling, so it takes me a moment to grab the menu out of his hand.

"Water," I choke out. Words are hard. "Water would be nice."

"Excellent choice," he says. "I'll bring that out while you dec—"

Before he can finish his sentence, another voice interrupts, "Um, excuse me!"

He and I both turn to see a girl stomping towards us. As she comes closer, I notice that she is roughly a foot shorter than he is but somehow seems way more intimidating.

"Are you taking my tables again?" she asks him accusingly.

His eyes shift from me to her, and then back again. "Now, would I ever do such a thing?" His voice implied that yes, he had, and many times over. I'm a little relieved—maybe he really isn't coming over here because he recognized me from last night.

The girl sighs then directs her attention to me. "I'm sorry, ma'am. Please ignore this little spat. You see, this is my section, and I'd be happy to serve you, but this…person…seems to enjoy stealing my tables. But I'm here now. What can I get you?"

"Um, excuse me, Amber," Aiden says, "but I've already taken her order."

"No, you haven't," I chime in.

Aiden swivels around to look at me with hurt eyes. "Wha…? How could you betray me?"

Amber laughs and pats my shoulder. "You, I like you. You're good people. But seriously, I'm sorry for all this."

"No need to apologize," I said, smiling genuinely for the first time in…I don't even know how long. "I come here for professionalism above all else."

They both laugh then. It feels good to make people laugh again. High school was like a stage to me, and Jenny was always a willing audience. I try to feel this familiar happiness for a few seconds without letting the sad sneak in and sting, as it usually does.

"Okay, okay," Amber says, waving her hands. "Back to work. I can get you some water, and then I'll come back to take your order in a moment."

As she turns to leave, she grabs Aiden by the arm and drags him away from the table. Aiden playfully fights her the whole way. I chuckle and lean back in my chair, stretching my legs out into the empty walkway. Is this what normal feels like? It has been way too long. I'd met a few people on my travels with Jak, but nothing ever blossomed. My evasiveness always seemed to get in the way.

Nobody wants a closed book like me.

Amber returns a few minutes later and sets a glass of water on the table.

"So," she says, "ready to order?"

My eyes widen. I'd completely forgotten to look at the menu since I let myself get lost in thought.

"I haven't even looked," I admit.

She sighs. "Was Aiden over here bugging you? Is that why? I'm sorry, he's such a—"

"No, no!" I exclaim. "It's not his fault. I'm just spacey today."

"Sorry. He's such a big personality to deal with sometimes."

"It's fine," I smile. "You two are a cute couple." Her lips twitch then, and a disgusted look immediately replaces her apologetic one.

"A-Aiden? God, no! He's my brother!" Her voice has reached a higher pitch, and it makes a man passing by jump. A couple of tables away, a group of teenage girls stare and giggle at us.

"Did I just hear my name shrieked? That's always cause for alarm…" Aiden says cautiously, walking over to us.

"She thought we were a couple," Amber responds. Then, to me: "No, sorry. It's just, you know…awkward."

"You couldn't handle me anyway, Amby," Aiden says, wiggling his eyebrows.

"Quit! That's gross!"

"Me? Gross? That's not what your mom said last night…"

"We have the *same* mother, you idiot!"

My eyes are watering from laughing so hard. As I try to take some deep breaths, I analyze the siblings. They don't look much alike to me. Otherwise, I wouldn't have said the couple thing. Aiden has messy, slightly curly hair, and it has a reddish tint to it. Amber's hair is dyed a crazy electric blue and cut short, with one side longer than the other. However, I guess they do have a similar build. Lean but not scrawny, though Aiden is much taller. Now that I'm finally paying attention, though, I do see one thing: they both have green eyes, like emeralds.

"You'll have to excuse my sister, uh…what's your name?" Aiden asks.

"Jackie," I say automatically. Jak and I chose our names long ago. They're purposely similar and easy to remember. I haven't given my real name in two years now. Even Jak calls me Jackie when we aren't in front of other people, the rare times he addresses me by name.

After Amber calms down, we all laugh off the awkward moment, and I order a chicken Caesar salad. The siblings go back to work, but Aiden still stops by my table a couple of times to chat. Amber watches him like a hawk, probably to make sure he isn't stealing her tables again. They seem like good people, fun and easy to talk to. I feel more comfortable around them than I have around anyone in months. Their dynamic reminds me a bit of Jenny's and mine in high school. I was loud and bold like Aiden, while Jenny was sensible and accepting, like Amber.

"Where are you from, Jackie?" Amber asks, setting my salad down in front of me. "We have tons of regulars, so it's rare to see a new face."

It's funny, since I was thinking the exact same thing about them. I'd never seen Amber and Aiden around town when I lived here.

"My dad's a truck driver," I say, pretending to be intensely interested in wrestling my silverware out of a napkin to avoid looking into her eyes, "so we travel a lot. I'm originally from Florida." I've rehearsed and used that lie so many times, it feels strangely comfortable and familiar, like wearing an old, favorite jacket.

"We just moved here a few months ago from Mississippi," Aiden chimes in, settling down in a chair beside me. "We're a little new ourselves."

"Uh, Aiden…?" Amber begins.

"Relax, I'm on break right now," Aiden says, cutting her off. "But yeah, we don't live too far from here. Traveling must be rough."

"Um, yeah. Hard to keep up or see anything, you know?" I shrug.

"Really? I mean, there's not much around here to see, but Aiden and I have found a couple of cool spots, if you want some tour guides," Amber offers.

"Yeah! Amber can take you to all the boring stuff, and then I'll take you to the actual fun stuff."

Amber elbows him in the shoulder. "That museum was not boring. You just have no class."

Before I can stop myself, I hear the words come out of my mouth: "I'd love that." They both smile, and I truly see the resemblance at last. Their smiles are the same.

"Great!" Amber says. "How long are you in town?"

"I'm pretty sure it will be at least until Sunday." Today was Wednesday, and Sunday was my next job, so Jak and I shouldn't be leaving until Monday.

"How about tomorrow, then? I'm off work, and Amber always works early on Thursdays, so she gets off at two."

"I can do that." Seriously, why is my mouth blurting these things out?

"Cool. We could all just meet here at two. I'll bring better clothes than my dumb ol' work outfit to change into," Amber says.

"What's your phone number?" Aiden asks, taking his phone out of his pants pocket. "I'll text you if anything changes."

I cough and drink my water to buy myself some time. This is happening too fast for my brain to comprehend. I can't give them my number.

"You told her?" I hear Jak's voice screaming in my head. Suddenly I'm back in the car with him that day, almost a year ago now. He found out that I told my friend Cadie about our business. I knew I could trust her, but he wouldn't listen. Due to me giving away our secret, he took my phone and gave me a new one. I was not to talk to anyone other than my parents, and he insisted on performing phone checks.

I close my eyes for a moment, willing the memory away. As I do, an idea dawns on me.

"Actually, my phone went to Phone Heaven a few days ago. I dropped and broke it. But you could email me." Jak surely wouldn't think to check my email. He doesn't know any of my emails nor any of the passwords, and I'll use my oldest one. Plus, it won't make any notification noises since I don't have any accounts synced to my phone. Aiden hands me his phone, and I type my email address into it.

14

I hope they don't notice that I am trying very hard to control my breathing.

As I hand the phone back, Aiden suddenly exclaims "Whoa! What happened to your knee?"

Amber looks down as well. "Ouch! That looks like it hurts!"

Confused, I glance down, and my heartbeat speeds up. My knee, all scraped and bruised from last night, showing clear as day through the huge hole in my jeans. The one I hurt last night, in front of Aiden. I fold my legs back under the table, though it's useless now that they've seen the injury.

Think, think, think.

"Um..."

Please don't connect the dots, Aiden.

"I fall a lot," I say, trying to laugh it off. "That's how I broke my phone. Tripped over my purse, I went down, and then the phone broke in the fall."

Aiden, please don't say anything...please.

Aiden opens his mouth, but he's interrupted by Amber joking. "A busted phone, a busted knee...we aren't in mortal danger hanging out with you, are we?"

"I'll try to control my clumsiness for the greater good," I say. Aiden looks at me for a moment, and I hold my breath. He's going to out me. He's going to-

"Break's done!" he announces instead, surprising me. "I'll send you Amber's and my email addresses. Need a to-go box?"

"Again, no, this is my table! And you aren't even clocked back in yet!" Amber scolds, following him inside.

A couple of minutes later, she brings me the bill and a box for my food. I pay in cash and try to tip generously. It's hard not to fumble or look nervous, especially when I could swear that Aiden is glancing over at me while he waits on his other tables outside.

As I step away from my chair, Aiden cheerfully calls out "See you tomorrow!"

I wave and fake my best smile. Does he really not know, or is he torturing me? My feet want to run, but I force them to carry on as casually as possible. Once inside the Book Nook across the street, I lock myself in the bathroom and finally freak out. How can one person screw themselves over so many times in a mere hour? Here's my greatest hits for today: I gave strangers a way to contact me, I agreed to see them tomorrow, OH, and also one of them happens to be a guy I

ran into after a meeting for my secret job, and he may recognize me now because I was too stupid to wear my not-ratty jeans.

Technically, I could cancel or just not show up. I've gotten enough practice…I could easily make up a lie or an excuse, but a thought suddenly bubbles up.

It forms slowly and floats to the front of my brain and pops: no, it says. I want this. I want to want things again.

Then: please.

Some inner desire is begging, pleading, a heartbeat drumming through me.

Please, please, please.

And I know that I can't cancel. I may not have much of a life, but it's still mine. Honestly, I have no idea what Jak would do if he caught me again, but I care less and less as the seconds tick on.

That is why desires are so dangerous. Wants tune out all reason, all worries. You concentrate only on that desire, that itch in your skin that tells you to go after it.

It consumes.

You develop tunnel vision.

All you see is what you want, and every step closer just makes you want it more.

You throw consequences out the window.

You become reckless and selfish.

…And then you may even betray someone you love, like I did.

Then- Jenny

I was by no means popular in school. However, I did have the advantage of living in the same small, Alabama town for pretty much my whole life, so I knew the same group of kids from elementary school through high school. They all came and went in their own ways, but the one that stuck around through everything was Jennifer King. We met when we were six years old on the bus on the way to Clayton Elementary. Palmsville sat on the outskirts of Clayton, and their schools housed two other towns' students.

From elementary school and on, Jenny and Cadie, Jenny's cousin, were like extra members of my family. Some of my earliest memories are of Jenny, Cadie, and I running around my backyard playing hide and seek and desperately trying to catch fireflies in our hands on warm summer nights. Sadly, Jenny's aunt Linda decided to move back to Georgia when we were thirteen, taking Cadie with her. We kept in touch, and Cadie would visit a couple of times a year, but it left a huge hole in our little group.

There were so many sleepovers and birthday parties throughout the years that they've all started to blur together. What night did we randomly decide to prank call everyone in my cell phone? Could we clearly recall the day the three of us had a huge shaving cream fight and got it all over Jenny's living room couch and her mom yelled at us and grounded her for a month? What about the time we went swimming at the public pool by the middle school, and we were so excited because a couple of cute guys spent the whole time talking to us? Phone calls that lasted for hours talking about nothing, countless notes we passed around in class, movies we could quote line by line, singing our favorite songs and changing the lyrics to make them funnier...I could take all the memories and stack them up miles and miles high with no possible end in sight.

Over our time together, Jenny and I developed this weird way of talking without talking. I had to learn how to communicate with her without words sometimes, since Jenny was such an introvert. Cadie is a lot more like me, maybe even more outspoken. Jenny wasn't as talkative as us, so I had to learn her tells. Thankfully, she wasn't great at controlling her facial expressions, which made knowing how she felt pretty easy. Plus, you can't not learn a lot about a person when you're constantly around them for eight or nine years.

Somehow, though, she always managed to surprise me.

Early in our junior year of high school, Jenny and I were eating lunch in the cafeteria together. It was like any old normal day. I was talking about some guy in one of my classes that I thought was cute, joking that he was so oblivious that maybe I should just walk right up to him and kiss him one day. At that moment, her face changed, ever so slightly.

"...What?" I asked.

Jenny's cheeks began to redden, and she shook her head.

"C'mon. You know I'll just keep bugging you until you tell me." I said. "I'll be obnoxious and annoy the heck out of you."

"So, the usual, then?"

"Jennifer Anne King!" I exclaimed. "Tell me what's going on!"

"Why are you middle-last-naming me?" she laughed. I gave her my best pleading, puppy dog eyes, and she caved, like I knew she would.

"Well, uh...what...do you think about...Laurie Henderson?" she whispered, looking over my shoulder. I turned my head, and there Laurie was, sitting a couple of tables away from us.

"She's nice enough. I don't have any classes with her," I admitted. "She's in all the advanced classes. You know I'm too dumb for all that."

"You aren't dumb," Jenny replied immediately. "I can't speak for your common sense, but..."

"All right, all right," I said. "Why do you care what I think of Laurie?"

"I wish you knew her better. That would help a lot. "

"What? You're confusing me."

"You're good at being brave," she said, leaning closer. "I'm no good at this. You said that guy you like is oblivious. I know Laurie's oblivious. What am I supposed to do...?"

For a second, my mouth flapped open and shut. ...Oh. Oh. As an idea formed itself in my head, I practically catapulted out of my seat and headed towards Laurie. Jenny's eyes widened so much, it looked like they were going to pop out of her head. As I approached Laurie's table, I prepared to perform the best acting I could muster.

"Hey, Laurie!" I said enthusiastically, sliding into the seat next to her.

"Oh, hi...Jayde, right?" Laurie greeted me, looking surprised. We had never really talked before now.

"Listen, Jenny told me you're amazing at math, and I'm not doing so well with my Geometry class. Can you help me study, maybe? Tutor? I could try to pay you..."

"Oh, uh...sure! I mean, you don't have to pay me. I can help, though," she smiled. "Who do you have?"

"Mrs. Bonner."

"Oh...oh, yeah. She isn't so great," Laurie said, shuddering. "I never had her, but my older sister did. Worst grade she ever got, and I know it wasn't her. She always told me horror stories about that class..."

Out of the corner of my eye, I saw Jenny staring me down. I couldn't decide if she was angry or intrigued. Maybe both. Either way, my plan was going exactly like I wanted. After Laurie and I agreed on when she could tutor me, I casually walked back over to my seat, trying not to look smug.

"What did you, why did you?" Jenny began in a rush.

I interrupted her, "What? I can't go ask a smart girl for some tutoring? You know Mrs. Bonner sucks!"

"You...what...?"

"She's helping me with Geometry on Thursday, after school. And you know, if you just happen to need some tutoring, too, I don't think we'd mind if you were there."

Jenny stared at me in disbelief, and I could tell that she was trying to decide if she should hug me or strangle me to death.

"You...I'm gonna kill you!" Jenny laughed, exasperated, shaking her head. "You're something else, Jay. I can't believe you did that..."

"Anything for you," I smiled. "And I really do need tutoring. So you see, it was all purely selfish."

Jenny threw one of her chips at me, hitting me right in the nose. She didn't have to tell me out loud, but I knew what she wanted to say: "Thank you."

Over the next few weeks, our study sessions went very smoothly. What's funny is they actually did help me quite a bit. Jenny and Laurie were another level of book-smart compared to me, so having their guidance every week raised my understanding of Geometry immensely. I guess it really is all about how the material is presented.

However, I never took my eye off of my true goal: Operation Jenny-and-Laurie. Laurie was a hard one to crack, though. I couldn't tell if she had any feelings towards Jenny. This was all for naught if I couldn't at least figure that out. Several times, I found excuses to leave the study sessions early: hair appointment, Dad said he wanted a family dinner, headache. Jenny knew what I was doing, but she was good at not reacting to it. Laurie would always just smile and say "Okay. See you later!" She was really sweet. I could see why Jenny liked her.

After a few weeks of study sessions, Jenny hadn't said a word to Laurie.

"Well," I told her one day at lunch, "this is the part I can't do for you. You must fly on your own, little baby bird. Fly! Make Mama proud!"

Jenny snickered in response. "You as a mom is a frightening concept."

"Jenny. Oh, Jenny. My bestie, my number one. Please allow me to ask you the simplest of favors: shut your face. Just shut it." Jenny was laughing too hard to make a comeback, so I shoved her. The seat next to her was empty, so she made the shove look way more dramatic and fell over into the seats. We were both giggling like crazy by then. Our classmates gave us different looks around the room: some, amused; others, judgmental. One I did notice more than the rest, though, was that Laurie was also staring in our direction. When she saw me looking back, she quickly averted her eyes.

"Hmmm," I said aloud. Jenny was still flailing dramatically on the seats. When she noticed that I'd stopped laughing, she sat upright.

"What's wrong?" she asked.

"Laurie was staring at us."

"She was?"

"Yep."

"No, she wasn't."

"Would I lie?" I said, draping an arm around her shoulders and pulling her closer.

"Uh, what are you doing?" Jenny and I weren't exactly the most physically affectionate people. We were definitely more in the "I call you awful names and insult everything about you because I love you" category.

"Just look," I said, gesturing with my chin. Laurie kept looking over at us, trying to be subtle. And I knew why.

"I caught you, girl," I grinned.

"WHAT are you talking about?" Jenny demanded, releasing herself from my grip.

"I'm conducting a scientific study!" I announced.

"Of…?" she leaned in, failing to keep the interest out of her voice.

"Every time I touch you, Laurie looks over at us."

"How do you know? I didn't see anything."

"You're not looking. One more time." And again, I draped my arm around her, giving her a tight hug. Finally, Jenny turned her head in Laurie's direction at that moment.

"Whoa," she said, breathless. "You're right."

"Now will you ask her out? Please?" She laughed and genuinely hugged me. That hug was saying "I finally have the courage to."

It was really nice to see Jenny so happy. Laurie had accepted Jenny asking her to the movies, where she told me they held hands the whole time. There were two whole months of Jenny gushing to me about her new girlfriend. She said she felt like butterflies were in her stomach constantly, and she would randomly sigh when she was thinking about Laurie.

I honestly was a little jealous. We were only sixteen, but by then, lots of people in our class already had a girlfriend or boyfriend, while I never had at that point. I'd been on two dates, if you could even call them that. One boy and I went bowling, where I felt I talked to myself since he mostly stared at his feet. The other time was a similar experience to Jenny's: we went to the movies, held hands, and I even got a kiss at my door. Granted, he practically shoved his tongue down my throat, but hey. A kiss was a kiss at that age. It was a steppingstone to (hopefully) better kisses. But neither of mine turned into what Jenny was experiencing.

One day, for some reason I can remember clearly that it was a Tuesday, she stayed out of school. She hardly missed class, but if she ever did, I usually knew why since we texted constantly. That day, she wasn't answering my texts, but I tried not to worry. Maybe she was sick and didn't feel like talking. Sore throats and coughs were going around the school at that point. Later that day, I passed by Laurie on the way into the cafeteria for lunch and waved. She didn't wave back, just kept walking. Why would she avoid me? Maybe she just didn't see me…right in front of her…as we locked eyes. I shook my head. Maybe Jenny and she had a fight. They had two months of bliss, guess it's about time something negative came up.

In Chemistry, my last class of the day, I felt my phone buzz in my back pocket. I was curious to see if Jenny answered me, so I slid it out of my pocket as stealthily as I could.

"Put the phone away, Jayde," Mrs. Abbott said.

"Whoa!" I exclaimed. "How could you possibly have seen that?"

"I've been teaching for a long time."

"No way, you definitely have some sort of superhuman talent. None of my other teachers have your eagle eye."

"Just put it away, or I'll take it from you," she commanded, but she was laughing.

I glanced down at my phone as quickly as I could before having to return it to my pocket. There was a text from Jenny that read, "Get home fast. I really need you. I've been crying all day." My body stiffened. What happened?

When the bell rang, I went into panic mode, shoving past everyone to get to the door faster. Sounds of protest were grumbled from my classmates. It was extremely rude, but my mind was in overdrive. The bus would be really slow. You have to wait in line, then wait for everyone to get on, then they stop a million times. I didn't live close enough to be able to run faster than the bus could make it, though.

Suddenly, a voice, then a hand on my shoulder.

"Are you okay?"

I turn. A boy from my last class had caught up with me, Parker Whitaker.

"Y-yeah…yeah," I stuttered, trying to maintain my cool.

"You seem really frazzled."

"That's because I am. Look, I have to go, okay? My friend needs me like now."

Somehow, Parker knew what I needed, because the next magical words out of his mouth were: "Do you need a ride? If you have to be somewhere in a hurry."

My desire to get to Jenny as fast as possible made me accept right on the spot.

"Yes, please. It's just a fifteen-minute ride, twenty tops."

He smiled. "No problem. C'mon, let's get going. Emergency, right?"

When we pulled up to my house, I saw Jenny sitting on my front steps curled up with her forehead resting on her knees.

"Parker, thank you," I said as sincerely as I could.

"It's no problem. I can see that she really needed you," he said, looking at Jenny through the car window. "Will you tell me how it goes tomorrow? If that's cool. I'll worry otherwise."

"Yeah, of course." He was so nice. On the ride over, he didn't pressure me into telling him anything, which somehow made me want to talk to him more. He only moved here a couple of years ago, and we didn't have any classes together until now.

As he drove off, Jenny finally raised her head. Her face was wet with tears, a heartbreaking sight. I'd only seen Jenny cry maybe three times in our friendship. I was the emotional one, always crying over a sad book I'd read or a sarcastic comment that my dad made that hurt my feelings. Not Jenny. The last time I'd seen her cry, her grandmother had passed away. That's way more of a reason to cry than anything I'd ever cried about.

She stood up soundlessly, and I walked past her to unlock my door. We headed to my room. My parents wouldn't be home for a while, but Jenny always said that my room was like a safe haven for us. I sat down on my bed next to her.

"Why have you been crying all day?" I asked.

"Mom saw Laurie and I kiss in my room and absolutely flipped out."

"Oh my God…"

This was a worry I carried in my mind when Jenny and Laurie started dating: Vivian, Jenny's mother. Unlike Bill, her father, Vivian wasn't the understanding or accepting type.

"Yeah…" Her voice was trembling. "Laurie and I were hanging out yesterday after school, and Mom barged into my room and caught us."

I swallowed hard. Just one moment, one little thing can make all the difference.

"We weren't even like making out or anything. I just happened to lean over and give her a quick peck. When Mom saw, she yelled at us. She said…she said…" Jenny squeezed her eyes shut. "…She said,

'What are you two girls doing!' And at first I was confused, but then I heard how she phrased it: 'you two girls.' Like how dare two girls do this thing."

I placed my hand over hers clutching my comforter. More tears began to slide down her cheeks.

"And she didn't stop there. She lectured us and lost her cool and she got loud, so of course, my dad came in when he heard her. Then she had to explain it all to him, right in front of us! Laurie's face was so red, it was embarrassing!"

"That's ridiculous! No wonder Laurie was acting weird today."

"She was? What did she do?"

"I waved at her…looked her straight in the eye. And she ignored me." I felt an immense sadness for Laurie, for what she sat through yesterday. I wished she had talked to me.

"Of course she did," Jenny said, her voice laced with anger.

"What do you mean?"

"She broke up with me last night after all the mess in texts. Said she couldn't do it, that it was too hard. That she wasn't even a lesbian anyway, that I had pulled her into this."

"Pulled her into…? You didn't force her to date you!" I exclaimed, perplexed at the accusation.

Jenny shook her head. "I don't think she was saying it to be cruel. I think she's just scared. My mom told Laurie that she was going to find her mother's number and call her, but my dad convinced her not to, thank God."

"Holy shit," I breathed. "That's cold."

"She may still, though. I don't know if I can trust her word." Jenny's eyes were intensely focused in front of her. "My parents slept separately last night. Mom was so mad at Dad for trying to defend me. He wasn't even mean about it, he just told her that I'm their daughter and I should love who I want to love. That it's okay."

I put my arm around her and squeezed tight. "Of course, it's okay."

Jenny looked back at me. "You…you accepted it without a thought. You accepted me."

"You're my best friend, and I love you for who you are. Why should I care who you want to date? As long as they're a good person and treat you right, that's all I care about."

"Aw, Jay…look at you getting all sappy," she chuckled through her tears.

"Oh, and you aren't allowed to love them more than me," I added. "I don't see how you didn't go after me first. I'm grade A girlfriend material. I mean, have you SEEN me?" I gestured grandly from my head to my toes for emphasis.

"Eh…" she hesitated. "You're not my type," she laughed.

"Good, because you aren't mine, either!" I replied, mock offended. Jenny pushed me playfully, and I shoved back. Her giggles made me smile.

"I do like guys too, you know," she said shyly. "Kind of sucks that I couldn't have just found a guy I like from school, and then this wouldn't have happened."

"Don't be dumb. Most of the guys at our school aren't exactly grade A material like I am."

"You keep telling yourself that," she smirked.

We were quiet for a moment then, absorbing everything we had just talked about. I wished I knew something better to say, but I was glad that I at least got her to laugh.

"…Jayde?"

"Yeah?"

"Do you think everything will be okay? Do you think my mom will stop loving me?"

"Hey, don't say that. Come here." She sank down and laid her head in my lap. More than anything, I felt she just needed to relax and try to put away the bad thoughts for now. She stayed that way for a while, until I asked if she'd like to take a nap. I felt her nod. Jenny climbed under my blanket and curled into a ball on her side, how she always slept. I sat and read a book at the foot of my bed until I was sure she was asleep. I heard my parents come home, so I decided to get up and ask them what we were doing for dinner. I wanted to make sure we had enough for Jenny. Before exiting my room, I stopped and squeezed Jenny's hand.

I felt regret, since I knew what I should have said when she asked if her mother would stop loving her: "How could anyone not love you?" I thought I'd tell her when she woke up. Sadly, I forgot to, and now, more than anything, I wish I had.

The next day, Parker asked me after class how everything went. I didn't give him many details since it was Jenny's business, but it was nice to talk about it with someone, if only vaguely.

"Hey, you want a ride home again?" Parker asked.

"I'd like that," I said, opening my locker, "but I don't want to leave Jenny alone on the bus. Maybe some other time?"

"Sure, the offer is open any— oh, hey." Parker was looking over my shoulder, and I turned to see Jenny standing behind me.

"Jeez, how long have you been standing there?" I asked. "You're stealthy."

"I just got here."

"You little ninja. Jenny, this is Parker. Parker, Jenny."

"You drove Jay home yesterday, right?" Jenny brought her eyes from her feet to look him in the face. "Thank you. That really meant a lot."

"It's no problem. I hope things get better," he smiled. "Anyway, I'll see you guys later."

"Well, ready to go?" I shrugged on my backpack.

"You should have ridden home with him," Jenny replied, frowning. "You shouldn't let me get in the way of your life."

"What're you talking about?"

"You didn't take his offer because of me."

"You really are stealthy," I said, laughing. "Listening in on me, appearing out of nowhere..."

"I'm serious!" Jenny wasn't laughing with me like I thought she would. "I'll be fine. Go catch up with him."

"Look, I'll ride with him tomorrow, okay? But let's get one thing straight." We walked through the double doors where the buses were loading up. I grabbed her by the shoulders to make her face me. "I like riding the bus with you. It's our tradition. You aren't getting in the way of my life, you make my life better. Do you hear me?"

A small smile played on her lips as she nodded.

I texted Jenny that Saturday and said she could come stay at my house to escape for a while. When she finally answered, she said she wasn't allowed, which threw me off. Since when was she not allowed to come to my house? Three hours and a few unanswered texts later, I decided that I was going over there anyway to find out what was happening. To my surprise, as I was asking my parents for a ride, my phone buzzed with a text from Jenny, stating that her father was bringing her over.

After midnight, Jenny and I lay in my bed in the dark, trying to sleep. She didn't eat much at dinner and would only shake her head if I asked what happened. We watched a couple of movies afterward. Jenny stared blankly at the screen while I shoved popcorn into my mouth to keep myself from pressuring her to talk. I usually could get her to spill, but this time, it didn't seem right.

I heard a sniffle beside me, and I knew she was crying. I rolled over and hugged her, and she squeezed back as she buried her face into my shoulder.

"Dad wasn't home, so I asked Mom if I could come over," she sobbed. "She said no, that the rules had changed."

My body stiffened. "What 'rules'?" Her house never had any specific rules that I could remember.

"She said that the friends I've made obviously led me down a bad path, that she'd choose who I hang out with from now on." Her grip tightened on me. "Then she started talking about conversion therapy."

"What the hell is that?" I asked, though I could take a guess, and my blood ran cold at the thought.

Jenny leaned up on her elbows and wiped her eyes. "From what she said, it will fix me. I won't be bisexual anymore."

I sat up quickly, throwing the blanket off me. "You don't need to be fixed!"

"That's what my dad said," Jenny replied, slowly sitting up with me. "He got home in the middle of our talk and told her that I didn't need therapy."

I sighed in relief. Thank God for Bill.

"He told me to go to my room, that he and Mom needed to talk." Her breathing was unsteady as she held back more tears. "I tried to keep my door cracked open to listen, but I think they went outside, so I didn't hear anything. Later on, Dad came to tell me that he'd bring me here if I still wanted."

We were quiet for a moment, sitting side by side with our backs against my wall.

"...So, what's going to happen?" I whispered.

"I don't know." Jenny's voice broke on the last word as she began to cry again. I'm not sure how long we stayed like that, her leaning into me with my arms around her. I couldn't imagine what was waiting for her when she eventually went home. My frantic mind wanted so badly to come up with some idea to save her, to steal her away to live with me, but the reality was that all I could do was this: be here, be the shoulder to cry on, be whatever she needed.

* * * * *

Two months later, right before we finished our junior year, Jenny's mother officially moved all of her belongings out of their house and began the process of divorcing her father. Jenny never stopped blaming herself for it. Bill tried to convince her over and over that they had already been having problems and things just blew up, but Jenny told me that she didn't believe him.

Summertime was usually exciting, since Jenny and I could indulge in some of our favorite activities, like bonfires in her backyard, swimming at the public pool, and the Kings' annual beach trip. Things were different that year, though, especially after her mother announced in June that she would be moving back to Georgia to live with Linda and Cadie. I couldn't imagine my mom living in another state, let alone believing that I was the reason she left. Jenny didn't smile as much, and she seemed to talk even less than usual. I would text her most days and not get a response, so I'd take it to the next level and ask my parents to drive me over there. My parents, sympathetic to my plight, would sit outside Jenny's house just in case she told me that she didn't want to hang out, which was often.

In July, my parents gifted me their old car and bought themselves a new one after I got my license. Excitedly, I drove over to Jenny's to surprise her. She agreed to take a ride with me, and for once that whole summer, she seemed to be enjoying herself by making fun of my driving and asking what I was going to name my car. It gave me a glimmer of hope: she's strong, and she will get through this. New things were on the horizon, opportunities for Jenny to concentrate on her own life: college, new people, and a home life that was sad now, but would improve and finally let her be herself without judgement. All the while, I'd be by her side, cheering her on.

Meanwhile, over those last few months, Parker and I had become better friends. It was definitely a new experience, being close friends with a guy. I had only really hung around boys at group birthday parties or in class, never this much and by ourselves. We went to loud concerts where we would dance and sweat the night away, our muscles taut and sore for a whole week after. He took me to dumb action movies that I would laugh all the way through since they were so cheesy. He'd pretend to be annoyed at me, but I could hear him chuckling under his breath. Parker loved trying new restaurants, so we ended up eating at any new places the minute they opened in town. On cooler summer days, we would take long walks at the park and stay until after the sun went down. Even after dark, sometimes we would linger to admire the stars.

One night, he took me up to a spot he had found, a hill that overlooked the whole airport downtown. You could see lights all the way to the horizon, and we spent a long time watching planes take off and land. The sight took my breath away. He told me I looked pretty in front of the lights and took a picture of me on his cell phone. I'm glad it was so dark, because I could feel my cheeks blushing an embarrassing red.

He also helped me drag Jenny outside on many occasions with us that summer, and she eventually told him the whole story about Laurie and her mother. After hearing the whole tale again, guilt settled in, making me wonder if I hadn't pushed Jenny towards Laurie, would none of this had happened?

"It wasn't your fault," Parker told me one afternoon. We were sitting on swings in the elementary school playground. It was early August, and our senior year was beginning in just a week. I had mentioned to Parker that her mother leaving was my fault. The sun's rays were highlighting his brown hair, and I could see the gold flecks in his deep brown eyes. I used to think that brown was such a boring color until I started hanging out with him.

"Of course it was!" I exclaimed. "Jenny probably would have never gotten the courage to actually go after Laurie if it hadn't been for me. And then her mom wouldn't have caught them, and then she wouldn't have left. I'm such a crappy friend..."

"Hey, look at me. No, really. Look at me."

His mouth was set in a hard line as his eyes met mine.

"You weren't the one who made her mom leave. Her mother obviously has issues, and honestly, I think things always happen for a reason. You helped Jenny see what kind of person her mom actually is. Would she really want someone in her life whose love was conditional?"

I had to keep myself from crying. That was something I had never thought of before, and relief flooded through me.

"I think you helped. Maybe it doesn't feel good right now, but you did what was best for her," he said, smiling at me. "You're a great friend."

My heart somehow sped up and melted at the same time. At that moment, I knew that I had fallen for him. I opened my mouth, ready to tell him how I felt.

"I'm really glad you're my friend, too." He looked down at his feet. "I moved here a couple of years ago and didn't really try to talk to anyone. I was too busy sulking over moving."

"Oh…I'm sorry."

"Don't be. I miss everyone back home, but I'm glad we met. I don't want to lose you as a friend if I can help it, so don't let me do anything stupid," he laughed.

I smiled, masking my disappointment. In my head, his words echoed: "I don't want to lose you as a friend if I can help it." Would telling him that I like him ruin our friendship for him? Would I be the one doing something stupid?

"You said all things happen for a reason, right? Maybe we met each other for a reason, too." I said instead.

He chuckled. Then: "I'd like to think so. C'mere." He reached for me, and we ended up hugging while watching the sun go down on that squeaky swing set.

Now -Scars

Aiden and Amber do, in fact, take me to the "boring" Clayton Art Museum the next day. It was a bittersweet drive to Clayton. I caught a glimpse of my old job's building, Downtown Art Supply. Despite what Aiden said, I don't find the museum to be boring at all, and I don't think he does, either. He seems to study the various paintings we walk by way more than me or even Amber. I have been here only a couple of times before on field trips when I was in middle school. I don't remember much, so it was almost like going somewhere new. Any art exposure I had was thanks to attending many of my mother's art shows over the years. Jenny and I always felt like we were super fancy, mingling with all the adults while they sipped their wine and spoke eloquently of the colors and textures of the pieces hanging on the walls.

When I was eleven, I walked around at one of my mom's art exhibits using the bottom of a cup as a monocle, making exaggerated "hmmmm" sounds as I studied the paintings and loudly commenting on the "lovely technique" and "vibrant colors." I was amazed that Jenny, in all her shyness, joined me in this charade until everyone in the room was staring at us. We were too busy laughing at ourselves to care, and it only stopped when my dad said that we were driving him crazy. However, I knew it was only for the benefit of all the other people, since he had a huge smile on his face and scolded us through chuckles.

"I don't know much about art," Amber admits, "but I try my hardest to come here and donate when I can. Our hometown didn't have any art museums, so when we found this one, I was so giddy."

I decide to tell a snippet of truth.

"I took an art class in high school. I wasn't always the best, but it was fun. It was a decent outlet for my teenage angst," I laugh.

"Wow, really? Could I see your art some time?" Amber asks, clasping her hands together.

"Uh, maybe. But it's like a couple of years old, so you can't judge the quality, okay?" I'd never had anyone so interested in seeing any of my artwork. Even Jenny didn't seem too interested when I told her I was going to take art for the first time, back in twelfth grade. I don't blame her though, since we were going through a rough patch at that point.

Amber stops by the restroom. I see Aiden staring at a painting down the hall, so I walk over to join him. He seems entranced by the piece until he hears my footsteps.

"What do you like about it?" I inquire.

"The brush strokes," he answers, as if he's just decided. "They suggest so much movement, and it makes it seem like the artist was pushing the paint around with all their might. Like they were going through something difficult and had to get it out."

"You know that's what art is usually about, right?"

"What do you mean?" he asks, his eyes still on the painting.

"Art is way more for the artist than the viewer. I'm not saying it doesn't benefit others, but it's a person's way to get things out that maybe they can't verbalize. I used to doodle all over my notes in high school, but I was just playing around. In my art class, though, I got real feelings onto paper. It helped me a lot." I've never said any of this out loud to anyone before, but it felt good to admit. It somehow felt easier to talk to a near stranger about this. Jenny always thought I took those classes for an easy grade and because of my mother's insistence, but really, it was so that I could express things that I couldn't say to her or to Parker. It didn't make the feelings go away completely, but it was a helpful distraction.

"Huh. That's cool. I never thought of it that way before. I guess that's why you feel things when you look at someone's art, because you're feeling what they felt." He turns to me. "What were you feeling, when you took those art classes?"

Amber walks over and interrupts before I can answer. "So I think we're just about done here. There's only one more section we haven't seen."

I'm glad that Aiden drops his question in favor of this distraction. My mind panicked, thinking of something to say, and it came up blank.

Next, we head for the Palmsville Shopping Center. It's actually located in Clayton, but since it's near the city lines, I guess Palmsville got the honor of claiming this area. It has more variety than we ever had in the past, including stores and restaurants that normally people would have to drive more than an hour away to find. The area in general is also lovely to look at. High arches were built at the entrances and exits, and there were large fountains spraying water. Children would beg for pennies to drop in so that they could make a wish. I've never dropped a penny in before, but because today has been great so far, I decide making a wish would be worth it. Amber and Aiden watch in amusement as I close my eyes, whisper my wish to myself, and then drop it in. I don't know if I actually believe in things like that, but what would it hurt, whether it works or not?

"What did you wish for?" Aiden asks.

"I can't tell you. Then it won't come true." He smiles in return.

Amber and I drag Aiden to a few stores to look at clothes, but he doesn't seem to mind much. When Amber tries on a bright pink, floral dress (memories of my flowery motel room come screaming back), Aiden tells her that she can't pull it off at all.

"You're an ass," she huffs as she stalks back to the dressing room. Before I follow her back in, I turn to Aiden.

"Man, you guys are brutal. I've only heard of sibling arguments, but I've never been in the middle of it."

"Ah, an only child, right?" he says, leaning up and clasping his hands together. "You never had to deal with any of this, eh?"

"I mean, I had friends with brothers and sisters, but they didn't pick at each other so much."

"We needed it," he responds immediately. "We helped each other toughen up."

I don't quite understand, but I shrug in response and join Amber in the dressing room. She chose the largest one in the back so that we could share the clothes we picked out. I tell her that I think she looks great in the dress, and she grins. Honestly, she could probably wear anything in this store and look amazing. As she removes the dress to try on a shirt I brought in for her, I notice a small but awful scar on her shoulder. I don't mean to, but the sight of it makes me audibly suck in my breath.

She looks at me quizzically, then follows my line of sight to her shoulder.

"Oh, that," she says, her voice flat. "Just something that happened, I don't want to talk about it and ruin our day. Put on the dress I just tried, I bet you'd look good in it."

I do as I'm told. Her tone suggested that the subject was off limits, move on, and so I do. I step out to show Aiden the pink dress that Amber just had on. Anything to get away from her pretending that nothing happened in there. Aiden whistles as I walk up to him, and I lightly hit his arm.

"Hush, don't make your sister mad," I tell him, though I feel slightly happy about the compliment, even if it was just a silly whistle.

He places his hand over his heart, mock offended. "But that's my specialty!"

I laugh half-heartedly. I plan to tiptoe around Amber for the rest of the day. That scar is a touchy subject, and while one part of me desperately wants to know, I also want to respect her boundaries. I've got secrets of my own. No reason to pressure her into telling me something when all I've done is feed them lies about myself since we met.

Aiden must notice my fake attempt at laughing, since he suddenly asks "Hey, you okay?"

"Yeah. Fine."

"Did something happen?" He leans forward, glancing towards the dressing rooms.

"Amber said she didn't want to talk about it, so we should probably drop it, right?"

"You saw her scar, didn't you." He says it so plainly, so matter-of-factly, I wonder if I heard him right.

"Yeah..." I admit. No use in hiding it now. He already knows.

"It's okay. She just doesn't like talking about it," Aiden replies, just as Amber walks up.

She asks, "I don't like to talk about what?"

"Your scar. She saw it, didn't she?"

Her eyes widen. "Can you just shut up?"

"It has been scientifically proven to be impossible, you know that," he says.

"Can we please not talk about this here?" she whispers furiously.

"Uh, guys," I interrupt. I hate seeing Amber so freaked out. "You owe me no explanation, I promise. If it's too weird now, we can totally split ways, that's not a problem..."

34

"What!" Amber exclaims, grabbing my arm. "No! We still have one more place to show you before sunset! We can't stop now!"

"You just seem so…"

"I'm not ashamed, nor do I not want you to know." Amber's voice is firm as she shakes her head, frowning. "This just isn't the greatest place, and Aiden here has no sense of appropriateness."

Aiden leans back in his chair smirking; he seems pretty satisfied with himself. I wonder what gives him that confidence. He reminds me of how I used to be.

"Anyway," Amber says, rolling her eyes. "Changing the subject. I think we'll have enough time to grab something to eat and head to the trails before the sun goes down."

"Trails?" I ask.

"Yep," she grins. "Our uncle Jerry showed us where some good ones are. I'm glad you wore decent shoes. The trails aren't too rough, but I wore flip flops the first time there, and believe me, it wasn't fun."

"I had to carry her sorry butt back to the car because one of her flip flops broke," Aiden laughs.

We pile into Aiden's Jeep after we eat to head to the "trails" that Amber mentioned. I assume they are heading towards the usual place for trails in town, the sports complex that is nestled across from the middle school. The park has two large baseball fields and a soccer field, along with trails that snake their way around them. It's always full of joggers, kids playing, and people on bikes. It's a place that reminds me of my old friends, in both good and bad ways.

However, my assumption is incorrect. Amber and Aiden actually take me to a place called Reid Mountain, somewhere I've surprisingly never heard of, though I can see why: it's hidden deep inside a residential area. I wouldn't have ever known that a hiking trail was back here. There aren't even any signs until you actually arrive.

The walk is long, and I can hear our breathing become heavier. Aiden comments on how out of shape he is, and Amber says that she isn't shocked, considering how much he pigs out at the restaurant. I smile, content with the sweat and my legs pumping against the ground, while an endless amount of sunbeams shine through the trees. The landscape is bathed in a golden color, giving everything a beautiful, dream-like quality, and I'm tempted to pinch myself to make sure that I'm not asleep.

We finally come to a clearing, and I inhale sharply at the sight. Amber and Aiden stand at the edge in front of the most gorgeous sunset I have ever seen. From here, I can see green treetops and fields for miles, and the silhouettes of nearby cities glow on the horizon. I walk forward in awe, amazed by the blends of yellows, oranges, and pinks that make up the sky. Aiden and Amber smile but stay silent as they make room for me to stand in the middle of them. As if by some weird sibling telepathy, they each simultaneously throw an arm around my shoulder, and their arms reach and lock around each other as well. We stand like that, linked, as the sun melts from the sky. It's so slow that I don't even realize it's happening until it's already gone.

We hike back through the woods by the glow of two flashlights that Amber has in her backpack. She even hands out water and granola bars, and Aiden and I eat and drink gratefully as we walk. Despite my protests, they insist on driving me back to my motel. I give them directions to a different hotel that's about ten minutes away from my real one. I could risk giving them an email address, but there's no way I could show them where I'm actually staying. Thankfully, they do not ask to come up to my room. I had no plan for if that happened, even though I tried to think of something the whole drive back. They tell me that we should hang out again soon and offer small waves as they pull away from the sidewalk.

I do not start walking to my correct building until I see them turn right at a stop sign down the street, the opposite direction from where I need to go. I drag my feet as I make my way back. I'm absolutely drained: from the hike, from being around people all day, and from all the memories that continued to flood my mind on the ride home.

Then – Friends

Once our senior year began, Jenny, Parker, and I became practically inseparable. My parents didn't mind including Parker as well in our "family dinners", and Jenny's dad always welcomed us in their home since we made her happy. Parker's mother was delighted to hear that Jenny was helping Parker with his schoolwork, so we usually planned homework sessions over at his house to show how hard we were working.

My crush on Parker had grown over time, but I couldn't decide what to do about it. He had pretty blatantly told me that he didn't want to ruin our friendship, yet my feelings for him wouldn't go away. We hung out and texted constantly, and other than Jenny, I was the only girl he seemed to pay attention to.

"I catch him looking at me all the time," I told Jenny one day. We were at her house, looking up songs from Chasing Jupiter's newest and sadly last album. I introduced Parker and Jenny to the band over the summer, and they fell in love with them as well.

Jenny stopped the music that was playing on her laptop. "Jay, I thought you said you two were just friends?"

"Well...I know...but..." My voice drifted off.

"But?"

"But I think he does like me," I finished, feeling deflated. My point seemed much stronger in my head, but now it felt silly.

Jenny frowned. "Well, ask him if he does. You encouraged me to be brave enough to ask Laurie out, so why not do the same with Parker?"

"Well, he…" I sat up from where I was lying on her bed. "He told me he just wanted to be friends."

"He actually said that?"

"It was more like, 'I don't want to do something stupid and ruin our friendship.' I was literally opening my mouth to tell him that I like him, and then he said that."

"I think that's kinda sweet," Jenny said, smiling. "A lot of people our age don't seem to care about friendship. They usually just jump into relationships without a second thought." She looked down at her hands and sighed. "Like I did with Laurie."

"Jenny…"

"I know, I know," she said, waving her hands dismissively. "Sorry, I'll stop putting myself down. What I mean is, if Parker's so worried about ruining your friendship, then he must really cherish it. Maybe you need to respect that and just be his friend, you know?"

I was silent for a moment. Parker's father passed away when he was a baby, and his mother moved them here from Virginia for a better paying job. All he had for the past two years was his mom and older sister. I couldn't imagine being that far away from everything I know.

"Yeah…he did say he hasn't made any friends here until now."

Bill appeared in Jenny's doorway as she said "That's sad. He's such a sweet person."

"Who's sweet? Me?" he said.

"Yes, we were in here gossiping about you." I laughed, rolling my eyes.

"I knew it!" Bill said triumphantly. Bill made the same face as Jenny when he was joking or being sarcastic—squinted, glowing eyes, trying to hold back a grin and failing. Of course, that wasn't surprising, given that she favored him already in so many other ways. They both had fair skin, red hair, freckles, and green eyes. Jenny had more freckles, and Bill was still a few inches taller than her, but that's about where the differences ended.

"We're talking about Parker, Dad."

Bill looked at me and shook his head. "I tell you, Jay, ever since you introduced that boy to Jennifer, he's all she ever talks about."

I raised an eyebrow and glanced at Jenny, but her attention was on her father.

"Dad…" she said through clenched teeth, a clear warning.

He stared back, dumbfounded. "Aw, come on. I'm just playing."

The doorbell rang, and Jenny hastily jumped from her chair. She brushed past Bill, who shrugged his shoulders and walked down the hallway towards his bedroom. I was left alone and confused. All she ever talks about? Was Bill just making stuff up and messing around, or was he telling the truth? I heard Parker's voice coming down the hallway, so I figured I would ask Jenny later about what Bill meant.

We decided to go to the sports complex, which was located near Clayton Middle School. The park didn't close until eleven, but nobody seemed to be there after dark. It was a huge place, and it felt amazing when it was empty, like it was all ours. We cut through a soccer field instead of walking along the road that snaked its way through the complex. It was a strangely warm November night, so we tried to stay outside as much as possible before winter came to stay. Rain had fallen earlier that day, and the water sparkled on the grass beneath our feet. I was too busy admiring how the streetlights illuminated the mist in the air, so I slipped and landed on my back in the wet grass.

Parker and Jenny laughed and laughed while I groaned "Great, now I'm drenched..."

They paused, looked at each other, and then mimicked my fall dramatically, screaming "Oops, look what happened!" and "Oh, no, I've fallen, and I can't get up!"

I couldn't stop giggling as they rolled around in the grass with me, and soon we were all soaked. I wondered how crazy we would have looked to anyone else. Jenny, Parker in the middle, then me: three teenagers all wet and muddy, with grass stuck to our clothes, hands, and even our faces. My heart sped up as Parker placed his hand in mine and squeezed. I turned my head to look at him, wondering what this meant. He didn't notice, since his eyes were closed, and he was smiling peacefully.

Jenny's voice rang in my head from our conversation earlier: *Maybe you need to respect that and just be his friend, you know?* He looked so relaxed in that moment, so happy with us, and I knew that she was right. My eyes trailed to the sky as I breathed in deeply, and a smile formed on my face, thinking of Parker and Jenny joining me on the wet, cold ground. I remember that moment being a reminder of why they were my best friends, because that almost perfectly defines what a friend does: they willingly join you in whatever you're going through, no matter how uncomfortable.

* * * * *

One month later, the week before Christmas break, Jenny begged me to sit outside with her for lunch instead of in the cafeteria. I protested, but she insisted so much that I finally followed her to the stone picnic tables, confused and wondering if she had truly gone crazy. We sat across from each other and began to eat. Jenny chewed silently on her sandwich, frowning, with her eyes downcast.

"Can you please tell me what's wrong? Why did you drag me out here?" I was already shivering as a burst of cold wind blew around us.

She swallowed and opened her mouth, then stopped and took a sip of her water. I sighed and took a drink of my own water, resigned to letting her take her time.

"Parker and I are dating," Jenny finally said, the words crashing into one another.

I wished I hadn't taken such a big drink, since I choked and began to cough.

Jenny started speaking quickly, so fast that if I hadn't heard her do this before, I may not have understood. "I know, I know, you've liked him for MONTHS. I'm a crappy friend. I am. It's just, he just, he's been so sweet about my mom stuff and didn't push anything on me and..."

"Whoa, whoa," I interrupted, still recovering from the water incident. Who knew I'd somehow drown myself while sitting at school? "Slow down."

"Okay," she said, drawing in a deep breath. "You probably don't remember, but I think things started to change one night when we were at the soccer field, like a month ago. Do you remember, you slipped, and we rolled around in the grass? He reached out and held my hand when we were all lying on the ground."

I felt my eye twitch slightly, and I balled up my fists in my lap underneath the table.

Of course I remember that night, that precise moment even, because he was holding my hand, too.

She seemed hesitant to continue; she could probably tell that I was about to cry.

"Jay, I'm so sorry..."

I cut her off. "Just...come on. How did it happen?"

I bit my lip, trying to keep it from quivering. I would not cry. Not here, not right now. I refused to become a spectacle for the entire school. But how could she do this to me?

"After that night, he said nothing about holding my hand. And you know me, I was so shy about it. But after a while, it started to bug me." Jenny smiled crookedly. "So I thought, 'What would Jayde do?'"

"...What would I do?"

"Yeah! I thought 'What would Jayde do? Would she drive herself crazy over a random hand holding, or would she do something about it?' And I knew...you wouldn't. You're so brave." She looked at me admirably, like I was something special. The kind of look I always loved getting from her, but this time, it just made my stomach turn.

No, that's not what I did.

Him holding my hand that night drove me crazy for a month, but I did nothing about it since I thought he only wanted to be friends. I didn't even tell Jenny that it happened.

"So I channeled you, and before I could talk myself out of it, I called him and asked to hang out. I think he was really surprised. I've never asked him to hang out with just me and so out of the blue."

As she talked, I distracted myself from crying by looking around, noticing tiny things that I normally wouldn't care about: a girl blowing her gum into a bubble as she walked out the door (even though gum wasn't allowed), a cracked window. I vaguely wondered how it happened. There was a weird back and forth going on in my head. On one hand, I was curious about how "they" began, but then on the other, I didn't want to hear any more at all. However, since I didn't reply, she continued.

"We didn't do anything big. Just grabbed something to eat and went back to his house to watch a movie. He asked about you."

That pulled me out of my trance. "He did?"

"Yeah, he asked what you were up to, joked that we were always together, so he was surprised that it was just me that day."

I looked down at my hands. He thought of me, even when he was with her. During this story of him getting together with her, I was on his mind.

"And I'm sorry, please don't be mad, but...I lied and told him that you were too busy with a paper that you needed to write for school. I wanted us to be alone so that we could talk about what happened."

I nodded and looked down at my hands, like my nails were amazingly interesting.

"So anyway, I kept trying to find the words, but I didn't know what to say. I mumbled something about how I wanted to hang out with him alone, and when he turned his head to hear me better, I just kissed him, right on the lips. I was being bold for once in my life." Jenny looked up then, and our eyes met. "I was being you."

I finally met her gaze, and she was staring, her pleading eyes drilling into me.

Forgive me, she was saying.

"…Then what happened?"

"Oh." Jenny didn't seem to expect that I'd want to hear more. "Um…we just talked. I mentioned the hand holding and said that I liked him, and he said he liked me too. The talk ended in us agreeing that we'd try dating and see how it goes."

"Since when have you liked him?" I asked, my voice sharp and accusing.

Her pale face went red, and the memory of Bill standing in her doorway came to my mind: *I tell you, Jay, ever since you introduced that boy to Jennifer, he's all she ever talks about.*

"I know I told you that I'm attracted to guys too, but I never really got close to any of them at our school until now. I've always felt more comfortable with girls, like when I was with Laurie. Parker really surprised me."

That didn't answer my question at all, but at that moment, I just wanted to get away and think alone.

"I…" I stood with my lunch tray. "I hope you guys are happy together."

Jenny stood as well and accidentally knocked her water over, but she kept her eyes glued to mine.

"Are you mad at me?"

I tilted my head back and squeezed my eyes shut, willing the tears away. Of course I was mad. I told her how I felt about him, how hard it was to hear that he didn't want to "ruin our friendship" right as I was about to confess my feelings.

Then it hit me: I didn't have a chance anyway. How can I be so angry when what I wanted wasn't even possible?

I set my tray back down on the table and sighed. "I am…but it's not fair that I am."

"You have every right to be!" Jenny's exclamation caused a group of students walking by to gawk at us.

"No…" I lowered my voice. "I clearly told you last month that he just wanted to be my friend. I didn't say 'Jenny, you can't date him because he doesn't like me.'"

Jenny's lip was quivering. Something wasn't right in her expression, but I couldn't put my finger on it. I knew she was upset, but I felt like she was holding back.

"I wish you had told me that you liked him, too," I said, wiping at her spilled water with my napkin.

She placed her hand on mine to stop me. "I should have, I'm sorry. You liked him so much and were so frustrated over him…I didn't feel like there was ever a good time to tell you how I felt."

"Just give me some time to get over it," I said. "Okay?"

We both shared a weak smile, and she finally let me walk away.

As I drove home from school that afternoon, I wondered what she would say to Parker about me, if anything. I was confident that she wouldn't tell Parker how I felt about him. There was no reason to make him feel awkward, and I had no plans to involve him in my drama. If he decided to date her, that meant that he wanted to, and I could only assume that they were both happy. They deserved some joy in their lives.

However, my stomach twisted in knots, knowing that she won Parker over by attempting to act like me. Maybe even a better, less cowardly version of me. Would things be different if I had made a move first? He held my hand that night, too, so clearly it wasn't a romantic gesture, yet they were together now because of Jenny's bravery.

Jealousy.

Such an ugly word.

Such an ugly feeling.

That was the first night I went home and actually did what I considered "real" art: not sketches on my class notes, not some silly thing to pass the time, but putting pencil to paper with a purpose. It wasn't much, and it didn't look very good, but I was actually a little proud of it. I hadn't done any kind of drawing or painting like this since I was ten years old, and even then, my mother helped and did most of it for me.

This…this was all me.

My mother saw the drawing later that night when she came into my room to ask if I had any laundry that needed to be done.

"Who drew that?" she asked, pointing. It was hard for her to miss since I taped it up on the wall next to my computer.

"Oh…I did."

"You did?" She stepped closer, eyeing the drawing with even more interest.

"Uh…yeah." I carefully pulled the tape off the wall and handed the piece of paper to her. Suddenly I felt self-conscious. My mother, the professional artist, gawking at my poor attempt. She tried for years to get me interested in anything artsy, constantly telling me that it was good for the soul. In middle school she noticed my class notes littered with little sketches, so she brought home a sketchbook and a couple of instructional guides one day. They're still buried in my closet somewhere, never used.

"The girl in your drawing looks so sad," she said, the last thing I expected. I was ready for her to tell me the anatomy was off or that the pencil was too smudged. She meets my gaze then. "Honey, are you okay?"

I thought she'd be overjoyed that I was drawing, but she asked me that instead. I didn't know if it was because she knew art or because she knew me, but she saw the meaning quickly. Tears had already escaped my eyes, and I wiped them away with my sleeves.

"No, not really."

"Did something happen at school?"

"I really like Parker, but I found out today that he's dating Jenny."

She frowned and sat on my bed. "I'm sorry, I know that's hard. Do you want to talk about it?"

"No, it's stupid. He doesn't like me, and they deserve to be happy. I shouldn't even be upset."

Mom came over to my computer chair and wrapped me in her arms.

"It's not stupid, and it's fine to be upset." She kissed the top of my head. "Your feelings are valid, and you're allowed to have them. It's what you do that matters."

When she turned to my closet, I knew what she was searching for without asking.

She set the abandoned sketchbook and drawing guides on my desk and told me "If you don't want to talk, that's okay, but you do need an outlet." She gestured with her head towards my drawing, now lying on my desk. "This is a good start."

I thanked her as she walked out of the room, then picked up the sketchbook delicately, flipping through the crisp, blank pages. I loved the aroma of it. It was half an old book smell, and somehow half a smell of…opportunity. It had purpose, to fill up all the blank space. I could bleed out all of my thoughts, I could share my secrets with these pages. They would hold them safely for me, so no one would ever know what was going on in my head.

My mother was right.

Art was a silent scream.

I could hide among those pages. Maybe then, I would feel less heavy, because my burdens would be elsewhere.

I texted Jenny and asked for some space for a while. Like my mom said, I'm allowed to have these feelings, but maybe some time away would lessen their intensity.

She texted back: "Of course, anything you need. But…how long?"

"Maybe until after Christmas break?" Two weeks. That would be a long time of not seeing each other or talking. "But we can still text," I wrote immediately.

"Okay. I'm here if you need anything," she said. Then another text right after: "I'll miss you."

I was crying again, but I had to stand strong.

"I'll miss you too," I sent back.

If Parker asked, it was a lot easier to make up an excuse. Jenny, though…she'd know all too well why I was avoiding her. I practiced drawing the whole two weeks of Christmas break. The books outlined ways to use basic shapes to draw pretty much anything you wanted. I sketched every example over and over. It's amazing what you can do if you obsessively practice every minute of every day.

That led to me wanting to sign up for an art class for my second half of my senior year. My school functioned on a block schedule: eight classes overall, with four classes each half of the year. I was signed up for a speech class, but I wanted to work on the kind of art I was doing at home. When I mentioned this to my mom, she came to the school on my first day back and asked if I could switch my class. The ladies in the office performed a miracle…or maybe it wasn't that hard to do, but either way, they found out that the first period art class wasn't full, and somehow transferred me to it. I walked into the art room with my head held high, excited that not only was I in there in the first place, but I would get to start my day like this for the next five months.

* * * * *

When I finally return to my hotel, I sit down heavily on the bed and sink my face into my hands. No matter how hard I try, my past life haunts me. It feels like it was so long ago, but it's only been two years. I stare at my feet, and when I get tired of that, I squeeze my eyes shut. Swirls of color flutter behind my eyelids, a brief escape from the dark.

I tried back then. I really did try. Jenny was my best friend, the person I trusted most in the world, and I was hers. She hurt me, but I tried to hold it inside, tried to forget it.

To distract myself, I decide to send Amber and Aiden an email to thank them for a great day. It triggered a bunch of sad memories, but it was worth it to be with them.

I see that I already have a new email from Aiden:

"I'm opening at the restaurant in the morning, but Amber's working a closing shift tomorrow night, so I'll be bored. Want to hang out and entertain me?"

Before I can answer, a new text pops up. It's from Jak.

"Emergency job, 10PM tomorrow. Will brief you tomorrow night."

I stare at the words, then flip back and forth between the email and text. I read once, a long time ago, that your body can somehow forget to breathe when you're anxious. At first, that sounded kind of strange, but ever since then, whenever I feel bad, I stop and take deep breaths. In through my nose, out through my mouth. In and out, slowly. I do this now, and it calms my shaky hands.

With that reassurance, I answer "Okay," to both messages.

Now - Glass

I wake suddenly, and my chest feels heavy. The dream I was having must have been stressful. I sit up slowly, feeling a headache sink in. It's only a little before ten o'clock, and I told Aiden I would meet him at the restaurant at two. With that knowledge, I lay back down. After tossing and turning for a while, I give up on more sleep and decide to start my day.

The motel doesn't offer much in the way of breakfast, but there's a small table with boxes of cereal, milk, and fruit. Fine by me and my grumbling stomach. I eat it quickly, feeling my headache getting better with every bite I take. I realize that I didn't eat much the day before while feeling so on edge with Aiden and Amber, trying not to slip up and tell them too much. They are ridiculously comfortable to be around, which meant that I had to keep my guard up even more than usual. I felt more like myself than I have in a long time.

It's another sunny day, and the light shines beautifully through the motel's windows. I smile, remembering how my parents always joked about how fascinated I was with windows. They claimed that even when I was just learning to walk, they would constantly have to keep me from scrambling over to one. Apparently, I would just stare at the sunshine, wide-eyed, and there was barely anything that could distract me from it. I tried to picture the scene: tiny me, wobbly on inexperienced legs, my wispy hair catching bits of light as I held myself up on the window frame.

There's a church located downtown that has towering stained-glass windows. Whenever my parents and I would venture around there to eat or to go to the concert center, I couldn't help but be entranced by the beautiful colors. I was ten when I got it into my head that I was going to paint my own windows to look like those. My mother caught me when I was rummaging through her paint.

"What on earth are you doing, Jayde?" my mother asked, an amused smile on her face.

"I'm going to paint," I remember responding matter-of-factly.

"What are you going to paint?" I felt a little bad, because she looked genuinely excited. I knew she'd always wanted me to follow in her footsteps and be an artist, but I had never taken much interest before that moment.

"My windows." I tried to sound more confident than I felt in the idea, now that she was staring me right in the face.

"Your...windows?"

"Yes. To make them look like stained glass."

My mother laughed then, and my dad walked in and asked what was so funny.

"Your daughter," she explained, "was about to use my paint to paint her windows. Wants them to look like those stained-glass windows downtown."

"Why is she only my daughter when she wants to make messes or break stuff, and only yours when she gets straight A's?" my dad chuckled.

"I've never broken stuff or made messes! At least...not big ones," I exclaimed. Ten years old or not, I wasn't going to be accused of things I didn't do. And technically, I hadn't messed up the windows...yet.

My dad took a couple of steps backwards, hands in the air. "Whoa, whoa, okay! Sorry! Didn't mean to offend! It's all your mom's fault, anyway. Yell at her!"

"I didn't yell!"

"Man, give me a break," my dad huffed.

"Face it, dearest. You're just never right." My mother smiled, and my dad put his arm around her, smiling back.

He turned back to me. "How about we make you a deal? You can't paint the real windows, but what if we go buy some kind of...plastic sheets or something that you can paint like stained glass and cover your windows with? Win-win."

"Really?" I exclaimed, then realized that I was yelling again and lowered my voice. "Really?"

"Yeah, we can go to the store. Just run stuff like this by us, okay?" my mother said, trying to look stern. "I don't want you changing the house without our permission."

My mother did most of the painting, but I convinced myself that I'd helped a lot. Dad then secured the plastic sheets onto my windows, and they colored the sun so many different shades as it shined through my window. I stopped closing my curtains so that I could wake up to an array of reds and yellows and purples. When Jenny came over a few days later, she gushed about how pretty it was and said she wished she could have something like that to match me.

When I told my parents how much Jenny loved my windows, they helped me make one for her, as she only had a single window in her room. I hid it in my closet and saved it for a whole month, until her birthday. I wrapped it as best I could, and I remember Bill bursting out laughing when he opened the door, seeing little me standing on his front porch with an awkward, flat present that dwarfed me in height. I loved Jenny's dad. He was quiet, sweet, and always beaming with pride over his daughter whenever he came to Meet-the-Teacher days or PTA meetings at school.

Jenny's mother, Vivian, was more angular, rough around the edges. With dark, chestnut brown hair (usually in a tight bun on the back of her head), a pointed chin, and always, always wearing red lipstick, she was a bit menacing. Don't get me wrong, she was usually nice. But she had this air about her, a vibe that made you straighten your back a little when she came around. I always felt, in a tiny way, like she was watching me closely, judging whether or not I was good enough to be her daughter's best friend. That didn't bother me much, but I never cared for the little jabs she would take at Jenny sometimes.

"Honey, we're going out to dinner. Couldn't you go put on one of the nice shirts I bought you? I'm sick of seeing you in hoodies."

"If you cared about the piano as much as you did about your father's ridiculous cars, you would be a master at it by now."

"I carried you around in my stomach for nine months, and you came out as only a little clone of your father. Is there any of me in you...?"

She would say them in a teasing voice, but I could hear the frustration underneath. It wasn't lost on her only daughter, either. Jenny spent a lot of her time doing things to please her mother while simultaneously trying not to lose herself.

So it was quite a relief, after her dad opened the door for me and Jenny came out of her room, to learn that her mother wasn't home. I suspected that Jenny's mom wouldn't be very ecstatic about this homemade gift. Jenny, however, squealed in delight when she opened it and asked her father if he could help us fasten it to her window. Bill smiled warmly, always happy if Jenny was happy, and quickly set it up for her.

I smile then, thinking of Jenny's reaction to my family's gift. I wonder briefly if it is still there now in her window, if she still enjoys the colors dancing around her room. I shake my head of the thought. Not today. Today is about regaining my composure.

I read in my hotel room for a while, wasting the day away until it was time to meet Aiden. It would be just the two of us tonight. Nervousness rises in my stomach and chest. What if he thinks of this as a date? I don't feel like it is. He didn't phrase it that way, but sometimes people don't say what they mean. I'm the queen of not saying what I mean. Vagueness has been a useful tool to me the last two years. Nobody questions you if you're vague and dismissive enough.

When I arrive at the restaurant at two, Amber is just clocking in to begin her shift. They must only have one car between them, as it seems Aiden was dropping her off for work. I wave hello, and Amber smiles.

"Jackie, good to see you again! Sorry I can't hang out," she says.

"It's okay, work comes first, right?"

"You mean money comes first," she corrects me.

"Well," Aiden says. "Ready to go? I'd say we could eat here, but...I eat here enough."

We climb into his Jeep and wave at Amber through the window. She looks around to make sure nobody is looking, then raises her middle finger at us and sticks out her tongue. We laugh aloud.

"That's definitely for me, not you. I promise," Aiden says through the giggles. "It's how she says, 'I love you.'"

"Man, any future romantic partner is going to be so confused by that," I joke.

Aiden asks if I like pizza, and I say that I do. He wants to take me to his favorite pizza place.

"It's a little pricier than normal places, but damn, it's worth it."

"Mmmm," I answer absentmindedly. It felt a little easier to have Amber there to fill the silences the day before. I'm not sure what to make conversation about. However, the quietness isn't awful. It's not like any awkward silences I've experienced before. Aiden is giving off a content vibe, not one that seems to be expecting a constant stream of chatter. I stretch my legs and try to relax.

"So you said you need to be back by nine, right?" Aiden asks me.

"Yeah," I say, ready to give my rehearsed answer when Aiden asks why…but he doesn't. He simply nods and keeps his eyes on the road. I wanted to be back a little early, just in case Jak stopped by to prep me before our "emergency job" tonight. Anxiety rises in my chest. Jak has never randomly added a client to our itinerary once our week was scheduled already. It makes me wonder why this one is so important. I've heard many bad memories that our clients desired to be erased; if this one needs to be done as soon as possible, I'm scared of what it could be.

When Aiden and I pull up to the restaurant, I'm pleased to see that it is a place I haven't tried before. My family's idea of pizza was always cheap delivery, but I'm not complaining. It was greasy and delicious, what you expect from pizza. We had so many movie nights huddled around the television, pizza boxes on the floor or on the couch, Jenny and I usually sharing our gigantic bean bag chair (which was really just two bean bag chairs that my father somehow combined with Velcro). My bean bag's side was blue, and hers was green, the colors we were obsessed with. You could always tell which of us picked something by the color.

The restaurant's tables are covered in red and white checkered cloths, and the walls are packed with all sorts of things: old-timey art of people eating pizza and dressed like they were from the fifties, lanterns hanging everywhere, random road signs that reference pizza (like a stop sign that says: STOP…in and have a slice). All the waiters are dressed in red vests and poofy white shirts. Some of them are wearing red checkered hats. The menu is printed on a heavy, wooden pizza board. I absolutely love it. We are seated next to an older man and woman who are quietly holding hands across the table, and behind us is a whole family: a husband, wife, and three little children who all look to be under five years old.

"What a handful, huh?" Aiden comments, nodding towards the kids. The oldest boy is out of his seat and tugging on his mother's menu, wanting her to read it to him. The younger two are coloring on kids' menus with crayons, another boy and a girl. The little girl tries to stick a crayon in her mouth, and the father gently scolds her.

I smile. "Yeah. I was an only child. I don't know what that kind of chaos is like."

"Oh yeah, I think I found that out yesterday. Amber and I were pretty chill kids."

"Really?" I ask playfully. "You, chill?"

"If you can believe it," he grins. "We were good kids."

"I don't know," I tease. "I imagine you like, running around terrorizing Amber, pulling her hair and stealing her toys, then somehow convincing your mom that you were the one who was wronged."

"Damn, have I made that bad of an impression?"

"You just tease the crap out of each other, but you do it more. So I figured it was always like that."

He seems to think about this, then nods slowly. "Sort of, yeah. Not so much at home, but wherever we could be ourselves. Like at school, and when we hung out a lot at this old arcade in town."

"An arcade?" I ask, leaning forward. "That's so cool! I never had any near me." The only arcades I've ever been to were in Florida during Jenny's family's beach trips.

"It was definitely a favorite spot for a lot of us," he says, peering down at his menu. "What do you think? Want to just split a pizza?"

We debate for a couple of minutes, since he wants pepperoni and bacon, but I don't like bacon, so I argue for peppers or onions instead.

"I can't believe I found the one person in the entire world who doesn't like bacon!" he exclaims. The argument finally settles on a half and half pizza so that we could each get what we want. After the waiter takes our order and walks away, Aiden continues: "I didn't know you people existed. You're like unicorns, you're not supposed to be real. Except you don't have a cool horn, you just have faulty taste buds."

"It's funny how upset everyone gets when they find out I don't like bacon." I cross my arms and sit back in my chair. "I've heard this same speech over and over…well, except the unicorn part, because you're…well, you know."

"I'm what?" he says, eagerly leaning forward, feigning intense interest. "I'm whaaaat?"

"Because you're a friggin' weirdo," I shoot back.

He balls up a napkin and throws it at me but throws it a little too hard, since it hits the mother of the family behind us right in the face. We both throw our hands over our mouths and apologize profusely. The mother scowls at us, glances at her children who are laughing their heads off, then nods at us with a fake smile on her face. No doubt, she was putting on a gracious adult act for her kids, and it makes me like her instantly. That kind of maturity is hard to find. Her husband is trying not to laugh and failing. I see her smack his arm playfully. We laugh then, too, and can't stop for a while. My stomach starts to ache from laughing. I don't think I've used those muscles in a while, and those few seconds of uncontrollable giggles make any awkwardness between Aiden and me disappear. We continue the rest of the meal that way: talking, teasing, can't stop chuckling like we're the funniest people alive.

At one point, he threatens to throw salt at me to cleanse me of my stupidity after I tell him that a movie he mentioned liking wasn't that great, but then I remind him that he'd miss me and salt the entire family behind us.

"But then they'd taste so much better!" he argues.

"You, uh…into cannibalism, dude?" I ask.

"I can neither confirm nor deny this."

"Well shit, why did you get pepperoni and bacon? Why didn't you ask if they had human meat?"

"You're a new friend, I didn't want to scare you off," he replies sheepishly.

I exaggerate a gasp. "You…you're just fattening me up so you can eat ME!"

He stares, then looks down and shakes his head, defeated. "You're too smart for me…I should have known you'd figure out my scheme…" He slowly raises a butter knife from the silverware on the table and threatens in a deep voice "Now I must kill you…"

I fake a squeal in terror and then realize that I'm in a semi-crowded restaurant. Thankfully, the couple and the family closest to us had been long gone, but others in the vicinity turn their heads to stare at us. Aiden doesn't seem to notice.

"Well," he says, wiping his hands on his napkin, "you done? Ready to go?"

As we walk out the door, I exhale in relief.

Aiden raises an eyebrow at me. "What's up?"

"Oh, nothing, just embarrassing myself in front of everyone in there."

"Pffft, fuck 'em," he replies, unlocking his Jeep. I burst out laughing. "No, really. Who cares? They're just people. They make their little judgments, and then we're gone. They probably don't even remember our faces by now."

He's right. I used to be like him—shameless. Nothing made me feel embarrassed to say whatever I wanted, to do whatever I felt like.

Aiden, thankfully, interrupts my thoughts: "Have you ever been trail riding?"

"Um…like…on a horse?"

"…What? No! I meant in a car, riding into the woods. This thing was made for trail riding," he says, patting the Jeep's dashboard. He pauses, then looks at me curiously as he turns the key in the ignition. "…Have you ever ridden trails on a horse?"

"Only once, but it was a bust," I admit. "I was twelve. My mom took me since she loves horses. My horse was pregnant and kept stopping to eat grass, so the person leading the group had to grab the reins for me and pull her along so that we could keep up."

Aiden cracks up. "I'm imagining it in my head now, and it's amazing."

"It was pretty funny, now that I think of it. But at the time, I was wanting an awesome horse-riding experience to tell my friends about at school, so I was cranky about it."

"I can see that. Bragging rights are of supreme importance for kids," Aiden says, nodding.

He pulls into a gas station across the street, but he parks instead of stopping at a gas pump. I follow him inside the little shop.

"Pick out a snack and a drink," he commands. "I want to show you a bunch of different trails, so you may end up getting hungry."

"But I'm so full of pizza!" I whine, holding my stomach. He narrows his eyes at me and points towards the shelves of chips and candy. "Fine, fine! Jeez!" I exclaim.

As he's checking out the drinks and I'm contemplating chip flavors, our eyes meet. He makes an "I'm watching you," motion with his hands, so I pick up a bag of sour cream and onion and shake them around in the air to prove that I'm going to buy something. The way he, Amber, and I naturally joke with each other makes it feel like I'm back in high school with Jenny and Parker, or even further back, when Cadie still lived here, goofing around and being kids. That's when I have a realization: I still am a kid, sort of. Twenty isn't that many years away from being in high school, but for some reason, I feel like I'm much older.

We climb into the Jeep after making our purchases and head off to the trails. The sun is bouncing off of Aiden's hair, and there are moments where it looks like he's glowing. I've always liked lighter hair colors, as they seemed more interesting to me. My hair is black— just a wavy mess of dark tangles. I sneak glances at Aiden. I can't quite decide what the color is. It's a random mix of red, brown, and blonde. The sun highlights the lighter parts, while the browns give it contrasting shadows.

"Why are you staring at me?" Aiden asks, clearing his throat.

I didn't realize that I had stopped glancing and became entranced in watching his hair change colors in the sun and shade as he drove.

"I know my beauty is endless, but come on…" He smirks.

"I—I was trying to figure out what color your hair is," I stutter, "and it's hard to because it looks like different colors in different light."

"Likely story," he says, squinting his eyes at me.

"Shut up, it's true. My hair is all dark and boring, so I like hair with lots of colors."

"Your hair isn't boring. It's pretty!"

"Oh." I'm surprised by the compliment. "Thanks."

"You're welcome. And my hair is the bastard child of every hair color known to man." Aiden abruptly turns off of the main road onto a dirt one. "Here's where the trail starts."

"Are we…allowed to be back here…?" I ask, glancing around. The dirt road leads down a hill and straight into the woods. Tree branches are hitting the Jeep on all sides now, a symphony of sound.

"I highly doubt it." He grins, keeping his eyes fixed in front of him.

It's strange to feel so far from a city, even when I know that I'm only a few minutes from the nearest road. We venture farther into the woods, Aiden with a half-smile and one hand placed lazily on the steering wheel. He must do this often. I wonder if Amber likes coming out here, too. Soon we come to a large clearing. There is a mix of orange and brown colored dirt, along with a few patches of grass. We are surrounded by trees on all sides, and I suddenly get the feeling of being trapped, like I wouldn't be able to find my way out if I needed to. I begin to open my door to get out, thinking this is where he wanted to take me, but he places a hand on my shoulder to stop me.

When I look back to ask why, I follow his gaze. A large, red pickup truck has made its way through the woods to our left, and it is heading our way. Aiden shifts the Jeep back into drive. His usual playful expression is stony now, keeping a close watch on the truck as he leads the Jeep straight to the other side of the clearing. It's slow going, and I want to ask what's up, but the moment doesn't feel right. The boy driving the truck looks younger than us. There are two other guys in the truck, along with quite a few others sitting in the truck bed. I count five as we pass, three other boys and two girls. They all stare at us, but I can't quite make out the expressions. Curious, angry? I can't be sure. Maybe both.

We finally make it to the other side, and once the trees swallow us and we lose sight of the clearing, I exhale.

Aiden seems instantly better, since he says "Yeah, sorry about that back there. I wanted to get away from them as soon as possible."

"What's wrong? You seemed tense," I finally ask.

"It's nothing major," he replies, taking a brief moment to look me in the face. "I've talked to them a couple of times, they're just kids who come out here to do stupid shit."

"They did look young." So I was right. They looked high school age, at the most.

"Yeah, the oldest of them I think is sixteen, since that's his truck. They bring beer and weed and whatever the hell else out here. It wouldn't be so bad if they didn't also steal their daddies' guns to come out here and shoot." He shakes his head, his stony expression from before back on his face.

"…Guns…?" I ask, unbelieving. My parents never owned a gun.

"Yep. I hung around with them one time. They were drinking, and they were kind of obnoxious, but whatever. I can accept that. But then when they started bragging about the guns and actually had some in the truck, it got a little scary. They started setting up the empty bottles as targets and got competitive but were too sloshed to shoot safely. I tried to talk them out of it, but…"

I didn't like where this story was going.

"One of the girls almost got shot. She was sitting by the bonfire they had made, chatting with her friend, and one of the guys shot the ground close to her, trying to hit a bottle that wasn't even near her. We heard the bullet bounce off the ground. She cried out, and everyone went silent. But because she was so far gone, she started giggling and everyone else started laughing and I just…didn't want to be a part of that. It was too close."

"Man, I'm glad I wasn't that dumb when I was a teenager," I joke, trying to give him some comedic relief.

He smiles. "You weren't that dumb? Really? You didn't think it was the best idea ever to get drunk and go into the middle of the woods where nobody would find you for days and shoot at your friends?"

"No, you're right. I don't know what I was thinking. I truly missed out on what would have been the best time of my life."

"The best time of your life...that would have ultimately led to your...untimely death?!" he exclaims, pausing for effect. I burst out laughing, and he grins, satisfied by his delivery. "Yes, yes, thank you, thank you! I'll be here all week!" he brags, waving and gesturing to an invisible audience.

"I never messed with that kind of stuff in high school," I say, once I stop laughing.

"I can't decide what makes people do it," Aiden shrugs.

He stops the car and looks around for a moment, contemplating. We had come to a choice between two paths, a perfect fork in the trails: left or right.

His decision is left, and as he turns, he continues: "There's this big debate on nature versus nurture in my head, you know? Like for some people, it's who they're surrounded by. If they have parents who do those things, or choose friends who smoke, or drink, or whatever, they start doing it, too, through that outside influence."

It's darker on this path. The trees above us are thicker, and it shrouds Aiden in shadows. "But then you have people like me, who avoided that crap because of those influences. My dad was a drunk and my mom couldn't find her way out of her drug addiction, so I vowed I wouldn't be like them. I purposefully found one of the very few groups of people at school who didn't indulge in all that. So it's a weird thing, like there's no clear answer."

I sit for a moment and process everything he just told me. It's hard to imagine since I grew up so differently. My dad had an occasional beer if we went to a restaurant; my mother would have sips of wine at Thanksgiving and Christmas. Jenny and I never went to any parties that had any drugs or alcohol by choice. We didn't want to deal with any of it. We had some acquaintances at school that would tell stories about times when they were "so wasted" or "so high" and it didn't sound fun, considering the next part of the tale would usually involve throwing up or doing something crazy.

"I think those theories can be wrapped up by the cliché but extremely true statement that all people are different," I say. "Some are more impressionable, while others are more independent. We all have unique ways of dealing with things, and our choices reflect that."

Aiden glances at me and nods in agreement.

"But mostly I think it's that a lot of people are dumb as hell," I conclude, which makes Aiden sputter and laugh.

"True that, sister!" he exclaims, reaching a free hand over to me for a high five.

Aiden then, in a seemingly random place, slows and parks. I look around, but nothing seems any different from what we had been driving through for the last twenty minutes: tall trees all around, and dirt interspersed with grass desperately trying to get whatever rays of sun that make it through said trees. He gestures for me to get out of the car. Once outside and away from the air conditioning, I feel how hot it is, even this late in the afternoon. I dressed smarter this time, though: no black shirts to soak up the sun, and I pulled my hair up into a messy bun. It's messy only because my wavy hair does what it pleases, regardless of how much I plead, fight, and wrestle with it. Tiny tendrils of hair always find their way out of the ponytail holder and tickle my face and neck, taunting me.

In the midst of checking out our surroundings, I see that I've fallen behind.

"C'mon, slowpoke!" Aiden calls out.

"You can't tell me what to do!" I shout. I decide to race him (without his knowledge, as that is the key to my success) and break into a sprint. I zoom past him as he makes a half-surprised, half-laughing sound. As I round a cluster of trees to gain more ground, I stop in my tracks. An old, rotting bridge stands tall in the distance. Metal beams reach high, probably once a bright green, now weathered and dilapidated. Cables run down to wooden planks to walk across, with a strong, concrete foundation dipping into a river below. That concrete must be the only reason it hasn't collapsed into the water by now. Absolutely haunting, a ghost bridge hiding in the middle of a forest.

"It's beautiful, isn't it?" Aiden has caught up to me, and his words shake me out of my reverie.

"It really is," I agree. I'm sad that I can't take a picture. Aiden isn't supposed to know that I have a phone, since I told him that it's broken. I was beginning to weave lies on top of one another, and they were slowly closing in on me.

"It's still safe to walk across," Aiden says, gently grabbing my arm to pull me along. "On really clear days, you can see all the way downstream."

"What is this place?" I ask, feeling an odd need to lower my voice, like I'm somewhere secret.

"My uncle Jerry told me that it used to be a park years ago," he says. "His wife has lived here her whole life, and she used to come to this park as a kid. She told me that the city started construction on it to add sidewalks and lights, even put a fence around it for a while. Look, there's still a couple of the light posts down that way, see?" He points to my right, and I see two of them in the distance. The sun twinkles off of their smooth, metallic surfaces. They look out of place, nestled among all the green.

We climb the four steps up onto the bridge. There are random holes in the wood, and one plank is completely missing on the side farthest from us. It looks like there used to be two sets of green handrails on both sides, but only one side is still standing. The other is lying flat on the ground, and I almost trip over it.

"So your uncle lives around here, too?" I ask, stepping over the fallen handrail. I'm curious about his family after what he told me earlier in the car.

"Yeah, he's how Amber and I got our jobs. He owns that restaurant."

"Wow, really?" I say, amazed. It's always been one of my favorites.

He chuckles at my reaction. "Yeah, really. I mean, I guess it's impressive, owning a restaurant. He used to live in Mississippi like us but moved here to be with Anita. That's his wife," he explains.

"How did they meet?"

"On the internet. Crazy, right? My uncle is kind of a homebody and stayed on his computer all the time. He met her in some random chat room. They were online friends for years, and I guess it eventually evolved into more. He told me once that my mom was so pissed when he announced that he was moving here to marry Anita."

How romantic it must have been for his aunt, for this man to stay in contact for so long and then move to another state just to be with her. Then to open a restaurant and name it after her? It's really sweet.

"It sounds like your uncle is a nice guy," I say.

"He is," Aiden grins. He climbs over the standing handrails and leans out over the water.

"Whoa, hey, you sure that's stable enough?" I reach out and grab the back of his shirt and pull on him.

He laughs. "It's fine, I do this all the time. Give the old girl some credit," he says, patting the rail. That small gesture reminds me of two nights ago, when I accidentally met him behind his uncle's restaurant, and he patted the garbage can that I knocked over. I still can't quite believe that I'm standing here with him in a forest. The wind is in my hair, and it tousles his gently as he looks at me and smiles. It's a beautiful day, a beautiful moment, but I feel like I don't deserve it.

"How often do you come here?" I clear my throat and turn to walk the rest of the bridge.

"At least once or twice a week. It's nice."

"Does Amber ever come with you?"

"She has before, but after I told her about those kids who were being dangerous, she's said no every time I've asked." He climbs back over the rails and jogs to catch up with me. "I don't blame her," he adds quickly. "She's a really anxious person, always tense."

"Why do you think that is?" I ask absentmindedly. My brain can't seem to come up with anything but incessant questions. Maybe if he keeps talking about himself, he won't ask me anything that I'll have to lie about.

"Because of our parents, probably. Ma left when I was eighteen and our dad would get drunk and hurt Amber when I wasn't home. I think that shit made her extremely tense all the time, even if nothing is going on."

I stop dead in my tracks. He takes a couple more steps and then turns back towards me, a confused look on his face.

"You...s-should you be telling me this?" My voice is wobbly, and my hands are shaking. How could he just tell me that? Why would he trust me? Nobody just...says those things, do they?

"Why not? If it happened, it happened. I'm not going to hide what we've been through." he says, shrugging his shoulders. However, when he sees that I don't relax, he continues: "Sorry for dropping a bomb you weren't prepared for. Amber always gets angry with me when I do that, like at the store yesterday."

The scar that I saw on her shoulder. It makes sense now.

"Then why do you do it?" I remind myself to breathe in, breathe out. I concentrate on steadying my voice. "I'm not mad, I want to get to know you guys. I just don't know why you'd trust me with such heavy information. Especially when Amber was clearly not okay with me knowing about her scar yesterday."

He looks down at his shoes, mulling over what I said.

"I can see what you mean." He takes a step towards me. "But I promise that Amber won't mind you knowing…" He hesitates. "Or…at least I think so. We moved here almost a year ago, but you're the first person she's reached out to."

I pause. I'm the only person she's reached out to in that long? I can tell that he's trying his hardest to show how sincere he is. Aiden always seems to be cracking jokes and goofing around, so seeing him look as serious as he does now, I believe he is telling the truth.

He runs a hand through his hair. "Let's keep going, okay? There's one more spot I want to get to before the sun goes down completely."

I nod. It's all I can do at the moment. As we walk back to the Jeep, we are silent. My brain is itching, crawling with wanting to know more, yet I'm not sure why. How am I so curious about these people I just met? I remember a thought from earlier in the day: I had the same feeling that I used to have when I would hang out with Jenny and Parker. Natural, easy, fun. Like we were puzzle pieces that needed to find each other and fit together. Amber and Aiden aren't replacements for them, nor am I looking for any. It is a new dynamic, but a very welcome one. I guess feelings, regardless of how strong, sometimes cannot be explained logically. All I know is that I have a desire to know them, even if I don't get to be close with them for very long.

"Since you said it's okay," I say cautiously, "would you tell me more about what happened to you guys?"

"I don't mind, if you want to know."

"I really do."

"One condition," he says, holding up his index finger.

I buckle my seat belt. "Uh…condition?"

"Yes. I'll tell you about us only if you promise to keep in touch with us after you leave. Amber will need a friend." He holds out his hand with the sweetest look on his face. "And of course, I'd like a friend, too. Deal?" So open, so vulnerable. Literally asking for a friendship, not scared of any possible rejection. I stare at his hand for a moment, and then I reach out and shake it. Our hands form a bridge between us, one that I know will be broken.

"Good. Very good," he smiles, clearly satisfied.

He drives silently for the next few minutes through the darkening woods; the sun is starting to set. I hear nothing but the friction of tires and the ground beneath them. It's strangely soothing, like we're the only two people in the whole world. I remember loving that feeling, like times Jenny and I would stay up really late when she would spend the night over at my house, and we would sneak out and take walks down my empty street. The night outside was quiet and eerie. We would speak to each other in whispers and giggles as we made up ridiculous stories about all of my neighbors tucked away in their houses. There were a couple of them that had to leave early for work, so they would see us as they walked out of their houses to their cars. They waved or nodded at us as we passed, as if seeing two teenage girls walking the streets at four in the morning was the most normal thing they would deal with that day.

I push away any thoughts of the nights that Parker made me feel like we were the only two people in the world. I locked them behind a door in my head a long time ago, complete with caution tape to seal it shut.

Aiden begins speaking: "Ma left after my senior year of high school. She didn't even make it to my graduation" It makes me jump a little. I had sunk down into my own mind again, getting lost in the memories. I forgot where I was for a second. "We found out later that she had been in and out of rehab a few times before she had us, bad drug addiction. I didn't even ask what kinds, didn't care enough to know."

"She just…left?" I manage weakly.

"Yep. Woke up one morning and—poof!—she was gone. Haven't seen her since."

Jenny had to watch her mother pack up her belongings, had to see her walk out the door. Her mom called every now and then, but she made a lot of excuses when it came to visits. She paid child support, but that seemed to be the most effort Jenny ever saw of her. Aiden never had to watch his mom leave, but to not even get a final word left me wondering which situation would be harder. I guess it doesn't matter, to be honest. I try to imagine not having my mother in my life: my supportive, sarcastic mother, the one who got me into art and taught me how to use makeup and encouraged me to stand up for myself. I can't bear to think of how different things would be…a huge hole that could never be filled.

"My dad wasn't always the best. He'd get drunk way too much and say really mean things sometimes. But he was the one who would go to work and support us. I thought my mom was a stay-at-home mom by choice, but later on, my dad drunkenly told us that she could never keep a job...which made sense after learning the druggie stuff."

"How did you not know she was having those problems?" I ask.

"Mostly obliviousness, I guess. We were kids, and we were close with Ma. She listened to our goofy problems, consoled us when Dad was an ass. I believed everything she said," he replies. I notice his hands tighten on the wheel. "She was my best friend."

Some physical, comforting instinct deep down inside of me reacts, and without even thinking about it, I reach over and place my hand gently over his. His knuckles are white from gripping the steering wheel, but I see them relax and gain some color back. He looks over at me and smiles warmly.

"Sorry, thanks. I guess it can be hard not to get a little lost in the memories. I know that's probably silly," he chuckles.

"No," I shake my head. "It makes perfect sense to me."

We come to another clearing. The grass is lush and tall here, an ocean of green. It scrapes the bottom of Aiden's Jeep as we drive over it. The spot he stops at is another lovely view: you can see for miles. The city's lights look like tiny dots from here. They must be switching on since the sun is going down.

"This is really pretty," I say as we exit the Jeep.

"Yeah, it's a little secret spot that I found. At least I think it's a secret, since I've never seen anyone up here."

"Well, I like it."

"Yeah? I thought it might be kind of lame compared to the epic sunset yesterday."

"No way. I never did this kind of stuff growing up," I admit.

"You missed out," he says, grinning. "Amber and I always liked exploring. We called them our 'Adventures.'"

"That...is friggin' adorable." I grin back.

"Amber came up with it. She said it felt like we found stuff that nobody else ever did." Aiden picks up a stick and throws it over the edge. We watch it but don't see where it lands. "That probably wasn't true, but as a kid...it feels like the whole world is yours, you know?"

"I definitely understand that."

We stand for a while, staring out over the city. The wind is cool up here. It feels good against the light sweat on my forehead. There are no sounds except for the rustling of leaves and grass. I see the first star of the night twinkling in the distance. Even though it isn't a shooting star, I almost close my eyes and make a wish on it. I want this feeling to last forever. This peaceful, far away from everything feeling. It's an escape from reality, the same thing I wished for yesterday when I threw a penny into the fountain at the mall. Maybe it wasn't realistic, but what wishes are? That's the whole point of those things: blowing out birthday candles, blowing on a fallen eyelash, wishing on a shooting star…It all stands for wanting to make unattainable desires come true.

"I'm really sorry about your mom," I say. I make myself look at him. "My best friend from high school, Jenny…her mom left when she was sixteen. I saw how bad it got to her, so I can only imagine how you must have felt."

"Damn. I'm sorry she had to go through it, too." He pauses. "And…thanks for that."

"Thanks? For what?"

"You told me something about your life," he replies, a slight smile on his face. "It's been all about me and Amber, you constantly ask questions."

Shit. So, he did notice my evasion.

"Sorry, again…" I say. "I'm just an inquisitive person."

"I see that." He looks me in the eyes for a brief moment, like he knows there's something more to it. However, he goes back to his story. "But anyway, I got off track. So, after Ma left, Pop seemed to drink more often. I don't really remember him without a drink in his hand, honestly."

I swallow hard. I know where the tale is going, and it makes my stomach churn.

"But aside from that, everything seemed relatively normal. Amber and I were sad, of course, but we got by. We had our friends from school, and I got a job at a car repair shop down the street. I made some friends there, and they taught me a lot of useful stuff. Even helped me pick out my Jeep back there." He gestures towards the Jeep with a wave of his hand. "A little while after that, I noticed that Amber was starting to get really reclusive. I'd come home to find the door to her room locked. When I'd knock, she wouldn't let me in sometimes. It was the weirdest thing, because we were literally always together before then."

He climbs the Jeep then and offers his hand to help me up to its roof. He pulls out a pack of cigarettes from his jeans pocket and holds the pack over to offer me one. I shake my head, no.

"My one vice," he grimaces. I bet Amber hates it, too. He takes a couple of puffs, and when he blows the smoke into the air, it blends in with the darkening sky.

"When I do see her outside of her room, she's really subdued, quiet. Would barely talk to me, and when she did, she always seemed either completely zoned out, like she was barely there...or extremely snippy. And I'm not talking about the silly irritating stuff we do all the time to each other, like it was legit anger she dealt me. For seemingly no reason to me at the time." He takes another puff, in, then out slowly. "I was late one morning to work. My alarm didn't go off, I overslept. So I'm running around, trying to get dressed, ran into the bathroom not paying attention, and I accidentally ran in on Amber. I apologized but noticed she had makeup in her hand, dabbing it on her arm. I asked her what she was doing, and she just froze."

"She was covering up bruises," I say in a low voice, more to myself than him.

"Yeah...when she didn't answer, I grabbed her arm, thinking it was something funny, and she winced. That's when I noticed the bruises. She had a few more on her back, and as you've seen, the scar on her shoulder"

"God," I exhale.

"She had no choice but to tell me. Apparently, it would happen when I was at work. My old man was a drunk but still somehow was smart enough to wait until then."

"So...he couldn't even make the excuse that it was the alcohol..."

"No. I mean, he definitely drank all the damn time, but he knew what he was doing." His eyes have become dead, staring straight ahead. "The scar on her shoulder was from a broken beer bottle that he swung at her. She was lucky he just cut up her shoulder."

Tears spring up in my eyes, but I fight to keep them from falling. Aiden didn't need me crying right now. He and Amber are the ones who need the comfort, not me.

"Why didn't she tell you before?" I practically whisper, trying to control my shaky voice.

"She was scared. She knew I'd want to beat the shit out of him for what he did to her, and believe me, I told her I was going to. She begged me not to, since he's...a much bigger, stronger man than me. I didn't care. He needed to pay." He smiles then, the saddest smile I've ever seen. "But she said, 'Please, I don't want to lose you, too.'"

I try to imagine Amber and Aiden then, standing in their bathroom together. Amber pleading, covered in bruises; Aiden furious, ready to get revenge. The people featured in this story don't seem like the same ones I met yesterday.

"We came up with a plan instead. We were both eighteen by then, so we could leave and Pop couldn't do anything about it. We made sure to never leave Amber alone in the house. She'd come hang out at the shop during my shifts. I got in touch with my uncle, and he helped us get over here as fast as he could. He gave us our jobs, and we moved out of his house after a few months of saving."

"Wow." I couldn't think of much else to say. "I'm really, really glad you guys had your uncle here."

"Same. Obviously," he says sarcastically.

I shove him. "Yeah, obviously. Or I would've met you in jail."

He laughs. "I wouldn't last a second in jail! I'm too pretty!" He shoves me back. "And how would you have met me in jail? What would you have done to end up there, huh?"

"I meant it as a hypothetical situation."

"Oh, so you'd only go to hypothetical jail."

"And be somebody's hypothetical bitch," I say. We lock eyes and then burst out laughing. It makes me happy to feel the tension slipping away.

"All right," he chokes through laughs. "Your turn."

"My turn to what?"

"Your turn," he says, lighting another cigarette, "to tell me something about you."

"But you said that I already did earlier," I protest.

"Oh, whatever. That was more about your friend. I want to know something about you." He pokes me on the nose with his index finger.

"Um...I like to read."

"What do you like to read?"

"Books."

"Whoa, really?" he exaggerates.

"Really. Amazing, right?"

"Come on," he says, looking serious. "Something real. I just spilled my guts over here."

I inhale deeply, then exhale. Something real.

"I was head over heels in love with Jenny's boyfriend, Parker, back in high school." I thought it would be hard to say the words, but now that they're out, it feels strangely good, so I keep talking. "I introduced them to each other, since I met him first and started spending a lot of time with him after her mom left. She would want to be alone all the time, and then I got lonely and felt helpless. But he really made me feel better and kept me company. He was sweet and not like a lot of guys at our school, who were only looking for sex. I fell for him, really hard, but I'm such an awful person, pining after him like that when he was with her." I look down at my hands, finally admitting it.

"Did Jenny know how you felt about him before they got together?"

"Yeah?"

"Then I don't think you were a bad person for how you felt about him," he says, an edge in his voice. "How did they get together, anyway?"

"Uh…well, one night we were all hanging out, and he held her hand at one point. I never told her, but he was holding my hand at the same time, too. But she took it as him making some sort of move, so she invited him to hang out without me and then kissed him." It was weird telling someone these things that had been bottled up in my head for so long. I had gone over them many times in my brain, until it became exhausting. Somehow, verbalizing feels more refreshing.

"She should have talked to you first," he says, "before making her move. At least that's how I see it."

"He'd told me one time that he just wanted us to be friends. I had no claim on him or anything."

"Still, that's what a real friend would do. She knew your feelings, and friends care about their friends' feelings. She had to have known that this would hurt you, unless she's just dense or something." His voice becomes even more intense. "You had no claim, but she also did something that hurt you, and you have every right to be hurt."

"Well, I did get upset and asked for space at one point." I continue. "And I sorta lied and avoided them when they were together, but I thought distance would help me get over it. I didn't want her to know how bad I felt. She had such a rough time after her mom left, her self-esteem was shot. I didn't want her to feel that bad ever again. As a friend, I'm supposed to protect her, right?"

Night has come. I look up at the sky, and the stars twinkle back at me.

"I was protecting her from me."

Aiden frowns, clearly disagreeing with my logic.

"Protecting the people you love is a noble thing to do. But you don't have to be a martyr. I felt incredibly guilty for not being able to protect Amber from the things that happened to her, but I couldn't let it drag me down. I had to keep going so that I could at least make sure that her future turned out better first."

I glance over at him, wondering if he's right. His face is outlined in moonlight now. Soft, white tones highlight his cheeks and eyes. The moon's glow on his hair makes the strands look almost silver. He turns to look at me as well.

"Thank you," I say again. "You're probably right."

"I'm always right," he smirks.

"I know this is supposed to be about me, but can I ask you one more question?"

"Yeah, sure."

"Why do you think your dad did that to her?"

It is a question that has been scratching at my brain, and since he has been so open, I wanted to hear his thoughts.

"Amber looks almost exactly like our mother." His voice is strained. It sounds like he has to push the words out. "Ma used to always say that Amber was her little clone."

I close my eyes and ball my hands into fists. The Jeep is cool underneath my fingers.

"That's…why I think Amber dyed her hair and cut it all off when we moved here. She probably wanted to look different." He takes another drag on his cigarette and then puts it out on the Jeep.

Their father was angry at their mother for leaving and taking it out on his own daughter, just because she was unlucky enough to be born in her likeness. My stomach turns. I do the only thing I can think of: I climb off of the Jeep and find the chips I bought earlier.

"…Chip?" I offer him.

He laughs, deep and genuine. "Yes, please."

We end our night together just like that: sitting on the roof of Aiden's car, barely speaking, passing a bag of chips back and forth while staring at the full moon.

I decide not to tell him the next part of my story. There's no need to ruin this pleasant moment, and selfishly, I prefer him thinking of me fondly like he does now, versus how he would feel if I told him what I did later that year.

Then - Secrets

"Seriously guys, it's okay. Just go without me," Jenny said, her hoarse voice barely audible over the speaker phone. Parker and I were huddled close to the speaker, trying our best to understand what she was saying since her voice was so weak.

"But this is one of your favorite bands! I'd feel bad if we got to see them, but you didn't," I protested. "We've had these tickets for months so that we all could go together."

I heard Jenny coughing distantly. She must be holding the phone away from her mouth.

"That's why you guys should go, Jay. You paid for our tickets." She coughed again, took a deep breath. "This is their last tour. Please go and have fun."

Crestfallen, I hung up and stared at my feet. I knew it wasn't the end of the world, but I introduced Jenny and Parker to Chasing Jupiter, one of my favorite bands, and they loved them. We made it a goal to see them together some day. Unfortunately, soon after Parker and Jenny started liking them, the band announced that they were breaking up. They had been recording albums and touring for twelve years, so it made sense that they wanted to move on to other things. When I saw that one of their farewell shows was playing in Georgia, I knew that this was our chance. The concert was in April of our senior year, and I had just started a job at an art supply store at the end of January. I used almost a whole paycheck to buy general admission tickets for the three of us. While I still wasn't happy that Parker and Jenny were dating, they were my two best friends, and this was something we vowed to do before they got together.

Jenny was extremely respectful and left me alone all of Christmas break. After we returned to school, I met her at her locker and said I was okay, although I really wasn't. But at the time, I saw no other option. If I acted how I really felt, what would happen with Jenny and me, or my friendship with Parker? She hugged me hard and wouldn't let go for a while, like if she did let me go, I'd change my mind or disappear. Parker walked up then and joined to make it a group hug, not knowing what was really going on.

I had to be fine, for all of us.

After that, I decided to get a job for two reasons: distraction and money. My parents were okay with covering my graduation and college expenses, but I wanted to help out with the costs as much as I could. As for the distraction part, the job would be something new to concentrate on instead of moping around about Parker. My solution to heartbreak: productivity. Once I convinced my parents that I felt I could handle school and a part-time job, my mother spoke to a friend of hers, Connie, that owned an art supply store in downtown Clayton (imaginatively called "Downtown Art Supply"). At first, the manager didn't have many hours to give me, but within a month, she had two employees quit. I picked up the slack and ended up working some weeknights and most weekends. In my rare free time, I tried as much as I could to only hang out with Jenny or Parker separately, but I did have to suffer some occasions with them together. The job, at least, gave me a valid excuse to get out of those group outings most of the time.

I enjoyed my time there immensely. It's one of the largest art stores that isn't a retail chain in the South, and that made it feel more genuine and friendly. I didn't even have to wear a uniform, just a red apron with the store's name printed across the front. I was a cashier at first, a fairly easy task to learn. Most of the customers were nice enough, and some even gave me tips on how to use certain tools or mediums they were purchasing if I asked. Connie really took a shine to me after the first couple of months, always commenting on how hard of a worker I was. Within my first three months, she had already shown me how to order stock and most of the opening and closing procedures for the store. I never closed or opened by myself since I wasn't eighteen yet, but Connie seemed determined to have me do so as soon as I hit that mark.

"Come on," Parker said, tugging on my arm. "We need to go if we're going to make it by the time the doors open."

I was taken aback.

When he saw my expression, he added: "She said to go. So we should go, right?"

I felt bad, but I climbed in the car anyway since he was right; she did say to go on without her. Parker turned the volume of the radio up loud, and I tried to lose myself to the beat of the drums and the strumming of the guitar. When I glanced over, Parker had a slight smile on his lips as he sang softly along to the song playing.

"How can you not be upset?" I asked him.

Parker looked over at me with a confused expression, turning down the volume.

"What did you say?"

"I said, 'How can you not be upset?'" I repeated. "Jenny can't come, and I'm bummed. How does that not bother you?"

He shrugged. "It definitely sucks, but we've known she's been sick since like, last week. I had a feeling this would happen."

"Yeah...I guess you're right. I was hoping she'd be better by now."

"Besides," he continued, "she doesn't even really like Chasing Jupiter anyway."

"What are you talking about? She loves them!"

"I mean, she's okay with them," he said hesitantly, "but she doesn't like them as much as we do."

"But...she told me that she loved them. She asked me if I'd make copies of all their albums for her months ago..." I was grasping, thinking that he must be mistaken.

He shrugged again. "She's told me a few times that the singer's voice kind of annoys her and that she's just not into it."

I opened my mouth to argue, but I know I couldn't. He would have no reason to lie about this. But on that note, why would she lie about something so silly in the first place? Parker glanced over at me and noticed how upset this news made me.

"I'm sorry," he frowned, "I didn't realize that was such a big deal. I thought it would make you feel better."

"How in the world would finding out that my best friend has lied to me—" The words stopped short in my throat, since I realized how hypocritical they sounded. I'd been lying to Jenny, too. I guess it served me right.

"You were feeling guilty about her not being able to go," Parker explained. "So if you know that she doesn't like the band much, then you don't have to feel so bad about her not coming to the concert tonight."

Again, I couldn't argue. Stupid Parker and his stupid logic. He always made sense, sometimes so much that it was infuriating. Whenever I wanted to be depressed or angry, whenever I felt like letting out an explosion of (admittedly) irrational emotion, he had a habit of swooping in and calming me down. That was honestly a major reason why I thought we would be good together: we completed each other.

"You're right…as usual," I said, rolling my eyes. He kept his eyes on the road, but I saw him smile. "But why would she tell me that she loves them? I wouldn't care either way."

Parker inhaled then exhaled slowly through his nose. His mouth was twisted to one side, an expression that I've noticed he seemed to make when he's thinking.

"Maybe she wanted to feel included," he finally replied.

"She's always included!" I protested.

"Well, yeah, but you know how Jenny is. She's always anxious and down on herself."

I struggled to follow his train of thought. Of course I knew that she had self-esteem issues, but why would that lead her to lie to me about a trivial subject? Who knew what else she'd told me that might have been stretching the truth.

Seeing that I was still confused, Parker continued: "Jenny feels left out sometimes with us. You and I have a lot in common, so she plays along to be included and feel like she's a part of the group."

My mouth flapped open and closed, reaching for something to say.

"And she…she told you this? Word for word?"

"I'm not using her exact words, no," he said. "But that's pretty much it."

"That's so…weird…" I mumbled slowly, though the more I mulled it over, the more it made sense in the context of what kind of person Jenny was. Over the years, we constantly had people point out that we were polar opposites from each other, but again, I felt that we completed each other. She was the calm weather to my constant storm of outbursts, the introvert to my extrovert.

The three-hour drive was much more peaceful once we made it through that conversation. While Jenny's lie still bugged me, I was able to set it aside and replace the bad anxiety with the buzzing excitement of seeing one of my favorite bands on stage. Parker played all of their albums consecutively, and we discussed which songs we thought they would play. It was extremely reminiscent of the summer we first started spending time together. I went to my first concert that summer, an outside event where everyone was packed tightly together, screaming at the top of their lungs and dancing. Throwing my hands up and singing along with them made me feel connected to every person in the crowd, knowing that while we may all be different people, we somehow became one during this short time. Towards the end, Parker grabbed my raised hand, and we sang together, hands clasped. My cheeks were already red from the heat, but they burned even hotter still when I realized what was happening.

The concert was everything that I wanted plus more. Parker and I sang so loudly that our voices were hoarse; even then, we still carried on singing through the discomfort. My feet hurt from jumping up and down, and I was coated in sweat. Parker looked over and smiled at me during one of our favorite songs, and we held our hands clasped together again. His fingers were wrapped around mine so tightly, it almost felt like he didn't want to let go. Some of the people around us began to push while forming a large circle in which they ran and bashed into each other. I was shoved into the turmoil, but thankfully, Parker pulled me away and shielded me from the mosh pit.

"Don't worry," he yelled into my ear above the music. "I won't let that happen again." He pulled me closer, his arm wrapped around my waist. We stayed wrapped together like that for the rest of the show, even when the crowd's energy slowed down and swayed gently to the final songs. I snuck glances at him, wondering if he knew that my heart was beating ridiculously, embarrassingly fast.

When we exited the venue, the night was cool with thin, grey clouds drifting lazily across the sky. Parker walked towards the driver's side of his car.

"Wait, hold on," I said. "You drove here, it's only fair that I drive back home."

"It's okay," he replied, unlocking the car. "I like driving."

"Dude, seriously, give me your keys."

"Dude, seriously…no," he grinned.

I reached for the keys, but he snatched them away and put his hands behind his back.

"You're gonna have to do better than that," Parker teased.

I held out my hand, but he shook his head.

"If you want them, you'll have to come get them." He jingled the keys out in front of him, wiggling his eyebrows along with them.

Never one to back down from a challenge, I lunged at him. Parker sidestepped me so that I almost smashed into the car's side mirror. I ran towards him and pulled him back by his shirt, but he held the keys high above my head. I jumped up to grab the keys. As soon as I had them within my grasp, Parker picked me up effortlessly, laughing. My legs were wrapped around his waist as he carried me to the passenger's side of the car. I heard him opening the door and began to playfully pound my fists against his back, urging him to put me down, that I won.

Ducking his head, he tried to place me into the seat, but I kept my arms wrapped around his neck, which pulled him down with me. I ended up splayed across both seats with Parker looking down on me, leaning on his elbows. Our breathing was labored from running and laughing.

"Fine!" I shouted. "You can drive!"

"Victory is MINE!!" he exclaimed, and it sent us into another fit of laughter.

I exhaled, catching my breath, and I saw him doing the same. Our eyes met, and it finally occurred to me how close we were; he was practically on top of me. I cleared my throat and gently nudged him so that he stood, which gave me room to sit upright. He didn't seem to notice my awkwardness, since he carried on as if nothing happened.

"Are you hungry?" he asked.

"Just...just thirsty," I croaked out.

"Me, too. I'll stop at a gas station."

Parker pulled into a gas station down the street. I stayed in the car and watched him shop. He grabbed two bottles of water, then contemplated soda before settling on two large cans of coffee that were almost as long and wide as my forearm.

"And how," I joked, once he settled back into the car "do you plan on drinking that much coffee?"

He shrugged. "With my mouth?"

"Such a smartass."

"Learned from the best," he smiled, pointing at me.

On the ride home, I closed my eyes and pretended to gradually fall asleep to avoid conversation. Parker was freaking me out a little. We were acting like we used to: flirtatious, touchy-feely. It had been quite a long time since we'd hung out alone, but that couldn't be the only reason why it felt different, could it? I willed myself to actually fall asleep with no luck.

Parker "woke" me up with a gentle shake a while later, telling me that we were back in town. I already knew that, as I'd been sneaking glances at the clock on his car's radio to see how long we had been on the road. I rubbed my eyes and stretched, playing up my role as the awakened passenger.

"I know you're probably tired, but do you think you'd be up for hanging out a little while longer?" Parker asked. "I'm wired from the coffee, and it's been such an awesome night. I don't want it to end just yet."

"It's like, one in the morning," I pointed out. "Don't you remember the last time you were out this late with me, when we went to that hill above the airport? Your mom freaked out and called a billion times, wondering where you were."

"Last time was different. I snuck out that night, remember? She had no idea I was gone." He smiled mischievously, seemingly proud of the first and only time he'd ever snuck out of his house.

I snickered. "You almost gave her a damn heart attack."

"I know," he sighed. "I hated how paranoid she was back then. All the questions, wanting me to call her every couple of hours, freaking out over the tiniest changes…" Parker shook his head. "But she's a lot better now, and she actually knows where I am tonight."

I was still hesitant, but what was another hour? I could handle that. Maybe I should see this as a great thing: I was reconnecting with a friend that I hadn't felt normal around in a while. He was dating Jenny, my other best friend, and I could try harder to accept that. He chose her, and she was one of the best people I knew, so it made perfect sense. What I could do instead was support them and make more of an effort to connect with them like I used to. Tonight had been incredibly fun, a night that will be a memory I'll look back on fondly when I'm an adult wishing that I could be a teenager again.

"Okay," I gave in. "What do you want to do?"

"You mentioned the hill by the airport. Let's go there. We haven't been since I took you last year."

When I agreed, Parker grinned and pulled a U-turn at the next traffic light. The road was completely empty. Even though it was the weekend, everyone in our town must be inside snoozing the night away. My mouth formed a tiny smile as a pleasant, secretive feeling swelled in my chest, like we were the only two people in our own little world right now.

"What're you smiling about?" Parkers suddenly asked me.

I decided to tell the truth.

"It feels like we're the only two people in the whole world right now," I admitted.

"It really does," he said in a low voice.

We arrived faster than usual at the airport since there was no traffic. The hill looked dangerous to drive up, but there was actually a path carved out from other cars. It made me nervous the first time I was here, wondering if there would be some strangers at the top. Thankfully, the spot was just as empty as the first time. Parker parked the car away from the edge so that no cars driving by, if there were any, would be able to see it. When we slammed our car doors shut, I winced. It was so quiet that the noise was disruptive, like we were disturbing the surroundings.

Parker and I walked side by side, our arms almost touching. We tried to follow a beaten down path where others had trod, since the grass was so tall and unkempt. I watched him out of the corner of my eye, wondering if he was doing the same. He stopped at the edge and closed his eyes, inhaling the cool air slowly through his nostrils. I paused as well to take in the sight before us: a blanket of tiny dotted lights of blue, red, and yellow, all laid out with purpose. The blue lights lined the runways, while all the red and yellow were from the surrounding buildings. Softly, the wind blew through the trees. It was a soothing sound, as if the wind was saying "Shhh," to quiet the world and comfort it into slumber.

"Have you heard from Jenny?" I inquired, breaking the silence between us.

"Oh, yeah," he replied, pulling his phone out of his pocket. "She texted a couple of hours ago to say she was going to sleep. I was driving, so I haven't answered it yet."

"Hopefully the medicine the doctor prescribed will help her feel better," I said, cursing myself for how lame it sounded.

"Are you still feeling bad about what I told you earlier, the whole her not liking the band thing?" he suddenly asked.

"Yeah, kind of," I sighed. "It just makes me wonder what else she hasn't told me."

Parker sat down in the grass, and I followed suit. When I looked over at him, he was staring at his red sneakers. One of his legs was bouncing up and down.

"She didn't mean to lie to you," he began hesitantly, "and I'm sorry for making it seem that way. She's just..." he paused, his gaze heavenward, searching for words. "She's just really, really self-conscious because she compares herself to you a lot."

I sucked in my breath. "But...why? She shouldn't compare herself to me or to..."

"Believe me, I've told her that," he interrupted.

"Why would she do that...?" My voice was practically a whisper.

Parker groaned and covered his face with his hands. The sound surprised me so much that I shifted away from him, my eyes wide.

"What...? What's the matter?"

"Agh! ...Crap!" he growled against his hands. "I shouldn't have gotten into this. It will just make you feel worse."

I leaned over and shook him by the shoulders, growing more irritated by the second.

"What will make me feel worse?" I cried. What other secrets were my friends keeping from me?

He sat silently leaning on his elbows, still covering his face with his hands. I reached over and gently grabbed his hands and moved them so that I could see his eyes. He sighed, defeated.

"Jayde, you just have to promise me that this won't get back to her and that you won't feel awful about this. But maybe you're right, maybe she should have talked to you about this instead of keeping it from you."

"I—I promise."

Parker's eyes searched my face, as if he was contemplating if I was telling the truth or not. However, he continued as he broke eye contact and shifted his gaze down to his feet again.

"Jenny's told me that she compares herself to you a lot because she feels like you and I would be a better couple than she and I are."

I swallowed hard. It's like she read my mind. I promised Parker that I wouldn't feel bad about it, though, so I cleared my throat and tried to remain calm.

"Why would she think that?"

"Don't freak out, okay?" Parker stared into my eyes, grasping my left hand in both of his. I nodded mutely. He blew air out between his lips.

"I had a major crush on you, since we first started hanging out. It makes her insecure, because she sees how much fun we have together. So she does silly stuff like pretending to like the same things we like so that she won't be an outsider. She wants to belong with me, with us. Does that make sense?"

My bottom lip began to quiver.

"Shit...what's wrong?" He widened his eyes, and his grip on my hand tightened, a sign that I, too, needed to get a grip.

"She knew...?" I said in what probably would be a comically squeaky voice if the situation wasn't so serious to us. "She knew that you liked me...?"

"Well, I mean...she asked if I did the night we decided to try dating. She wanted to make sure that she wasn't a second choice, you know?"

"I can see why she was worried. If you liked me, why did you agree to date her?"

Parker bit his lip. "I really wasn't expecting anything like this with either of you. I was just so happy to have friends again. But then Jenny kissed me and told me she liked me. It opened up this new...opportunity, if that's the right word. I didn't have a reason to say no. I liked you a lot, but at the same time, Jenny is great, and we get along really well. My mom always says to take chances, to give people a chance. So I did."

Things started clicking together in my brain. That's why she acted so guilty when she told me that they had gotten together. She must have suspected that he felt the same way about me as I did about him, but she wanted him, too. When she felt he had made a tiny move by holding her hand, she went for it. However, her insecurities were driving her crazy: how can one feel absolutely secure when they know that their boyfriend hangs around a girl that he had feelings for such a short time ago?

Jenny's words to me that day in the cafeteria floated through my mind:

I just kissed him, right on the lips. I was being bold for once in my life. I was being you.

I wondered if she asked him how he felt about me before or after she kissed him, though it hardly mattered at that point.

Meanwhile, Parker tried to fill in the silence.

"I know this is a lot of information to take in all at once. But I promise, promise you that I wasn't just hanging around you because I wanted to date you, and Jenny wasn't some second choice or anything. I want more than anything to be your friend. Please don't let this ruin our friendship, okay?"

I swiveled my head to look him in the eye. We were worried about the same thing, about ruining our friendship. I didn't want to chase him off by expressing my romantic intent, and it seems that he felt the same way.

"You've done so much for me," he said, releasing my hand.

"What do you mean?" I asked, surprised. "You're the one who's done way more for me."

"Are you kidding?" he scoffed. "Do you know what I was like before I started spending time with you? I was so quiet and shy to the point of having no friends for two years."

"There's nothing wrong with being shy," I argued.

"Well, yeah," he agreed. "But it truly hindered me. That's why my mom was always so worried about me after we moved here. I was always alone." He shook his head, pulling at the grass beneath us with his fingers. "When you and I started talking, it freaked me out. You were this pretty, outgoing, amazing girl. I didn't want you to realize how much I didn't deserve to be around you."

"Parker, you deserve so much better than me! I've been so petty and jealous!" I cried.

Realization dawned on his face.

"I was wondering why you didn't hang out with us much anymore," he frowned. "But I don't think it's petty. It was probably weird to hang out with a couple all the time."

I nodded, even though he didn't seem to grasp the whole reason why. I guess Jenny kept my secret at least; he still had no idea how I felt about him. We sat in silence for a moment, then turned our heads at the sound of an airplane behind us in the distance, getting ready to land.

"I really am a lot better after meeting you," Parker said. "I'm happier. I speak up more at school, and I'm not as nervous anymore when I have to do presentations in front of my classes. So my grades are better, too."

"That's because of Jenny," I said, wiping my eyes.

"Sure, partly. She tutors me in math, mostly, but before I knew her, hanging out with you gave me a better attitude. I started finishing all of my homework, and I think that helped me when there were quizzes. I wanted to keep up with you and be great."

"W-why?" I couldn't fathom that. It had to be Jenny, right? He chose her, not me.

"Come on, Jayde. When you walk into a room, everyone takes notice. You act silly in class and show up the teacher, but they actually like you for it. You're beautiful and brave and I'm so damn lucky to be close with you." He paused. My heart was frantically beating, and I felt my cheeks flushing. "The day I actually worked up the nerve to talk to you the first time, when I drove you home...do you remember?"

"Of course I remember," I answered softly.

"I was so nervous," he chuckled. "I had kinda admired you from afar for a long time, heard rumors of things you'd said and done around school."

For some reason, I had never thought about the fact that my classmates would talk about me in school. It wasn't something I was ever concerned about.

"Then, junior year, we had chemistry together, and I got to see that all the stuff I heard was true. It was cool to know that at least some rumors could actually be good things." He'd made a collection of grass he pulled on the top of his sneaker. I'd never seen him act so fidgety before. "That day, when you were trying to get to Jenny, I noticed how fast you ran out of class, pushing and shoving through everyone. It was weird. I knew something had to be wrong."

I nodded. That afternoon stands out as a blur of worry and panic in my head, a moment when everything changed for Jenny.

"I never knew how to approach you, and you were always busy talking to someone. So I summoned up bravery I didn't know I had and asked you if you needed a ride home. Imagine my shock when you actually took my offer." Parker laughed and shook his head, like he still couldn't believe it.

"Thank you again, for the ride home. And for talking to me when I needed it." I didn't know what else to say, but upon remembering that day, an overwhelming feeling of gratitude rushed through me.

"You're welcome, obviously," he said, smiling. I think I loved that particular smile of his the most: wide and genuine, the right side of his mouth a little higher than the other, eyes sparkling. It made him look older somehow. Parker stood and brushed his jeans off with his hands.

"I guess we've been here long enough, huh? Let's get you home." He offered his hand to me, and I took it, leaning my weight into him as he pulled me up. My legs were wobbly from sitting on them for so long. As he began to walk back to the car, I glanced behind me; the plane was closer now. Parker turned back to see what I was doing and followed my gaze. A few seconds later, he was by my side again, and we watched the plane fly over our heads together. Even from thousands of feet away, the sound was deafening.

"You said 'had.'" I said, my eyes still on the sky.

"What?" he asked. I don't know if he didn't hear me, or if he didn't understand what I meant.

"You said you 'had' a crush on me. Does that mean you don't anymore?"

I couldn't believe I just said those words out loud. I couldn't believe that I was finally standing there, awaiting an answer to a question that I should have asked months ago. Parker opened his mouth, then closed it, then opened it again. A dumbfounded look was plastered all over his face, and it made me nervous, because it could turn into all kinds of bad things: anger, dismissal, or even a refusal to give me an answer. We stared at each other for what seemed like a long time as the wind still blew and the lights still shined below. The world carried on as it usually did. Meanwhile, my world had changed with one question.

Parker cleared his throat.

"What do you mean?" he chuckled nervously.

"I'm asking you a question," I said, faking confidence. "It's simple, yes or no."

I took a step towards him, and we were so close that we were almost chest to chest. He turned his head to the right and blew air out between his lips.

His shoulders slouched, and with great effort, he replied: "Yes. I still like you." Looked up, met my eyes. "You can't just make that kind of thing go away completely."

I swallowed, clenched and unclenched my fists. My heart was soaring. How long have I been waiting to hear those words? How much have I wanted this more than anything else? When I didn't immediately respond, he continued to sputter: "Again, though, please don't feel weird or mad or anything, okay?"

I saw his lips moving, but all I could hear was Jenny's words:

I just kissed him, right on the lips. I was being bold for once in my life.

I leaned forward and lightly pressed my lips to his. His body stiffened for a moment, but then he slowly melted into the kiss and wrapped his arms around me.

I was being you.

We kissed slowly at first, finding a rhythm. His hands worked their way into my hair, and I lightly traced his face with the tips of my fingers. As we pulled back, our eyes locked, but soon we went back for more. He pulled me so close that our bodies were pressed together, and my arms were wound tightly around his neck. The kisses became more intense the longer they went on, a mutual desire finally being satisfied. When we pulled away to catch our breath, smiles lingered on our faces. We held hands the entire ride back to my house, and then we kissed even more in my driveway. It was like we couldn't get enough. My lips were still tingling as I entered my house, and for once I was saddened that I didn't have a sibling to gush about my night to.

I didn't think of Jenny again until the next morning, when I woke up gasping, a nightmare on the edges of my mind. That really happened. I really did kiss my best friend's boyfriend. I cried bitterly, throwing myself back down onto my pillow. There had to be a way to fix this without us losing Jenny. Will Parker break up with her for me? Should we tell her together that we messed up?

Either way, I hated myself, since my mind was already made up: I wasn't letting him go.

Now - Emergency

About an hour later, Aiden pulls up to the hotel I directed him to the previous night. We didn't talk much on the drive back. I think we were mulling over our conversations, and his silence makes me wonder if he regrets telling me those personal stories.

"Here we are," Aiden says, shifting the Jeep into park at the hotel's glass doors. "And...right on time!" He checks the watch on his wrist with a flourish.

"You are truly a master of time," I reply, clapping sarcastically.

He changes the subject. "You said you and your dad will be leaving by Monday, right?"

"Yeah?"

"Well, how about one last day with us before you go? Amber and I are off tomorrow."

I'm thankful that he doesn't ask about Sunday, since that's my next job. However, hearing "one last day," is immensely disappointing.

Does he know that I was lying when I said I would keep in touch with them?

I don't want to hurt them. It pains me to think that I can't build any sort of friendship upon these last two amazing days. I know I'm being selfish. Aiden said that we can't be martyrs for our friends, but he has no idea what I've done. I'm paying my dues, both literally and figuratively. I can't mess around and make things worse. Who knows what Jak would do if he found out that I was in this car right now? He has the power to hold up and wave my terrible mistakes around like a giant flag for all to see.

"Sure," I answer, stepping out of the car as casually as I can. He rolls down the window and I lean inside. "Just email me the details like we've been doing."

"Will do," he says, smiling. "See ya tomorrow." He holds his hand out for a knuckle pound, and I return it.

I enter the hotel doors and wait for Aiden's Jeep to disappear down the street, then once again set off towards the place that I'm actually staying. It isn't a long walk, but somehow, it's incredibly lonely after being around Aiden for a while. His voice, boisterous and lively, fills up every room. He even made the dark, quiet woods seem less scary. Hearing Amber and Aiden bicker yesterday while I could peacefully sit and laugh, not thinking too much or wallowing in guilt for hours at a time...it's a feeling that I forgot about. The heaviness in my chest was replaced by a lightness, a child-like giddiness as I delivered comebacks to Aiden or made Amber smile with compliments about how she looked in the clothes we tried on. When I think about tomorrow as "one last day" with them, it makes my heart sink.

I climb the stairs to the third floor of my hotel and swipe the card used as the door's key. Feeling inspired, I suddenly wish I had a sketchbook with me. I haven't felt like drawing since the summer after my senior year. Now my hands have that familiar itch, a need to feel the weight of a pencil against paper. I long to smell colored pencils and paint. Instead, I lay down and close my eyes, allowing my mind to wander with ideas. Swirls of colors fly through my mind, until they all mix and form a dark background. Stars come into shape, and I see Aiden's silhouette against the moonlight and his cigarette burning in the dark. I want to take a mental picture of that image, save it, and draw it. Amber, too: in the pink dress from yesterday, contrasting against her intense blue hair and green eyes. I want to draw her happy, smiling, carefree...how she deserves to be.

Just then, a knock comes at the door. My eyes pop open, and I sit up quickly. When I answer the door, it's Jak. I breathe a small sigh of relief: I got back here just in time. When I open the door, his expression is solemn. Our jobs make him just as unhappy as they make me.

"I came by earlier," he says, "but you didn't answer the door."

My heart jumps up in my throat. "Sorry. I fell asleep reading."

"Get ready, I want to try to be a little early for this one. The client is a seven-year-old girl." He pauses, letting that sink in. "Her mother signed the contract, but I want us to speak to the girl directly and hopefully get her to understand and sign as well."

"Will there be repercussions if we don't get the little girl to sign the contract?" I ask. This is the youngest client we've ever had. Before this, the youngest was a girl who was my age at the time, nineteen.

"I highly doubt it. Parents can make most decisions for their children until they're legally adults." He hesitates. "I just think it would be best to talk to the actual client directly. I've only spoken to her mother." There is an awkward silence until Jak speaks again: "I'll be waiting in the lobby."

I shake my head. Tonight, I decide to wear a brown dress that I bought at a thrift store two weeks ago. It has one strap and white frills running down the middle. I wrap an orange scarf around my neck and pair that with an orange wrap over my usual blonde wig. My goggles are always the last touch. They are a deep brown-gold color with a heart drawn over one eye, along with a silver wing attached to the right side. I bought them with Jenny years ago at an anime convention we were able to attend. Now they serve a dual purpose: a disguising function and a reminder of who I'm doing this for.

Once I'm dressed, I take the stairs down to the lobby. I let my feet pound heavily to work out some nervousness. Jak turns as I appear on the bottom floor, and I keep silent and follow him as he opens the front door. The motel receptionist raises her head for a moment as we pass. I notice her eyebrows shoot up when she sees what I'm wearing. I'm honestly surprised that she notices, considering that at every other place I've ever stayed, the receptionists barely ever acknowledged us whenever we passed by.

"Costume party," I shrug, and she smiles and nods in understanding. It's a good excuse, especially since Jak always looks a little strange as well. He usually wears some variation of a suit, but they're always brightly colored or have some ridiculous pattern. Today, he has on a grey coat with deep, black pockets that all have oversized, clunky zippers. The shoulder pads are large and bulge out. His pants are the same grey as the coat and have zippers that run from the ankle to the pockets. I briefly wonder where he found such a weird suit. Coupled with a brown, messy wig and bright, yellow contacts, he looks like a confusing cross between goofy and intimidating.

The car is a different rental from earlier in the week. It's a black four door hatchback, shiny and new. As we climb in, the awkwardness is stifling. I can't ask him about the job; I know he won't tell me any more than he wants or needs to. I certainly can't talk to him about Amber and Aiden. There's no need for small talk about the weather or how he's doing. And absolutely, one hundred percent, I can't ask him about Jenny. That's the number one thing that I'm not allowed to talk about with him. So instead of talking, I fix my eyes dead ahead as he drives.

It takes a little over twenty minutes to arrive at our destination. This neighborhood isn't doing so well. The houses look old and worn down, like they're tired and leaning over. I see an assortment of random items piled up in one yard: two shredded tires, several towels, and what looks to be a table with two legs missing. There are empty fast food containers and beer bottles lying in the closest ditch. Jak instructs me to wait five minutes before entering as he steps out of the car. I watch him walk around the house to where I assume there is a back door. I don't see him again, so he must be inside. The glass in one of the windows on the house is cracked so much that I wonder how it hasn't fallen out of the frame by now.

The darkness is starting to get to me. It's heavy and surrounds, like it will eventually swallow me up. I notice that only two streetlights are burning, while the others seem to be out. A forgotten neighborhood. I look down at my phone, half-grateful that it's been five minutes, and that I can go inside and away from the sight of this sad street. The other half of me, though, carries a dread down in my stomach as it always does when I'm about to meet a client.

I find the back door that Jak must have used, since it is still standing open. My eyes adjust slowly to the dark as I take careful steps through the kitchen. I see a faint light at the end of a hallway to my left, so I follow it. When I come to the source, a woman, a little girl, and Jak all look up at me simultaneously. The woman and child are sitting on a couch against the wall, while Jak has taken a seat on a stool across from them. The woman has her arm around her child, holding her close, almost defensively, even though she was the one who invited us here.

"I like your goggles," the little girl says to me.

"Thanks." The muscles in my back lose a bit of tension. "I like your bunny." The girl is clutching a tattered, grey bunny tightly to her chest. Its eyes are shiny black, and it has a little pink nose.

"His name is BunBun," she answers, smiling proudly. "I took him to show-and-tell at my school."

Jak clears his throat to keep me on track.

I sigh. "What are your names?" I ask, reaching my hand out.

"I'm sorry. This is all so weird to me, I didn't properly introduce myself," the woman says, shaking my hand weakly. "I'm Cathy. And this is Lizzy."

"Elizabeth," her daughter corrects, shaking my hand, a serious expression on her face.

I swallow, trying to get the lump in my throat to go away. I did the same thing when I was younger. My parents would always shorten my name to "Jay," and I would correct them, telling them that "Jayde sounded more grown-up."

"What do you want to forget?" I say, looking into Elizabeth's eyes. However, her mother is the one who answers.

"She's been through a lot," Cathy says. "There's been some traumatic issues concerning a family member, and I think it would be much better for her future if she could forget it."

Cathy is pronouncing every syllable carefully, reminding me of a robot. She must be trying to conceal her emotions to seem more professional. This is, after all, technically a business transaction.

"I apologize, Miss Calhoun, but she will need more information than that." Jak's mouth is a flat line.

"Why? I don't want her to have to relive the—"

"It's okay, Mommy," Elizabeth interrupts. She places her small hand on her mother's. "I don't want to do this anyway."

We all stare at Elizabeth. Even Jak's jaw is hanging open in shock.

"Young lady," Jak begins, then stops, rubs his forehead. "…You signed the contract just a few minutes ago."

"I'm sorry," she answers. "I just didn't want to make my mommy mad."

"Oh honey, why would I be mad at you?" Cathy says, running her fingers through her daughter's hair. It is wavy and wild, a golden blonde.

"Because this is what you want, right? For me to forget?"

We are all silent for a moment. Elizabeth is looking up into her mother's eyes, pleading, wanting so badly to do what her mother says, to make her happy. The way she's looking at her makes my heart squeeze in my chest. The love of a child, the purest love.

"It would be better for your mental health in the future," Cathy explains. She's using a voice that I've heard a lot when someone speaks to their child. Light but firm, and always with a slight high note at the end of every sentence. "Remember what we talked about? About how you have to treat your body when you're sick? Same thing goes for your mind, too. And forgetting is the cure."

Elizabeth looks down at her hands, contemplating. It's so much for a young child to digest, the complicated differences between physical and mental health. One can affect the other, and while she may not feel it now, she may later on in her life. Cathy is trying to protect that precious future. I can understand why she feels that this is the best option for her daughter.

I step forward and get down on my knees in front of Elizabeth.

"How old are you?" I ask gently.

"Seven," she says shyly. We are eye-to-eye now, and I think that flusters her a bit.

"Old enough, then, for big girl talk. Right?"

"Right!" Elizabeth exclaims, sitting up straighter. She leans closer to me, putting on a comically serious face.

I smile. "Okay. So how this works is, I can make you forget those bad things that happened to you. I have some kind of weird power to do that."

Her eyes widen. "Powers? Like a superhero?!"

All three of us adults can't help but chuckle. I haven't heard Jak laugh in a long time…it's nice to hear.

"I'm not a superhero or anything, no. But I can make you forget, if you want. You and your mom would need to say out loud the exact thing you want to forget. It's so I can hear it and start concentrating on those exact words and only those words."

Elizabeth's eyebrows crinkle in thought.

"So that you won't make me forget all my memories? Just the ones I say?"

"Exactly. You're a smart girl," I praise. "But then you, and your mom could help with this, would need to write down the exact memories too."

"Why?" she asks, leaning forward. She's completely enraptured in what I'm explaining, as if this was some exciting story I was reading to her.

"Well," I begin, "the paper is how I do it. If you write stuff down and I tear it up, then whatever you wrote on there is what you forget."

"But if the paper is how you do it, then why do we have to tell you out loud? Shouldn't you just be able to use the paper?" She has a slight lisp, and it's so adorable that I almost want to hug her right then and there.

"I...made a mistake, a long time ago." I glance at Jak, and he nods as an encouragement to keep going. "A friend of mine had me burn stuff she wrote on, and it ended up making her forget everything."

"Everything?"

"Everything," I confirm. "Memories are all connected. Do you know what I mean? One thought leads to another, one person reminds you of another person. So say if I burned a paper that you wrote your mom's name on, you could possibly forget anyone you ever met through your mom, or anything your mom ever taught you."

"I don't want that!" Elizabeth cries.

"I know. So that's why there's two steps. To protect the rest of your memories while getting rid of the bad ones." This was almost a rehearsed speech, as I've had to explain this many times to clients. Even after paying and reading the contract that Jak wrote, they were often nervous and needed some reassurance. Somehow, it was easier to explain it to this seven-year-old than to the adults.

"That's neat," Elizabeth smiles.

"I'm glad you think so," I frown.

"Then it's settled," Cathy speaks up. "I have a notepad on this desk right here. Want me to help you write it?"

"So this is what you want, Mommy?"

Cathy is taken aback. "Don't you want to forget, sweetie?"

"No," Elizabeth says in a small voice. I sense that she's not used to telling her mother no.

"But...why?" Cathy has tears at the corner of her eyes.

My lip quivers. I shouldn't be here. I shouldn't be witnessing this.

"They're my memories in my head. I want to keep them. They're mine."

Elizabeth says it so confidently, her little voice firm, unrelenting.

"Baby," her mother says, pulling her closer. "If you keep them, you'll have a difficult time. You've had nightmares, remember? Things will be harder for you."

"It's okay," Elizabeth nods. "I can do it."

I try to hold my tongue, but the words burst out of me: "I think you can do it, too."

Cathy gives me an agitated look, but I don't care. Elizabeth needs someone to believe in her, even if it's just some random girl wearing goggles that she likes.

"Lizzy," Cathy begins, using a firmer voice. She places her hands gently on her daughter's shoulders. "This is for your own good. I promise it will make things much better. The bad dreams will go away, the bad stuff will all be gone. And then you can move on with your life."

"But I already am," Elizabeth retorts.

Cathy opens and closes her mouth, clearly struggling to find something to counter that response with. She looks at us with pleading eyes, but we can't argue with her. She makes a good point, and it isn't our place to convince her. Then surprisingly, Jak speaks for the first time since the beginning of the conversation.

"Young lady, are you sure about not going through with this?"

"Uh-huh," Elizabeth nods furiously.

"Look me in the eyes," Jak commands, leaning forward.

Elizabeth squirms. I can see why. Those yellow cat eye contacts are a little off putting. However, she takes a deep breath and stares him down.

"If you want to break the contract, that's fine. I want to treat you as an adult. So you decide."

Elizabeth stares into his eyes fiercely and says "Yes, please. I want to keep my memories, bad and good."

"Then it's settled." He picks up a piece of paper on the coffee table in front of him. I hadn't noticed it in the dim light, but I briefly spy a child-like signature underneath a loopy cursive one at the bottom before he rips it up.

"B-but she..." Cathy stutters weakly.

Jak looks at her with sympathetic eyes. "I'm sorry, Miss Calhoun. We cannot, in good conscience, take this child's memories without her consent."

Cathy breathes in deeply and exhales slowly, pushing the air through pursed lips.

"I understand." She takes her daughter's hand and smiles at her.

"Thank you, Mommy," Elizabeth smiles back. "I promise I'll be okay."

Jak produces a wallet out of an inside pocket of his jacket.

"Here," he says, taking a paper check out of his briefcase and handing it to Cathy. "I haven't cashed it yet. We did not perform a service, so we won't be needing payment."

"Are you sure there isn't something I can do for you two? You came all this way..." Cathy insists.

"We'll go," Jak says. "If there's anything else we can do for you, just let us know."

Elizabeth stands from the couch and runs over to me.

"Can I see your goggles up close? Just for a minute?"

I bend down until we're eye-to-eye again. She squints her eyes, studying the goggles on my face. She traces the wing on the side gently with her fingers.

"I'm gonna make some for me," she announces, "just like yours. With the heart and wing and everything. But I want mine to be purple."

"Why don't you just keep mine?" I ask.

Elizabeth's eyebrows shoot up.

"Really? I can keep them?"

"Sure, if you want." I don't know how I'm saying these words, how I'll feel once I part with something that reminds me of Jenny…but it feels right.

"But you need them to be a superhero!" she says, balling up her fists and shaking them. "Every superhero's gotta have a mask."

"Thanks," I say, patting her head. Her hair is ridiculously soft.

"I'm gonna start right now!!" she exclaims. She runs past me and down a dark hallway to the right. I see a light flick on. That must be her room.

Cathy shakes her head. "She's going to be up all night, that crazy girl."

"She seems like a wonderful child," Jak says, peering down the hallway.

"She really is," Cathy agrees. "And I'm not just saying that because she's my kid."

We laugh. It's so weird to be standing in a stranger's living room, laughing during such a bizarre event. I don't think I've ever laughed during one of these jobs before.

"No," Jak replies, "I'm sure you and her father aren't biased. You can clearly see what a good person she is."

Cathy leans against the wall connecting to the kitchen. "Oh, definitely. Lizzy's dad and I divorced a few years ago, but it wasn't a huge fight or anything. We got married because I was pregnant, and we were young. We had no idea what we really wanted then." She looks down at her feet. "But that still led to a lot of changes. Her father helps as much as he can, but sometimes my dad would help out and babysit her when I had work shifts or just needed a break. After a while, though, Lizzy…she started refusing to go. I'd practically have to drag her over to her own grandfather's house."

I look down the hallway at the rectangular box of light, trying to imagine this happy little girl throwing a fit, crying, refusing her mother anything. It seemed next to impossible.

"I made her go a few more times, I mean…I had to work, you know? And she could never explain beyond 'I don't wanna go to grandpa's house,' so I thought she was just being fussy, like all kids can be. But…finally, the last time, she just blurted out 'Mommy, he does weird stuff to me, and I don't like it!' And it finally, finally dawned on me that maybe this was something way bigger."

Jak's hands form fists at his sides. I try to control my jaw clenching. Poor, poor Elizabeth. How does a child get that kind of message across when they don't even understand what's happening? She tried, she really tried.

"All of the aftermath has been so damn complicated, and I didn't know what to do for her. She's started having nightmares recently, waking up crying and sweating. So when I found this random ad online about successful memory wiping, I just…I had to try. I wanted to save her from having to live with this for the rest of her life."

Online? I always wondered how Jak got the word out about me, but I guess I know at least one way now. She looks meaningfully at Jak, then at me.

"I hope you can understand. I wasn't trying to force her into anything. I just wanted to protect my little girl, because I couldn't protect her before."

"We understand completely," Jak says, holding his hand out to shake. "It was a pleasure to meet the both of you."

She shakes our hands, and I can tell she's forcing a smile. To her, we were a miraculous fix for a horrible issue, but now we are walking out of her house without actually doing anything. It wasn't our choice, but I still feel somehow responsible as we step outside. I turn back towards the house one last time and see that Elizabeth is at her window, waving at me. I wave back.

The drive to my motel is still quiet, but it isn't like before. The air feels more pleasant, somehow. I think Elizabeth made us both feel good. When we pull up to the front doors, I open the car door and climb out. Before I can shut it, Jak surprises me by calling me by my real name:

"Jayde."

I freeze.

"You…you did good tonight. For both of them. I think you gave that little girl the bravery to speak up for herself." He looks at me, and I feel like it's the first time he's seen me as an actual person in a long time. "Elizabeth was quiet the whole time I was in there, signed the contract, nodded her head to everything her mom said. But somehow, seeing you and talking to you sparked her courage. You prevented us from most likely doing irreversible damage."

I nod, holding back tears for the millionth time that night. God, I wish I didn't cry so easily. I need to get my tear ducts removed.

Jak hesitates. "So…thank you. For that." It is a thanks that he doesn't want to give me, so I appreciate the hell out of it. Kind words about me from him are rare.

I nod in response. It's all that I can think of to do. As I climb the stairs back to my room, random snippets of the last two days swirl through my head: Aiden laughing, Amber's scar, the dilapidated bridge, Elizabeth running up to me, smiling. Elizabeth may be a child, but she decided to bear the pain and take the world head on with no magic fixes. I have met so many adults in the last two years that used me as an escape, yet here was this seven-year-old who knows what I can do for her and still chose to keep the terrible memories because they are hers. She's accepted what happened to her and is already becoming stronger for it.

Amber and Aiden, too, are doing the same. They have been through so much, and yet they continue on as best they can. They saved themselves from a bad situation, found a good environment to surround themselves with, and are being productive and moving forward. In these two short days, I have grown to admire their strength and humor.

I've been so afraid for such a long time of owning the things I have done. I've hidden away out of shame and regret. While that has spared me the pain that I'm so terrified of, it has also taken more than I could ever imagine away from me. I've chained myself to a fate that I don't have to endure out of guilt and sadness. If I am going to move on from my past, repressing it and trying to forget are not the answers. I have to hold my head up and own it, as Aiden, Amber, and Elizabeth have, and perhaps I will find some peace. It may take an extremely long time to feel normal or happy again…but I have to try.

I decide right then and there, sitting in my flowery hotel room, that after my next assignment on Sunday night, I am going to tell Jak that I can't do these jobs anymore. Jak will tell my parents and Parker how much I've lied to them, as he's threatened. Will he let them know the real reason for Jenny's memory loss? I'm not sure what all he will do; I've already lost Jenny since she doesn't remember me, and Parker probably already hates me since I abruptly cut off contact with him years ago. There's nothing left for me in Palmsville, since Amber and Aiden know "Jackie," and I couldn't continue to live here and pretend to be this other person while being their friend. I'll move away from Palmsville, I'll start over, and hopefully my parents will still want to talk to me. They will most likely never trust me again, and I don't blame them.

I don't think Jak would ever reveal that I'm the Sin Eater to the police. On the news, I saw that there have been copycats, people who have used our "Sin Eater" moniker to get into people's houses and steal from them. It's only been two occasions, but it's out there: the authorities are aware of our existence. He has no proof, but I have no way of showing that he was involved, too.

I should tough it out for Jenny. I should, since her circumstances are my fault. But maybe I could get a regular job somewhere and still send what little money I make to help her, continue to be the anonymous contributor somehow. It won't be nearly as much…but I still want to help.

Despite how terrified I am, I will face everything that I've been avoiding and move on with my life, no matter how hard or painful, no matter what comes my way.

It's the only way to feel human again, and not like the shell of myself that I have become.

Then - Burn

Late in May two years ago, our graduation had come and gone. While it was a big event in our lives, Parker, Jenny, and I spent it in a relatively simple fashion by going to have dinner with our parents at a steakhouse afterwards. Jenny's mother actually showed up during the ceremony, but she declined going to the restaurant with us. Jenny stayed quiet at dinner as she pushed the food around her plate. Even then, almost a whole year later, her mother's actions hurt her.

It had been strangely easy to sneak around with Parker the last two months of our school year. We would mostly spend late nights together, sneaking out of our houses or lying to our parents or Jenny about where we were. My parents trusted me fully, and Parker's mom had eased up on him since she really liked Jenny and me for helping him keep his grades and spirits up.

Meanwhile, Jenny had been dedicated to finding the right college for her. She took the ACT twice to get the best score she could and wrote essays for several scholarship opportunities. All the hard work paid off, since she received a full tuition scholarship to Hartsville University in Texas, where she planned to major in accounting. All of her classes would be covered thanks to her GPA and ACT scores, so all she'd need to worry about would be living expenses and supplies she may need, like textbooks. Jenny worked ridiculously hard, despite the fact that she could probably pass any class with her eyes closed. I always admired her intelligence, the quiet type that didn't brag or show it off, yet somehow it was completely obvious the moment you heard her speak.

"I've read that long distance relationships rarely work out," Jenny said to me one day while we were hanging out at her house. It was a week after graduation, and she had asked me to help dig through her belongings to decide what to take when she moved, though she wouldn't be leaving for another two and a half months. She had already started sorting some things out when she got her acceptance letter back in April: what she wanted to donate, what she wanted to leave or keep. The last step was her closet, filled to the brim with plastic totes of clothes, old books, even some toys from when she was a kid that hadn't ended up in their attic. Anything Jenny didn't have a place for, it was all in here.

"You read that where? The internet?" I asked.

She blushed. I apparently nailed it.

"I'm kidding," I said, dragging a box from her closet. "But really, don't worry too much about internet statistics. Go with your gut feeling."

"I...don't know..." Jenny's sentence trailed off.

"If you aren't sure, then maybe you should go ahead and break it off," I advised. A little voice in my head started whispering to me:

You're a horrible friend. You're just telling her that for your own benefit.

"You think so?" Jenny asked, surprised.

"Yeah, like ripping off a band-aid, you know?"

You're a horrible friend.

"Maybe it would be better in the long run."

You're just telling her that for your own benefit.

Jenny sank into a quiet contemplation while I cursed myself in my head. Any guilt that I should have felt for those past two months suddenly hit me all at once. How could I do this?

"I understand where you're coming from, Jay," Jenny finally said, "but I think I'd like to give it a try. I love him."

I'm glad her back was to me so that she didn't see me wince.

Something had to change soon.

Later that night, Parker and I went to a theater that's thirty minutes outside of our town to see a late movie. We always tried to meet away from the usual hang out spots of the people who knew us, just in case. He had been visiting his sister that day to celebrate his graduation, but I insisted on seeing him that night, no matter what time he got home. The first hug when we met up gave me a faint hope. We can do this, I thought. We could fix it somehow. I barely paid attention to the movie, and as we were walking out afterwards, Parker could tell that there was something wrong with me.

"You okay?" he asked. "You've been kinda quiet tonight."

We reached the edge of the sidewalk. The parking lot was temporarily flooded with people who just came out of their movies, and they stepped around us on the way to their cars.

"We need to talk," I said.

"C'mon," he said instantly. He took my hand and led me to his car, which was parked on the side of the building. He had reversed into the spot, so when we slipped inside, I was staring out at the rest of the small parking lot. I watched people through the windshield pass by laughing, holding hands, a carefree night except for us. I could tell that he was feeling apprehensive. The air had shifted, a nervous energy that couldn't be ignored.

"We need to talk about Jenny." I forced the words before I had a chance to chicken out. "We said you would break it off with her after graduation. It's after graduation now."

"Yeah, I've been thinking about that, too," he sighed. "She and I haven't had any time alone this week."

"I know. But we really need to figure this out." I placed my hand on top of his, avoiding eye contact. "She...she told me that she loves you."

Parker blinked rapidly. "She's never told me that."

"Well, that's what she said today, and I felt like such a shitty friend. She's sitting there saying that long distance relationships usually don't work out, so I tried to hint at her to break up with you so that maybe you wouldn't have to..." I trailed off. Recounting the conversation made me feel nauseous.

Parker blew air between his lips, his eyebrows raised.

"You did that for me?"

"Well yeah, I thought it might save you some trouble. Maybe you wouldn't have to be the bad guy. My mistake was trying to find the easiest way out of a complicated situation because I feel so damn guilty."

Parker pulled me closer and wrapped me in his arms.

"It will be okay," he whispered. "We've been trying to do the right thing. Don't give yourself such a hard time."

I lifted my face to his. "How can I not give myself a hard time?"

"By realizing that this was the only way to make everything easier on her," he answered. "I love you, and if I suddenly announced that months ago, it would have destroyed her. She may have cut us out of her life. Who knows, her grades might have gone down, and then she wouldn't have gotten that scholarship."

I fell silent. How can someone simultaneously be right and wrong at the same time?

"I'll break it off with her soon, the next time we can actually be alone," Parker said. "I'll tell her it's because she's moving. If she's already mentioned to you that she's worried about us because she's leaving, then it shouldn't be a surprise if I feel we should break up over it."

I nodded against his shirt. It did make sense. Jenny's a sensible person, way more sensible than I've ever been. She will understand. She has to.

"Then when she's officially moved, we can tell her that we want to be together," I replied, feeling more confident in this plan. "That gives her a couple of months to digest the break-up, and she'll be far away at college with way more to think about than us."

I felt lighter than I did at the beginning of the night. This will work. We have it all figured out, and I knew Jenny was strong enough to get through it. I could be with the boy I loved and still keep my best friend. In my relief, I leaned in and kissed Parker deeply, both of my hands tangled in his hair. He pulled me closer, and I got lost in the embrace and the feeling of his lips on mine. When we pulled away, flushed and smiling, I turned and noticed someone standing a few feet in front of the car, staring at us through the windshield.

It was Bill, Jenny's father.

Shit.

His face was locked in surprise with his mouth hanging open, and it looked like he'd frozen mid-step. A woman approached him. I saw her glance over at us, then back at Bill. She lightly touched his shoulder. His lips barely moved to mutter something to her, his eyes still on us. A tight smile played across her lips, a look of uncertainty, but she walked forward to a car and unlocked it to get inside. Bill began walking toward Parker's car more confidently, as if he'd made up his mind about something.

Shit, shit, shit. No, no, no.

Parker swallowed. I could hear his shallow breathing, in and out rapidly. We didn't say anything to each other, and we instinctively retreated as far apart as possible to our opposite ends of the car. When

Bill reached the driver's side, Parker inserted the key into the ignition so that he could lower the window.

"You will break up with my daughter tomorrow," Bill said the instant the window was down.

"...S-sir?" Parker stuttered.

"You will break up with my daughter tomorrow," Bill repeated. His fury was only evident in his voice; the rest of his face was convincingly stoic. "And you."

His eyes settled on me. I felt myself crumple, wishing to disappear from his intense gaze.

"How long has this been going on?"

My lips were quivering. I wanted to lie, to claim it was just a one-time mistake that happened tonight. He wouldn't believe me, though. Why would he, after what he saw?

"Since April," I answered weakly.

"You will tell her," Bill commanded. "You will tell her everything. You have tomorrow. If it isn't done by then, I will take care of it for you and make sure she never sees either of you ever again."

We nodded in unison, unable to look at him.

"Jennifer deserves far better company," he spat at us. "So at least do the right thing by telling her the truth."

He walked away stiffly and didn't look back. Parker and I stared straight ahead and watched Bill as he climbed into the passenger side of the car the woman entered a few minutes ago. Even after they were gone, we continued to sit in painful silence. I was so shocked that I couldn't even cry, despite how much I needed the release. I wondered who the woman was, what they were doing all the way out here, but the answers to those questions were ultimately meaningless. All that really mattered now was the inevitable storm before us, a guaranteed chaos that we were being forced to walk into.

"If you break up with her tomorrow, I'll tell her about us after," I said. My voice sounded hoarse. It hurt to push the words out.

Parker turned toward me, the first time he'd looked at me in ten minutes.

"What? ...Are you sure? Shouldn't it be both of us?"

"I'm sure. The breakup part is going to be hard enough for you to deal with. It's two big punches in one day," I explained. "So I figure it's fairest to split it up."

"But...Jayde, that doesn't make any sense," he argued, but I interrupted him.

"Please," I said, closing my eyes. The tears finally formed and slid down my cheeks. "I know we both had a hand in this, but I should talk to her alone. I started this, and I think it's only right that I finish it, too."

I shifted in my seat to look him in the face.

"I know it's dumb," I admitted, "but I just want to share this one last thing with her. To get a chance to really explain."

He smiled, a brittle and bittersweet one. "It's not dumb at all."

I sniffled. "Thank you. Though it all seems ridiculous anyway, because...because..." I stuttered for a moment, and a sob made me shudder all through my body. "Because I know that no matter what, I'm going to lose her."

I began to cry softly, feeling the loss and heartache of what I know was going to happen. Parker pulled me into his arms and ran his fingers through my hair. Normally, this was comforting, but I felt the urge to pull away. However, I forced myself to stay. It wasn't his fault that I was feeling so horrible. I never wanted to be this selfish, yet there I was, and look what it had gotten me. My stomach was in knots, and I was vaguely reminded of being a little kid that was caught in a lie about something trivial, like sneaking an extra cookie or breaking a vase. It was a shameful feeling, knowing that my parents were disappointed, being lectured by adults when I thought I was smart enough to make my own decisions.

"Let's get you home," Parker said in a soothing voice.

But it wasn't soothing at all. For the first time in my life, I didn't want to go home.

Instead, I wanted to run away and never look back.

* * * * *

The next day, as promised, I went to Jenny's house after Parker called to tell me that he had broken up with her. Bill let me inside and informed me that Jenny was in the backyard. I stood in front of the door leading outside and stared at the doorknob. Just open it, I thought. Do it, you coward. Bill was sitting a few feet away at the kitchen table, sipping coffee. When I turned my head, our eyes met. He was watching me.

I don't want to do this. It felt wrong, but I knew it was only because I was afraid of the consequences. Somehow, I never envisioned this moment, because I was so sure that our plan would work. What an idiot I was.

Finally, I closed my eyes, took a deep breath, and reached to open the door. I spotted Jenny in the yard by their makeshift fire pit. Jenny and I begged for a bonfire at her house after our school had one for Homecoming our freshman year. We weren't allowed to attend, since it was only for the juniors and seniors. Bill, as usual, did exactly as Jenny wanted, and immediately built a small fire pit in the backyard. It's really only a big circle of bricks stacked up on one another, but it has served us well. We've sat around fires on cold nights, made ridiculously melty S'mores, and even had a sort of camping night where we stayed in a tent, but we eventually came inside at 2:00AM once the fire died and we got too cold.

She had a tiny stack of papers and two small notebooks sitting on the bricks, and she held a lighter in her hand. When she heard my footsteps, she turned abruptly with an irritated look on her face. However, when she saw that it was me, her eyes lit up. She always looked happier when she saw me, and that made me sad, knowing that what I was about to confess was going to make her hate me.

"Jay? Were we supposed to hang out today?" Jenny asked. She looked exhausted. "I totally forgot, I'm so sorry."

"No, no," I said, stuffing my hands into my pockets. "We didn't have plans. I just came to check on you."

"I guess Parker told you."

"Yeah…he did."

"And what did he say?" She sat and handed me one of the notebooks on the fire pit. "Here, tear out all the pages in this," she commanded as she ripped pages out of the other one. She stacked them haphazardly next to her, and some of the pages trembled as the wind blew. I had never seen her so angry. I did as I was told and started ripping pages out as well, making my own little pile.

"He said you guys broke up," I replied. I wasn't sure what else to say at the moment. My brain was working in overdrive trying to find the best words, but those didn't exist in situations like this.

"Correction: he broke up with me," Jenny said.

I treaded carefully. "Did he…tell you why?"

She huffed. "Vaguely. At first he tried to say that it was because I was going away to college soon. But when I told him that was a crappy reason, he told me some cliché bullshit about how we don't have much in common and how we just 'aren't clicking'…whatever that means."

She bent down to pick up some pages that had fallen on the ground. "But when I told him to give me the real reason and to stop making up excuses, he just froze. He kept babbling that he just wasn't 'feeling this anymore' and that he didn't want to lead me on any longer."

"Um, sometimes people can fall out of love, right? Maybe that's what happened?" I didn't know why I was saying this. I should have been telling her the truth, that's what I was there for.

"No, he's just fucking me over like every other thing that's happened in the last two years," she growled, throwing the lighter down.

In all the years I'd known her, Jenny had never cussed. I've tried to goad her into it at times, because I thought of how funny it would be to hear her sweet, little voice say a curse word. I never thought I'd hear them for the first time like this: me standing and staring, frozen in fear of what would happen, her anger tearing through me with every word. She would surely rip me to pieces, just as she had done to all that paper. I finally looked at the notebook in my hands and had a realization.

"Are these…your diaries?" I asked, stunned.

"Yes," she said. Exhaling, she reached for the thrown lighter, then smoothed her hair down. "I'm going to burn them."

"You can't be serious!" I cried. "Don't you want to save them? I know I'd be upset if something ever happened to my journals."

"No. Why should I save them?" She held up a page. "These are just reminders of everything. My mom's gone and barely acknowledges me, Laurie acts like I don't exist, and now Parker's leaving me, too?" Her eyes filled with tears, and she slumped back down on the bricks. "What is so wrong with me that everyone keeps leaving?"

I embraced her tightly, wondering how the hell I was supposed to break this girl's already broken heart. I turned my head and saw Bill standing in the window, watching us.

"There's absolutely nothing wrong with you. Do you hear me?" I said, and she shook her head. "You're the best person I've ever met, Jenny. Really. All of them, they don't deserve you." I took a deep breath. "I…I don't deserve you."

She let out a half laugh, half sob, then suddenly stood up again.

"Jay, you and my dad have been the best people in my life for as long as I can remember. Now shut up with that nonsense and help me set this shit on fire."

What could I do? I was in a daze, desperately wanting to do what she desired, to make her happy. How could I possibly drop this bomb now, after what she's said? But how was I going to explain if I didn't say anything? It would be better coming from me.

Being lost in my thoughts zoned me out for a moment, and she had been talking still. I barely caught the end of what she was saying: "—just rained, though, so I don't know if we could make a big fire or anything. The ground is still wet."

She tilted her head, looking like she couldn't decide if she should be angry with me or not for neglecting to listen in her time of need.

"Uh…Jay? Hello? Where are you right now?"

I finally snapped back into complete awareness. "Oh! I'm…I'm sorry. It's just…I'm surprised."

"About me and Parker?" She shrugged. "When he was saying that we 'weren't clicking' or whatever, I figured that you would have been able to predict it before it even happened."

"What do you mean?"

"Duh, you're our best friend. You know us both better than anyone, you probably saw this coming from a mile away." She smiled sadly. "Maybe this is my punishment, for doing this to you. I'm so sorry. It was wrong of me to go after him in the first place."

"Jenny, no…"

She held up her hand to silence me. "I know you dealt with it. I know you forgave me. But it still doesn't excuse what I did. You deserve better, and I deserve for him to leave me."

I stared down at the ground and wiggled my toes in my shoes. She really was going to hate me. It was like standing on the edge of a cliff, and I knew I needed to jump soon. I figured I may as well go down after helping her one last time. Honestly, burning things sounded fitting, like maybe if we burned those pages together, it could be a cleansing memory we have of each other, a bittersweet finale of heartbreak for the both of us. I stood and grabbed the lighter from her.

"There's my girl," she said proudly. She picked up a few papers from her pile of diary pages and handed them to me. "I just want to be done with all of it."

I touched the flames to the edges of the paper, taking my time. I wanted to see every tiny bit turn brown slowly and watch the smoke rise in a white, thin line.

"There's so much more out there, you know?" Jenny continued. "College, new people, jobs...you really like your job at the art store, right? I bet I'd like something like that..."

I heard the words, but her voice suddenly took on a muffled quality, as if she was speaking through a thick cloth. The paper continued to burn, and my eyes were fixated on the flame making its way to the ink. My heart was beating in my head, pounding relentlessly, and my hands shook. Jenny droned on, and I tried to make myself listen. I didn't want her to think I was ignoring her, but it was hard to hear her at that moment.

When the fire began to eat away at the ink on the page, she said:

"Jayde...I just want to forget all of it, everything. I want to start over."

Her voice reverberated in my head, and I felt it in every inch of my body, all the way down to my toes. Jenny's eyes glazed over.

My last thought as the whole page turned to ashes, as Jenny was falling to the ground:

Please...don't forget me.

I stared at her crumpled body, frozen in fear. Tears ran hot down my cheeks, but I didn't wipe them away. There was a surge that ran through my body, electric and terrifying. Right after that, all of a sudden, Jenny fell to the ground.

Bill was outside now, pushing by me to get to Jenny. He felt for her pulse as he dialed 911 on his phone, half-cried his address into the receiver, pleaded with the operator for help.

He looked up at me with wild, worried eyes, like he just realized that I was still standing here.

"What happened?" he demanded.

"I don't..." I hesitated, stuttering through tears. "I don't know!"

The ambulance was there within minutes, and I watched as the paramedics loaded Jenny onto a gurney. They let Bill ride in the back with her and informed me of what hospital they were taking her to. I ran to my car, confused, worried, wondering what the hell just happened.

Please be okay, Jenny. Please.

Now- Fall

"Uh…hello?" I hear. Then again: "Hello? Earth to Jackie?"

…Jackie?

Oh. That's who I am right now.

I blink my eyes rapidly until they focus again. I'm standing in front of a food truck that specializes in fancy grilled cheese sandwiches, and the man in the window is tapping his fingers on the counter, awaiting my order. The voice who woke me is Amber, and she's laughing. She pushes me forward.

"Come on, or he'll spit in your food!" she jokes.

The man's expression softens. "I only do that to the rude customers." He grins at Amber. "I'd never do that to a pretty young lady like you."

Amber clears her throat.

"Jackie," she says, her voice too loud, "will you order your food so this nice man can do his job, please?

"Aw, you're pretty nice yourself, sweetheart. If your boyfriend weren't sitting over there, I'd snatch you up." The man grins and winks at her. Amber keeps her composure as best she can, but I see her shifting to stand behind me as his eyes wander over her. He's got to be at least twice our age, if not older.

"Uh…the garlic provolone, please," I say.

The man barely acknowledges me as I hand him my debit card. Amber is turning red and staring behind us, pretending to be intensely interested in Aiden looking at his phone a few feet away. It's kind of cute, her blushing. She doesn't seem like the type who would blush so easily. I don't say that to her, though, since she isn't liking the attention she's receiving already. The man tells us (and by us, I mean Amber) that our sandwiches will be ready in a few minutes. As we walk away, Amber loops her arm through mine and exhales dramatically, as if she had been holding her breath.

"God, that was awkward!" she says.

"What was awkward?" Aiden looks up immediately from his phone. I can see his ears practically twitch in excitement at possibly hearing a story that is embarrassing to his sister. I suspect he will hold this over her head for quite a while.

"The sandwich dude was being all creeptastic over Amber," I answer as we sit down with him at a picnic bench. This park is across the street from the elementary school playground that Parker and I came to together years ago, where he told me that he believed that all things happened for a reason. I can even pick out the exact swings that we sat in from here. Thankfully, the siblings chose to sit at the concrete picnic tables over here on the other side, next to the tennis courts. Amber sits across from Aiden, and I slide in beside him.

To my amazement, Aiden doesn't laugh, but instead goes into protective big brother mode. "I could stab his face with that plastic fork on the ground over there."

"No!" Amber laughs. "It wasn't that bad."

"If you say so," Aiden shrugs.

I need to concentrate on what's happening in front of me versus letting my mind wander, as I did earlier in front of the food truck. My nerves are completely shot since I decided that tomorrow will be my last client with Jak. I keep worrying over what to say, how to say it, his reaction, what I'll do after it's all over…

No, brain. Stop it.

Concentrate on the people in front of me…right here, right now.

"Orders up! Numbers 56, 57, and 58!" the food truck man calls out.

"Wow, that was fast," I say. Amber and I stand to grab our orders.

"No, no, you girls stay here. Allow me," Aiden smiles deviously. Amber and I hand him our receipts and watch him walk up to the truck. I think I see a flicker of disappointment on the man's face. Aiden balances the three sandwiches and three bags of chips on his arms masterfully. I guess being a waiter helps you learn such things, as I would have dropped them after the first two steps.

"That dude is old enough to be our dad, Amber," Aiden says when he gets within earshot.

"Yeah, it's kind of gross," she replies, a disgusted look on her face. She opens her chips and pops one into her mouth. "But it happens a lot."

"Same with me," I say. "I always wondered if I'm just a magnet for the older men, but it seems it's a thing that happens everywhere."

"You should see all the creeps I have to save Amber from at the restaurant," Aiden says after he swallows a bite of his sandwich.

"Uh…'save me from'? I think I do fine on my own," Amber protests.

"You know all those times when you're dealing with a table, and I call you back for something? Usually you complain that I didn't really need you for whatever I'm asking. That's when I'm trying to do you a favor and pull you away from someone being too 'friendly' towards you."

"Wait…" Amber says. "So like last week, when you asked me to come to the back because you couldn't find more salt for the tables?"

"Or that time," Aiden begins, barely containing a laugh, "when I called you all the way to the back just to show you a picture of a sloth I found."

"Aiden!" Amber exclaims. "You don't have to protect me all the time! I'm only a year younger than you, I'm not that helpless!"

"So this sloth picture," I interrupt, "was it like, a funny one, or something at least related to a past conversation or anything?"

Aiden laughs harder, slapping his hand on the table. "That's the best part! It had nothing to do with anything!" He takes a deep breath. "I was like 'Amber, I really need your help back here!,' and after she followed me to the back, I pulled out my phone and said 'You HAVE to look at this sloth hugging a teddy bear…' The LOOK ON HER FACE, it was the best. Holy shit, she was so mad."

"Congratulations, you are a real-life troll," I say as I pat his shoulder.

"The internet kind and the bridge dwelling kind," Amber smirks.

"It would be the most tastefully decorated bridge, that's for sure," Aiden says. He eats the rest of his sandwich in a single bite, while Amber and I are only halfway done with ours.

"Speaking of guys old enough to be our father," Amber says, "Aiden told me that he regaled you with the fun little story about our father last night." She glares at Aiden, then turns towards me. "Thanks for not running the other way."

"Run? Why would I run?" I inquire, baffled.

"Because people have before," she shrugs.

"If people run away from real problems, then that's their flaw," Aiden declares. "I don't get why you're so secretive about it. You're internalizing it."

"I'm not-" Amber pauses, inhales slowly. I again feel like I'm witnessing a conversation that I shouldn't. "I'm not internalizing. I've dealt with it, I'm over it. Broadcasting something like that just freaks people out, and I'd prefer to concentrate on my future versus recounting my past to everyone I meet."

"It didn't freak me out," I chime in sheepishly.

"It did a little." Aiden's smile is crooked and teasing me, but I don't feel like being teased on this topic

"I was just surprised."

"Jackie, don't feed the troll. You're fine," Amber reassures me. "You have a right to whatever reaction you had. The fact that you came out today means that you still want to be friends with us despite our damage, which is really cool of you."

I smile and take a bite of my sandwich.

"See? It all worked out in the end!" Aiden takes his empty container and bag of chips to a trash can a few feet away.

"This sandwich is really good," I say, attempting to change the subject. "I didn't realize how good pretzel bread could be as sandwich buns."

"Right? It's amazing," Amber nods. "They're my favorite food truck around here, despite the older guy trying to flirt with me every time."

I chuckle. "He probably thinks you come to his truck so much because you're totally into his grey mustache."

"Oh yeah," Amber says, rolling her eyes. "I'm all for guys who were probably in their thirties when I wasn't even born yet."

"You two are slower than, uh…" Aiden hesitates. "Something really slow. Like that sloth I showed Amber."

"Good one," I say.

"Give me a break, I didn't sleep very much last night." Aiden places his hands on his hips, imitating a superhero pose. "My wit is not invincible, as most would believe."

Amber mouths "wit" to me and does air quotes.

Aiden shouts "I saw that!" while sticking a finger into her mustard, and he reaches across the table to try to give her a mustard mustache. When she backs away just in time, he turns to me instead. Before I know it, he has an arm wrapped around me and is smearing mustard on my face. I shriek, attempting to wriggle free, but he's too strong. When he releases me, I sputter and grab napkins from our pile in the center of the table.

"What was that for?" I shout.

"You were giggling, that makes you just as responsible." He grins, so proud of himself. I take a sizable glob of mustard onto my finger and smear it on his face when he looks away.

"Why, you little…!" He grabs my hands and wrestles with me, trying to make my face even more of a mustardy mess. Amber clears her throat.

"Excuse me, children. Can we go now, please?" she laughs.

Our next stop after lunch is Fox Creek. It's a place I've been many times before, so I have to pretend to not be as familiar with the area. Despite that, I'm still excited. The creek is deep, wide, and lined with slippery rocks. Many people come to swim and sunbathe, but most like to test their bravery; there's a long, cylinder-shaped collection of rocks with a stream of water running down that is used as a slide. It can be a bit dangerous. If the person sliding leans over too much, they could fall a few feet into the water, possibly headfirst. Some people don't even bring a float, so they gain a ridiculous amount of cuts and scrapes on the way down. I've seen some people show off their injuries after sliding, though I don't understand how hurting yourself is impressive.

When I was five, I begged my mom to let me slide like all the other people, but she said no. I can hear her voice clearly, even now years later, gently telling me "You can when you're older, honey. It's too dangerous." I waited until she wasn't looking and sprinted towards the slide. She shouted my name and chased after me. I pumped my legs furiously but clumsily, since I wasn't weaving my way very skillfully through all of the other visitors. Right when I reached the edge, ready to take the plunge, my mother scooped me up and away from the slide. Some onlookers seemed amused, while others had a face of pity for me. Poor little girl, they probably thought, not mature enough yet to take the fall.

As we pull up to the creek, the slide is in view. I watch a younger boy and girl crowd onto a small float and coast downwards. The boy is even brave enough to wave his hands in the air. I think about that childhood moment, of me being so young and courageous, running willingly up to an edge...while now, I'm nervously thinking of the impending job tomorrow with Jak and how I'm so unwilling to take a fall now. Even in Jenny's backyard, when she was burning her diaries, I was too scared to jump, to accept whatever consequences that might have come.

It is a beautiful day. White, fluffy clouds float lazily on the skyline while the sun peeks out from behind. The rays shine through the trees and into the water, causing it to sparkle. I breathe in deeply, enjoying the earthy smell of everything around us. The relaxing rhythm of the creek's gushing waters becomes louder the closer we get, and my heart beats slower, calming at the sounds. Aiden carefully leads us around other people's towels and belongings, then instructs us to get in front of him to climb a rugged set of rocks to reach an empty spot above us.

"It's not a fun climb," he tells me as he gently places a hand on Amber's back to keep her from falling, "but it's got the best view of the whole place."

He's right, it is quite a rough climb in our flip flops, but I understand what he means. Nobody wants to come up this far, so we have the top of this massive rock all to ourselves. Our belongings won't be bothered, and we can scout out the best places to swim from up there. We reach the top with a celebration of high fives and victorious whooping. Some others below hear us making a ruckus and clap and cheer back. Amber leans over to give them a thumbs up, which leads to more cheering. Meanwhile, Aiden lays out our towels to warm in the sun. The water here is usually cooler due to all the shade from the surrounding trees, so having a nice, toasty towel to dry off with will be heavenly.

I had to dig through all of my usual luggage, but thankfully I found the one bathing suit that I carry around with me in case I feel like swimming at my hotels. It's also my favorite: a pair of deep blue shorts with pink buttons, and a white and blue striped top with pink strings to tie around my neck. I hadn't used it in a while, but I was grateful to find it. Amber offered to let me borrow one of hers when I mentioned I may not have a suit to swim in, but I wouldn't fill it out as well as her. Amber is taller than me, and she has curves that I wish I had. I remove my shirt and shorts that I'm wearing over my bathing suit, extremely aware of how fit she looks, while I am mostly skin and bones. Her vibrant blue hair looks amazing in the sun, and it makes her green eyes stand out even more. Maybe someday I can try to emulate her style a little and dye my hair. We weren't allowed to have "unnatural" colors in school, but maybe once I get my life in order, I could dye my hair some crazy color.

We carefully climb back down the rock once everyone is ready to swim. On the way down, Aiden places his hand on my shoulder.

"You look great, you know," he says in a low voice.

"How did you...?"

"Sorry if I'm assuming wrong," Aiden says quickly. "It's just...I've seen that same look a million times before on Amber's face, and then she always sighs and says 'Gosh, I wish I was pretty like her...'"

Upon hearing her name, Amber turns around and waits for us to catch up.

"Well, you're not assuming wrong," I shrug. "Just a passing thought, not a big deal."

"What's not a big deal?" Amber asks.

"Damn it, Aiden," I say, pushing him.

"I should have known it was his fault somehow," Amber smiles knowingly.

"Actually, dear sister, it is not. I just happened to notice that our friend here is feeling self-conscious."

I let out a frustrated sigh. "It's really not that big of a deal."

We have reached the bottom of the climb. Amber and Aiden exchange a glance, then shrug in unison. Aiden walks ahead of us then, leading the way to an empty place in the creek we saw while standing on the rock. Amber lingers behind with me.

"I'm sorry you're feeling self-conscious," she says. I can tell that she is treading carefully, not wanting to upset me.

"Oh, no, it's fine!" I smile, hopefully a good sign to her that they didn't hurt my feelings. "It's just been a while since I've worn a bathing suit, and you look so good in yours. I'm jealous!" Amber doesn't answer right away. I wonder if she's not used to those kinds of compliments.

"Thank you," she says.

I decide that I need to summon an old skill I used to have in high school: pep talking. Jenny was always so down on herself, and part of me believes it was because of her mother. I always took special care to notice and make energetic conversation about any sort of change she made to her looks, since she was often too scared to do so. When she dyed her hair for the first time one summer and almost cried, I sat her in front of a mirror and showed her how much the redder color brought out her eyes and freckles. When she tried out fake nails and broke them almost instantly, I insisted that this happened because her natural nails were too beautiful to cover up anyway. On the extremely rare occasion that I saw her in a dress, I would gush over how jealous I was of her nice legs. It always seemed to cheer her up, and I didn't even have to lie. Jenny was beautiful, inside and out.

Jenny is beautiful. Present tense, is. I'm sure she still is, even though I haven't seen her in two years. She never seemed to acknowledge it, so I became her cheerleader.

"What do you do to stay in shape?" I ask. "You've got some muscle. It's the perfect amount."

I think I see a slight, proud smile on Amber's face, but she's trying to hide it.

"Oh, not a lot. I joined a gym when we moved over here, and I've been taking kickboxing classes."

"Not a lot? That sounds exhausting to me!" I laugh.

"It is," she admits, "but you get used to it. It's a lot of fun, I promise. You just have to make sure to explain to them that you don't want to do kickboxing competitively. My instructors have been bugging me about joining their teams lately."

"That means you're really good at it, though!"

"Oh, she is," Aiden chimes in. "She could kick my ass with her kickin' kickbox kicks."

"I don't think you get points for alliteration if it's the same word over and over," Amber jokes.

We reach the unpopulated edge of the creek, where the talking and splashing of all the other visitors are only distant sounds. I dip my toe in; it sends shivers up and down my body.

"If you're good, why don't you join any of the teams?" I ask Amber. Aiden has already started to wade slowly in the water, making exaggerated sounds of suffering from the cold. I turn to face her. "Hone the skills, literally kick some ass...sounds cool to me."

"I'm not a competitive person," she says. "I do it for me, that's all I need."

She brushes past me, and I know that the conversation has been gently but firmly ended. She doesn't have to say it for me to understand, as I can infer why she takes the classes: the helplessness she most likely felt at the hands of her father, and not wanting to ever feel that way again.

I see that Amber is now wading in after Aiden, so I take a deep breath and follow. The water isn't as bad as I thought it would be, but it takes quite a few minutes for my body to adjust to the temperature with every step. Aiden and Amber have stopped a few feet ahead, their backs to me and heads bent over something.

"What're you doing?" I ask through chattering teeth.

"Aiden brought this bag that's supposed to protect your phone in water," Amber answers. "We want to make sure it's sealed correctly before we dunk it."

"Looks fine to me," Aiden declares. "Let's do this thing!"

He tosses his phone into the creek a few feet away. I gasp.

"What if you lose it?" I cry.

"I won't," he chuckles.

We spend quite a bit of time taking videos and pictures underwater with Aiden's phone and studying the results. Sadly, we discover that the water is far too murky to get any clear shots. We can see down to the bottom with our naked eye, but a phone in a bag moving around rocks and dirt? Not so much. After all the shuffling and movement, I suddenly realize that I'm not cold anymore. In a rare moment of bravery, I hold my nose and submerge myself completely under the water. I stay under for a few seconds, feeling the coolness tingle all over my body. Any sounds are muffled now, and my hair flows gracefully in all different directions. When I was little, I always imagined that this must be what a mermaid feels like at all times: lightweight, smooth, carefree, and beautiful. I wondered if they ever got sick of listening to swishing water and if they could talk to the aquatic animals.

When I reemerge, Aiden exclaims "Go Jackie! You took the plunge!"

I smile slowly, the corners of my mouth still quivering a bit from the cold water.

"Yeah...I did."

"Well, guess we should follow her example," Aiden says, looking at Amber. "On a count of three?" Amber nods, and they begin to count down together: "Three...two..."

Before reaching one, Aiden hops over and dunks Amber into the water.

She comes up sputtering and screaming: "You...you jerk! I should've known!" Aiden runs away, sloshing and slipping over the rocks on the riverbed, laughing so loud that I'm pretty sure I see a few heads turn in our direction in the distance. Amber begins to chase him, and I join her. We manage to tackle him into the water, our justice served. Aiden is somehow still laughing as he surfaces.

"I just swallowed," he gasps out, "so much water. Oh my God." He shakes his head like a dog, and the water flies everywhere, sparkling in the sun.

"That was such a Baywatch moment," I say, making a little frame with my pointer fingers and thumbs. "Wish I had recorded a slow-motion video of that."

We spend an embarrassingly long amount of time trying to perfect slow motion runs in the water while shaking our glistening, soaked hair. I can barely breathe from all the running and laughing. Finally, we agree to take a break and settle down on some rocks nearby. Aiden and Amber find a larger rock to sit on together, but I decide on one that is half submerged so that I can have most of my body in the water. I want to keep myself used to the temperature of the water so that I don't have to readjust once we start swimming again.

The siblings are using each other's backs as a prop to lean against. Another drawing mood strikes in my head looking at them. Their pose and the scenery would be interesting to draw: two people, back-to-back, one looking up towards the sky (Amber) and one looking down at his feet (Aiden). Jagged rocks surround them, which are then contrasted by the smooth water running over in gentle streams. I would make sure to draw the little details, like the ripples at Amber's feet and the water dripping from Aiden's hair. From my angle, they're blocking the sun, so they're slightly silhouetted as well. Some large, dark shadows, but just enough light that you can see their expressions, which is satisfying to me since I love drawing faces.

Once we get back to swimming, the second half of the day is much more relaxing. We practice floating down the creek on our backs, arms and legs splayed, watching the clouds drift by. I catch glimpses of wildlife everywhere: squirrels scurrying up trees, tiny fish swimming with the current, two frogs croaking away on the banks. Aiden even finds a group of turtles, all no bigger than the palm of my hand, resting on some rocks farther down the creek, away from all the people. Amber expresses the desire to lay out and tan a little before the sun starts to set, so we eventually make our way back to the towels. Sadly, we didn't anticipate how hot they would be, but we deal and lay on them anyway.

I don't know why, but I've always loved the feeling of slowly air drying after swimming. It's almost like I can see the drops of water evaporating from my skin. I breathe a sigh of relaxation. The towel underneath me is fuzzy and soft, and the occasional wind feels heavenly. I don't notice until I suddenly come back into consciousness that I drifted off to sleep. My head is killing me, and I clutch it, groaning.

"Good afternoon, sleeping beauty," Aiden jokes. "Did you have a nice cat nap?"

"How long was I out?" I ask.

"Like thirty minutes or so. We have everything packed up," Amber says, folding a towel and stuffing it in her bag.

I'm having a hard time concentrating. My head is swimming, and my stomach lurches with nausea. All I can think to do in response is turn on my side and curl into the fetal position, my arms hugging my stomach.

"H-hey, you okay?" Amber asks in a worried voice.

"I feel...hot...sick..." is all I can manage to say.

Suddenly, I'm being lifted. When I open my eyes, I see that Aiden has picked me up. His face is calm but serious.

"Let's get you back to the car, okay?" Aiden tells me soothingly. There's a part of me that wants to protest, say that I can walk on my own, that I'll be fine...but a bigger part of me is really enjoying being taken care of. I loop my arms around his neck and rest my cheek against his chest, letting my eyes close again. The motion of being carried on the uneven terrain feels a bit like being rocked. The movement relaxes me into a half-conscious state, and I don't even have the clarity of mind to feel silly, like I'm a baby being rocked to sleep. Once we're back at the Jeep, Aiden gently places me in the backseat. I stretch out, appreciating the sizeable, plush cushions. I hear the air conditioner turned on high, while Amber rouses me long enough to get me to take a few sips of water.

A few minutes into the ride, I manage to sit up more to let the cool air blow on me. Amber sees that I'm up and hands me her bottle of water, warning me not to gulp it down fast or it might make me feel sicker. I follow her advice and take small sips while my whole body starts to finally cool down.

"I think you got a little sick from being sunburnt," Aiden says. "You're pretty red on your shoulders and your back."

I bend my neck to study my shoulders, and he's right. Sunburn. I sit up straighter to see my face in the rearview mirror. My cheeks are a little flushed, but overall the only difference is that I have more freckles from being out in the sun. However, it looks like parts of my legs and arms didn't fare as well, since they're as red as my shoulders. No wonder I feel so bad.

"I'm so sorry," Amber frowns. "I forgot sunscreen."

"It's not your fault," I reassure her. "I forgot, too. I don't play out in the sun as much as I used to."

"How're you feeling now?" Amber asks.

"A little woozy and sick still. The water is helping, but my stomach is still churning."

"Let's go by our restaurant," Aiden says. "We can grab some food to hopefully settle your stomach. The sun drained me too, I'm feeling hungry myself."

I lay back and close my eyes, satisfied with this arrangement. My skin is becoming increasingly itchy, and it's hot to the touch. I was never one to get a nice tan; sunburn was always a part of my summers. Even though it's uncomfortable, it's a strangely nostalgic feeling. Various memories flood my mind all at once of summers long past: family trips down to the beach, swimming and biking, afternoons spent outside until the fireflies came out. I float among those warm days filled with the people I love, like I'm still there beside them.

I miss my mom and dad.

I miss Jenny and Parker.

I miss the familiar smells of my old house, of Parker's cologne, of Jenny's candles she always had lit in her room.

I miss being able to share what I was going through with Cadie, even if only through texts. She knew everything that happened and still wanted to talk to me.

My eyes begin to water, and I feel a tear escape and slide down my cheek. I swipe it away as casually as I can. Somehow, these things insist on bubbling up to the surface the more I time I spend with Amber and Aiden. I feel the car turn, and Amber points out a parking spot. Slowly, my eyes open, and I'm thankful that we have arrived at our destination. As we exit the vehicle, I realize that I'm still in just my bathing suit, as are the siblings. We slip on our shorts and T-shirts in the parking lot, while a family walking past glance at us curiously. Aiden is cracking up at the sight of us, since we all have wet spots everywhere from the bathing suits soaking through our clothes.

The restaurant is cool inside, just what I need, though the combination of wet clothes and sunburn makes me shiver. The hostess standing up front smiles widely at the siblings as we enter. Her name tag reads "Hollie."

"You guys just can't stay away, even on an off day." Hollie jokes.

I think Amber gives her a brief summary of our dilemma, since I see Hollie look over at me with a sympathetic frown. I don't hear what Amber says, as I'm too busy trying to keep my teeth from chattering. Hollie leads us to a table closest to the kitchen, but when I look behind me, Aiden is gone.

"Devon will be with y'all in a second," Hollie says. I see her take her place in front of the doors. Aiden enters the restaurant again, though I don't even know when he left. The girl leans over the podium she's standing behind, brushing wisps of hair behind her ear. A flirtatious stance, from what I can tell. A small bit of jealousy dances in my stomach and works its way into my throat. I'm surprised at myself, then disgusted. That girl is allowed to flirt with Aiden, and Aiden liking her back is perfectly fine. She's pretty, and she seems very nice. I turn stiffly to look at my menu, feeling ridiculous in my envy over how well-adjusted Hollie seems, how he deserves someone normal like her. Suddenly something is dropped on my head, and everything goes dark. When I pull it off of me, I see that it's a hoodie.

"Sorry that it isn't clean," Aiden says to me. "It's all I had in the back of the Jeep." I stare at him quizzically, so he continues: "You looked cold."

"Oh." I don't know what to say. "Thank you." The hoodie is soft and smells like a mix of cologne and grass. He must have worn this outside a lot last fall, probably on all of his trips into the woods that he mentioned yesterday.

Amber and Aiden already know what they want to order, which makes sense. They must have tried the whole menu by now. I knew what I wanted from the moment I walked in as well, but I pretend to read through it slowly, like it's still new to me. They think I've only eaten here once, just a few days ago. Hollie stops by again, and I have to duck my head farther behind my menu so that I won't linger on the fact that she squishes against Aiden in the booth when there's plenty of room on the other side with Amber. She has to leave right after, though, since a family is at the front waiting to be sat.

"She's trying a little too hard today, isn't she?" Amber remarks, eyeing Hollie when she walks away from our table.

"Ah, c'mon, she's a nice kid," Aiden says.

"She's only a couple of years younger than you," Amber counters.

"She just graduated from high school. That's a kid, in my opinion." Aiden keeps his eyes locked on his phone.

"You know she looooves you," Amber teases.

Aiden shrugs. It seems like he would prefer to drop the subject.

"Um. So do you guys like working here?" I ask. Not the most subtle way to get Amber to leave this train of thought, but it's all I can think of. Amber looks at me with crinkled eyebrows and a crooked, knowing smile.

"You're trying to save him, huh?" she says.

"Or maybe," Aiden cuts in, "she really is interested in our thrilling restaurant business lives."

"Ha! Thrilling. Right."

"It is thrilling," Aiden argues. "Why, just the other day, I almost dropped a whole tray of food on the ground…but then I didn't."

"There you have it, folks," I exclaim, using my hand as an imaginary microphone, "Aiden the Tray Slinging Champion does it again!" I cup my hands over my mouth and mimic a crowd shouting and cheering while Aiden lifts his hands in victory, addressing the imaginary audience with fake humility.

"To be honest, I did drop a ton of stuff when I first started here," Amber confesses, shaking her head. She begins to tell me about how she had been fresh out of high school and never had a job before, so that nervous energy often made her clumsy when she was training. I'm just glad that she isn't discussing Hollie with Aiden anymore, and I can tell that Aiden is grateful too, as he mouths "Thank you," in my direction. Devon, our server, interjects every now and then to ask if we need anything. It's an incredibly pleasant dinner, filled with stories from the siblings while I eat my delicious wrap (filled with a fresh salsa, cheese, rice, and vegetables, ordered off their Latin half of the menu). This was one of Jenny's favorite meals here, so I enjoy it as much as I can. She always wanted me to try it.

When I'm finished eating, I excuse myself to the restroom. I look in the mirror; the sunburn is really showing and is brightest on my shoulders. I blow my bangs out of my eyes, accepting that there's not much I can do about it now. All I really want to do at the moment is to lay down and fall asleep, but I need to savor this day with Amber and Aiden, no matter how I feel. Hopefully the sunburn will stop stinging soon, or maybe I'll be able to ignore it with time.

I come out of the bathroom to discover that the siblings have paid my bill.

"Let me pay you back," I say, opening my wallet.

"It's our tour and you're the guest, we got you," Amber smiles. "We're also taking you to the store to get some aloe gel. That should hopefully help your skin cool down."

"Well…thank you for the delicious meal! At least let me buy the aloe."

I feel a little silly, since I didn't even think about aloe. Suffering in silence was my strategy, but Amber seems to think of everything.

…Well, except sunscreen. I don't make that joke, though, since she looks so worried about me.

"Think you'll be all right for what we have planned next?" Aiden asks me as we step out of the restaurant.

"That depends on what it is," I tease.

"It's a surprise!" Amber whines. "So seriously, how are you feeling? We'll get you the aloe, but we can take you back to your hotel if you're still feeling crappy."

If I were to be completely honest, I would tell her I still feel pretty sick to my stomach, that I think I ate too fast. Plus, nothing sounds better at the moment than just closing my eyes and letting my head swim into unconsciousness. However, there's not a chance that I would choose sleeping over doing whatever it is that they have planned. I don't know when exactly I'll be able to see them again after today, so every minute counts. When I tell them that I'll be fine and that I'm having an awesome day with them, they both grin that same, wide, teeth-baring smile. Once we reach the grocery store down the street, Aiden volunteers to run in and grab the aloe gel for me. I peel my T-shirt off so that I'm just in my bathing suit top again, since I'll need to reach my back and shoulders. Amber lays our towels along the backseat to make sure that the gel won't rub off into the cloth.

When Aiden returns from the store, he surprises me by telling me to turn around, that he was going to help rub the gel onto my back. I glance at Amber to make sure he's not joking, but she's rooting around in the back of the Jeep, grabbing water bottles from the cooler. I obey and turn my back towards him. The gel is extremely cold at first, so cold that I gasp when I feel it on my skin. His hands are the tiniest bit rough, I guess from working on cars or maybe in the restaurant. It's somehow soothing, though, and I have to force myself not to close my eyes and lean back into him. I distract myself by taking a portion of the gel and gently layering it onto my red cheeks.

Once we climb back into the car, I ask "How long will it take for us to get to this mysterious place that I can't know about yet?"

"Mm, about twenty minutes," Aiden answers.

"Actually, probably a little longer with traffic, since we have to go through downtown. So more like thirty," Amber says.

"And now that I think about it, it's Saturday…so I bet the traffic will be a little backed up," Aiden adds.

"Mind if I grab a power nap, then?" Car rides have always been relaxing to me. I know that if I lean back and allow myself to, I'll drift off and snooze the time away.

"'Course not," Aiden says. "We'll wake you when we get there."

As I close my eyes, I hear the volume of the radio go down. They must be doing that for my sake, and I smile with appreciation. The sounds of the traffic around us begin to fade as I drift further into my slumber. I feel that I'm both awake and asleep somehow. My comfort increases since I can still register the car's movement, when it makes a turn, the tires beneath me, yet it's like I'm dreaming, floating in some unknown place. The dark begins to distort and swirl, forming a rectangle in front of me. I recognize the familiar object: a door. Upon closer inspection, I notice finer details: the bronze doorknob, chipped black paint. My eyes slowly examine my surroundings. I'm on a porch. A sad-looking fern is hunched over next to me, unable to hold itself up. I feel its long leaves brush my arm as I reach to open the door.

When I enter the house, it is dark except for one light burning down a short hallway. I must be here on a job for a client. Sucking in a deep breath to calm my nerves, I push myself forward. There's no turning back now. Jak is standing in the living room with his arms folded behind him. Our eyes lock when I step in. He nods slightly. The client is sitting in a chair in front of a lamp, silhouetted against the backdrop. Their posture mimics the fern's outside: bent and frail, like it could snap and fall over at any moment. I open my mouth to speak…

A loud THUMP travels its way to my ears, and I'm thrown forward, hitting my face on the seat in front of me. I sit up quickly, holding my throbbing nose. Aiden is swearing under his breath, and Amber is holding onto a handle above her for dear life. When I look out the window, all I see are fields of grass. Aiden brings the car to a stop and jumps out all in one motion, while still muttering.

"I told you this was a bad idea!" Amber calls after him, leaning towards the open door.

"What...what happened?" I ask, rubbing my eyes. I am a strange mix of half-asleep and alert. My eyes are heavy, but my heart is beating frantically.

"I think we hit a big rock or something," Amber replies.

"Everything looks fine!" Aiden shouts from outside. He gets back in the car and shuts the door. "I'm glad I didn't bust a tire."

"We would have to learn how to survive on eating dandelions and drinking dew off of grass," Amber says.

Aiden swivels his head around, like he forgot that I'm still here in the backseat.

"Oh shit, that must have freaked you out. I'm sorry," he says to me.

"It freaked me out too, you know," Amber pouts.

"Hey, at least you were awake and had your 'Oh, Shit' handle to hang on to. Jackie got tossed around back there. I felt her hit my seat."

"Excuse me," I laugh, "what's an 'Oh, Shit' handle?"

Amber pulls on the handle that she was previously holding onto.

"This. A lot of cars have them. I'm sure they have some other intended use, but we always figured they were handles to hold onto when you're scared for your life. And what do you do when you think you're going to crash?"

Amber and Aiden simultaneously grab their respective handles and shout "Oh, shit!!"

I laugh pretty hard, despite the pain in my nose making the action unpleasant.

"So...where are we?" I finally ask.

"You'll see," Amber says. "We're almost there, but we had to take a detour."

"There was a cop at the red light where we would normally turn to come up this hill," Aiden explains, "so I took another back road. A cop saw us come up here a few weeks ago, and he followed and told us to leave. I guess we aren't supposed to be here."

Aiden drives cautiously while Amber presses her nose up against her window, watching intensely. I'm happy to see that we hopefully won't have another impact like we did a few minutes ago. The grass underneath the Jeep is tall and unkempt, so it feels like we're on a boat sailing through a sea of undulating green. We make it over the large hill, and I spy lights on the horizon.

My stomach drops.

We're at the same spot that Parker and I went to together, the one that overlooks the airport. I curse myself for not realizing sooner, but he only took me twice. I couldn't have recognized it immediately.

I don't know I'm crying until I hear Amber exclaim "Jackie, are you all right?!"

My hands touch the side of my face, wet with tears. Aiden shifts the Jeep into park abruptly and turns to face me in his seat. Blurry yellow, red, and blue lights are shining in the distance from the airport.

I'm here. I can't believe I'm here again.

"…Jackie?" Aiden says as he hands me a napkin from the glove compartment. Somehow, I will my hand to take it from him, but my mind is still trapped in a fog. Surprisingly, my hands are covered in tiny water droplets. I briefly wonder how long I've been crying.

"Did something happen?" Amber's words drift into my ears. They couldn't have known. Hell, even I didn't know that coming here again would affect me like this. It's like my brain suddenly shut down all at once, and now I'm slowly regaining consciousness. I try to talk, but all that comes out is a strangled sound, which makes me cry even harder. Something hurts deep down. I can't pinpoint exactly where it hurts: my head, my chest, my heart? A chorus of anxieties and guilt flood through me, voices whispering of my betrayal, how I acted on my base desires, which resulted in betraying my best friend.

Parker cheated on Jenny for two months with me. He was finally forced to break up with her, but then she fell into a coma that same day when I erased her memories.

I didn't even have the guts to tell her the truth, that I was the reason for their break-up, that we'd been together behind her back.

Amber and Aiden are still staring at me, wide-eyed and concerned. I can't bring myself to explain yet. My breathing is ragged and labored while my brain keeps shouting "I'm suffocating, I'm suffocating!" Taking deeper breaths is difficult, as if my lungs are refusing the air. I have to get out of this car. It's caving in, it's too small, all eyes are on me, and I can't take it.

Hastily, I grab the car handle and tumble out of the car. The outside air is refreshing; grass and dirt, even the faint smell of lingering gas fumes from a car driving by. My eyes are firmly shut. I can't look at that same horizon without becoming more upset. I feel a hand on my shoulder. Amber is crouching next to me.

"What can we do to help?" she offers.

"Just...c-can't..." I manage to blubber out.

"Can't breathe?" Aiden finishes my sentence for me. He kneels down on my other side, so that I'm surrounded by the siblings. "Would you prefer us to leave you alone?"

"N-no," I sob. "Don't leave."

"Physical contact okay?" he asks. I nod. Amber's hand stays on my shoulder, while Aiden's hand rests on my back.

"I know this sounds s-stupid," I say, "but can you guys just not look at me for a bit?"

I hear them shifting around, but they maintain contact with me. When I glance up, I see that the siblings both have their backs against the Jeep with closed eyes. Their faces look almost peaceful, like they could be drifting off to sleep. Aiden's hand is gently rubbing my back, up and down. I concentrate solely on that motion, letting it take my mind to another, more relaxing place. Steadily deeper breaths fill my lungs, and the sobs begin to lessen. After several minutes, I finally find the strength to turn myself around so that my back is against the Jeep as well. I see Amber's eyes flutter open, but she doesn't turn them towards me. Aiden remains motionless, his mouth slightly open and taking soft breaths. I gingerly wipe my nose and eyes, not looking forward to the inevitable interrogation. A huge part of me wants to talk about it, but I don't want them to think badly of me.

"You'll just hate me," I say, staring at my lap. Aiden's eyes shoot open.

"What do you mean?" Amber asks. She doesn't turn towards me, still trying to respect my wish to not be looked at.

"When you guys eventually get around to asking why I'm crying, when you hear the reason...you'll think I'm an awful person." My voice is strangely steady and firm.

Aiden and Amber glance at each other over my head. They seem to have the ability to communicate without speaking, like Jenny and I used to.

"You don't have to tell us," Aiden says. "It really isn't our business. We just want to help you feel better."

"Not that we aren't curious," Amber confesses, then she quickly adds: "But it's only because we care!"

I chuckle despite myself at her honesty, and with that, some of the tension dissipates. Sighing, I pull myself away from the Jeep to stand up. Turning towards the horizon, I soak in the familiar sights. From what I can see, everything looks the same. The wind rustles the trees as they always have, and the grass is as wild and tall as ever. Even the air smells the same as it did back then. Might as well pull off the band-aid.

"Aiden, do you remember what I told you yesterday? About my best friend and her boyfriend?" I hear him stand and brush himself off.

"Yeah?"

"We have a...similar hill like this where I used to live," I say, barely remembering to lie about that part, "and my friend...she was dating this guy, and I kissed him there for the first time." Breathe in, breathe out. "We snuck around behind her back for a couple months. I still feel horrible about it. The hill reminded me of what I've done, and it overwhelmed me."

Aiden clears his throat. I turn to face them and see that Amber is standing as well. She looks concerned but stays silent.

"So, uh..." Aiden hesitates, scratching at his beard. "When you said yesterday that you were feeling guilty about liking him while he was with your best friend..."

"Yeah," I interrupt. "I omitted a big part of the story." And much more than that. "I'm sorry."

"Don't apologize," Amber speaks up. "You don't owe us anything. It was brave of you to tell us the truth."

"I agree," Aiden says. "Are you feeling okay now, or would you want to go somewhere else?"

I pause, wondering why they aren't berating me. I did something awful, so why aren't they telling me that I should feel bad about it?

"Wait," I say shakily, "why aren't you guys mad at me?"

Amber and Aiden glance at each other, confused.

"Should we be...?" Aiden asks.

"I-I..." I stammer, unable to comprehend what to say in this situation. I laid out one of my worst mistakes, and these people just shrugged it off and asked if I'm okay. Are they pretending to be nice until they can drop me off and never contact me again? Tears form at the corner of my eyes. I try to hold them back, but two small drops slide down my cheek. Amber reaches out and places her hand on my shoulder, but I take two steps backward, giving myself some space.

"I don't deserve your sympathy," I say.

"Why not...?" Aiden asks, drawing out the questioning tone at the end. He's looking at me like I'm a timid, wild animal that could lash out at any moment.

"I did a horrible thing to someone I love. You should tell me that what I did was awful."

"Okay," Aiden shrugs. "What you did was awful." He pauses, looks at me intently. "But that doesn't make you an awful person."

Amber nods. "I agree. Jackie, everyone does crappy things sometimes."

"But I...I can't forgive myself. Why did I do that?" I'm shaking, on the brink of yet another breakdown. When I try to revisit those memories, my brain acts like an old television: unclear and full of static. Making sense of what I did is impossible.

"Because you were younger and less experienced," Amber suggests.

"Because your best friend knew you had feelings for someone and started dating him anyway," Aiden adds.

The trees are swaying together in the wind, dancing about with no cares in the world. I envy them.

"But I can't forgive myself," I repeat. "That still doesn't excuse what I...what we...did."

"You keep saying you can't forgive yourself," Aiden says, his voice coming out as sharp as a knife. "But do you really mean you won't? You're holding yourself in a cage of your own making." I stare back at him in shock as my heart sinks down into my stomach. Amber lightly touches his shoulder, and it's like he breaks out of some sort of trance. He shakes his head.

"I'm sorry, Jackie. I didn't mean that to be as harsh as it came out."

"It's okay," I say. "I mean, you're probably right."

"How about this?" Amber says, stepping forward. "What about your friend? Has she forgiven you?"

The words are rocks scratching my throat as they come tumbling out.

"I haven't told her."

"That's why you feel so bad about it!" Amber exclaims. "It's eating you up. I know it will be hard, but you should tell her the next time you see her."

"I haven't seen her in two years," I say quietly.

Aiden steps forward and breaks his brief silence. "Why?"

Their inquisitive eyes drill into me. I resist the urge to run.

"She was...in the hospital for a while and diagnosed with amnesia," I say. It's the closest to an accurate diagnosis that the doctors could make. Her case baffled everyone for quite some time. With no head trauma or psychological distress to speak of, Jenny's memories seemed to disappear into thin air.

"Wow..." Amber breathes.

"I decided to start traveling with my dad," I continue. My hair blows wildly around my head, as if it's pushing me to stop this charade of lying and half-truths. "I couldn't bear to be around her after what I'd done, and then her losing her memories...so I left."

Amber bites her lip and looks down at her feet. Aiden holds eye contact, his face a mixture of sympathy with an odd hint of understanding. I'm not sure what telling them all of this will accomplish, but I feel like I owe them this much after my breakdown in the car. They've told me so much about themselves, it would feel wrong to leave them in the dark. I'm surprised I haven't tripped up yet, that I'm not confused by the tangled webs of lies that I've weaved.

"How's she doing now?" Amber asks.

"I'm not sure," I admit. "The last time I heard anything was before I left my hometown for good. I know that she's awake and did some physical therapy at the hospital."

"Wow..." Amber says again. "But...if she was in a terrible condition, somebody would have told you about it though...right?" Amber asks. They're both staring at me with pleading eyes now, so sincere and caring that it makes my heart hurt.

"Yes, someone would let me know," I say. Because at least that's the truth.

Silence settles between us. I can tell they're searching for things to say. Before we stretch this uncomfortable conversation further, I find it in myself to make a joke: "So does eating ice cream still fix sad stuff, or was that law changed recently?"

Their expressions soften, and Aiden speaks up after being unusually quiet: "There was a long debate at the White House about trying to vote ice cream out in favor of cookies for times such as this, but ice cream still won by a landslide."

I laugh. It feels good. "Thank God, because I could really use some ice cream right now."

"Your chariot awaits then," Aiden says, gesturing towards his vehicle.

Once we're all in the car, I lean back and close my eyes, letting their voices wash over me. The rest of the night is a blur of an ice cream shop and Aiden and Amber's usual bickering, but it's extremely obvious that they're joking even more than usual to try to cheer me up. I plaster a smile on my face, despite knowing that it's unconvincing. When they drop me off at the hotel after, I'm stumped on what to say.

"Email us soon, okay?" Amber says. "You're leaving tomorrow, right?"

"Tomorrow or Monday, I'm not sure which," I answer. Always keep it vague, my own little motto…and it matters now more than ever, given that I don't know what or where I'll be after tomorrow.

"Well, you remember our promise, right?" Aiden asks. "You said you'd keep in touch. Don't leave us hanging." He smiles, but there's a serious tone underneath.

My heart squeezes. He knows that I'm not going to. I can tell by the way he's looking at me, like he knows that this is actually a goodbye, not an "until next time."

They hug me as best they can from the front seat, and then I step out of the car slowly, wishing the night didn't have to end. As soon as the Jeep is out of sight, fresh tears come pouring out of my eyes. I trudge back to my hotel with blurry vision, half-wishing that I'd bump into someone that would ask me what's wrong, why am I crying? Suddenly I feel as if I could talk and talk for hours.

I didn't tell them enough.

I want to tell them everything.

But there's no use in it. Would they even believe me?

So my real name is Jayde, and I helped my best friend's boyfriend cheat on her with me, but right when I was about to confess that to her, I erased her memories with some weird-ass powers I have somehow! Now I have this creepy job where I erase strangers' memories for money to pay for my friend's hospital bills! Anyway, you want to go get some pizza?

Oh, God. I can't even imagine the looks on their faces.

I flop face first into the hotel's bed when I arrive in my room, and I switch the lamp off beside me without looking. Once the whole room is plunged into darkness, my heart rate slows down. The pillow is wet and gross from my tears, but I don't care. I'm sinking now into slumber, floating downward into oblivion, a place of dreams, an escape from reality.

*****

Parker and I had sex during that time, just once. We both agreed that we wanted to be each other's firsts. My parents were out one night for dinner and a movie, so Parker and I made a "date" of our own. He brought me flowers for the special occasion. I tried to play it cool, but it made me melt inside.

Sex was what I expected in some ways and what I didn't expect in hundreds of other ways. It was awkward but intimate, scary yet breathtaking. We knew we didn't have much time until my parents would be home afterwards, but we laid together anyway for what seemed like a deliciously long time. Parker's breathing was steady and reassuring, and I wanted to stay wrapped up with him forever.

"I love you," he whispered in my ear. I noticed that his heart started beating fast, in time with my own quick pulse.

I turned towards him, my forehead pressed against his.

"I love you, too," I whispered back. He kissed me then, sweet and deep, a kiss of both relief and happiness.

I remember thinking that surely what we were doing wasn't wrong if it was for love. Parker didn't love Jenny, he loved me. We agreed that it wouldn't be fair for him to break up with her until after graduation, so that she would be able to keep a stable head during final exams and while applying to colleges. Then we could wait a couple of months after the breakup to reveal to Jenny that we decided to be together. We figured that she wouldn't be happy at first, but then she would eventually be supportive. That's what friends do.

Things would eventually be okay in the end…because love is never wrong, right?

And it was all downhill from there.

Then- Ritual

The nurses at the desk on the third floor knew me by sight back then, so they offered smiles and waves as I walked by. It was the fifth day in a row that week I'd gone to see Jenny in the hospital. My dad said maybe I should stay home for a few days, take a breather. I understood his concern—I'd been pretty much going from work to the hospital, back to work, then the hospital for the last two weeks now. Home was only for sleeping and the occasional meal. I couldn't do that though. After Jenny fell that day, the ambulance rushed her here to the Clayton Medical Center, and if she was here, that's where I would be, too.

I turned the usual left and almost ran into a girl as she was stepping out of Jenny's room.

"Jayde!" she exclaimed.

"Cadie…?" I said as she enveloped me in a tight hug.

"Of course, who else would it be?" she laughed, holding me at arm's length. "You look great!"

"Sorry, you do too! You just look so different than the last time I saw you."

"Oh…right." She picked up one of her low pigtails, the hair now blonde with purple tips versus the usual chestnut brown that I remember. I admired her impeccable make-up as well, all dark shades of purple and heavy eyeliner.

"C'mon, we have to have lunch and catch up! It's been too long," Cadie said, pulling me down the hall.

"I'm up for it, obviously. But I'm going to go see Jenny real quick, if you don't mind waiting."

She shook her head, like she just remembered where we were. "Of course, duh. That was stupid of me. Meet me at the cafeteria whenever you're ready, just text me if something changes!"

Cadie blew me a kiss and strolled away, humming to herself. I forgot how good it felt to be around Cadie. She brightened up this dim hospital for a moment, but sadly, that couldn't last as I trudged into Jenny's room.

Her face was frozen, expressionless, almost like she could be sleeping. Even though I saw her chest rising up and down, I gently placed my hand there to feel her breathing. Her thin, red hair was spread out on her pillow, mimicking the color of the fire we used to burn her diaries.

There were two chairs in the room, one on either side of the bed. I pulled one up close and slowly lowered myself into it. I felt like I hadn't functioned properly since she fell that day, as if a big part of myself went down with her. I would have given anything for her to be getting ready to go to college, for her to be awake. Even if she wanted nothing to do with me, at least she would still be moving on with her life and not stuck here.

There was a soft knock at the door. I expected Bill or Vivian to enter, but instead, I looked up to find Parker standing next to me.

"Hey..." I said.

"Hey."

We were silent for a couple of minutes, staring down at Jenny together.

"How's she doing?" he asked.

"I'm not sure, I just got here. I don't know where Bill is right now."

"Ah." Parker put his hands in his pockets. "I ran into Cadie. Did you see her?"

"Yeah. Wait...you haven't met her before, have you...?"

He chuckled. "No, but I guess Jenny showed her pictures or something, since she surprised me in the hallway by jumping me for a hug and introducing herself after."

I laughed too. "That's Cadie all right."

Parker grabbed the other chair and placed it next to me.

"How are you holding up?" I asked him.

"As best as I can," he sighed. "You?"

I looked down at my hands. "I'm sorry. I know this is all stupid small talk."

He shrugged. "Still valid conversation. I really am wondering how you're doing."

My right leg bounced up and down. I wanted to get up to pace the room, but his gaze kept me in my seat.

"Why are you being so nice to me?" I whispered.

His mouth was a hard line. "I understand why you need space right now. I've called because I want you to know that I still care about you. But there's no pressure to answer or to hang out."

I bit my lip. Could Parker and I ever feel normal or…right, after all this? Since Jenny was admitted into the hospital, Parker's and my relationship seemed to feel worse and worse. Every time he held my hand or hugged me, I felt nauseous.

"I just don't know how to feel when she's like this, you know? What if she never wakes up?" I finally said the forbidden words that have been in my head, in everyone's heads.

"C'mon, we have to keep hoping," Parker said, scooting closer and wrapping his arms around me. "She's strong and healthy. Even the doctors confirmed that. She'll be back with us soon." He lifted my face with his fingers to look at him. "Jenny needs you to believe in her."

I lowered my head and nodded into his chest. Being in his arms, right in front of her…even though she wasn't awake, it still didn't feel right. I didn't break away immediately though, since I knew it would hurt his feelings.

"I have to go meet Cadie," I told him instead, both a truth and an excuse.

"That's good. I'm glad you get to see her."

"Yeah, it's been…three years now? Jeez, three years since I've seen her." I sat up and stretched. "If Bill comes in and tells you anything, will you let me know?"

"Of course." His smile was weak.

Parker rose and walked out of the room with me, almost like he was escorting a guest from his home. As soon as the door was closed, he took my hands in his.

"Take all the time you need, okay?"

"What if…" I paused and took a breath. "What if this never feels better? What if I can't…"

"Then at least still be my friend," he interrupted, his voice almost a whisper. "I don't want to lose you." He glanced toward the door. "Lose both of you."

I blinked back tears as I nodded, speechless. If I tried to talk, I would cry. He squeezed my hands, and somehow, he seemed relieved and was smiling wider.

"Okay," he said. "Okay."

We stood in the hallway like that, my hands in Parker's, until I felt my phone buzz in my pocket. I took it out, and a text from Cadie was waiting: "You still coming?"

"Cadie," I choked out, holding up my phone.

"Right," he said, releasing my hands. "Do you think…maybe you could handle texting at least? Can I text you tomorrow and check in on you?"

"Yes."

"Will you answer? It doesn't have to be much…"

"Yeah, I will." I managed to smile.

"Have fun with Cadie," Parker replied. He opened his mouth, then closed it and shook his head. "I'll see you later. I think I'll stay with Jenny until one of her parents gets here."

After one last wistful gaze at me, he entered Jenny's room. I wondered what he was going to say before he changed his mind.

The walk down to the cafeteria was a chance for me to pull myself together before I saw Cadie. Her cousin was in the hospital, and I didn't need to give her one more thing to worry about. Parker was right though; we should at least remain friends. It wasn't fair of me to shut him out. I just wish I could make us feel better, so that we could be there for each other. Either way, he didn't deserve for me to ignore or avoid him.

As I entered the small cafeteria, I spotted Cadie immediately. Her hair was so bright, there was no way I wouldn't notice her. The room was set up half like a high school cafeteria and half like an actual restaurant. There was a choice of booths and tables, and the menus were hung all in row over what looked like a professional kitchen. Thankfully, it was a quiet, empty time. When I came in a few days ago, there was so much noise from the numerous people crowding in line that I couldn't think straight. I walked through and asked for an order of fries, something small that I could snack on to hopefully calm my nerves.

"So when did you and Linda get here?" I asked Cadie as I sat down across from her at a booth. I immediately stuffed a fry into my mouth.

"Just a couple of hours ago," Cadie answered, stealing one of my fries. "Her and Aunt Vivian are out at lunch with Bill right now."

"Man...that must be awkward."

Cadie laughed. "God, I bet. I feel the worst for Bill though - he's outnumbered." Cadie leaned forward and grabbed my hand. "But enough chit-chat about the catty adults. I want to know about you."

I stopped mid-chew. "What about me?"

"How long have you known? I'm so happy that I'm not the only one anymore!"

"...Known what?"

Cadie narrowed her eyes at me, assessing if I really was clueless or not. I shrugged in response.

"So you really don't know," she said, deflated. She sat back and crossed her arms.

When I shook my head, she sighed and came over to sit beside me.

"You were there, in Jenny's backyard. You were helping her burn her diaries."

"Uh...didn't you say there was something I didn't know? I know all this, because like you said, I was there."

"Jenny was wearing a grey T-shirt and green sweatpants the day she went into her coma. Flip-flops, too." Cadie was staring into my eyes and leaning closer. "As you burned your first page, Jenny fell."

I stared back, confused. Who told her all this? Most of the details made sense for Bill or her mom to pass on, but why would they tell her exactly what Jenny was wearing?

"I guess you really don't know," Cadie concluded, "but that's good! That means you didn't do it on purpose."

"Do...what...?" I said each word through clenched teeth.

Cadie smirked, then leaned in closer. "You're a Sin Eater."

My left eye twitched, and I couldn't keep the disgusted look off my face.

"Is this some sort of cult you're in? Because if so, I'm not joining."

"Listen to me," she demanded, sounding exasperated. It was pretty funny that she was annoyed, since she was the one who was speaking in riddles. I turned to face her and sat back against the wall, gesturing for her to continue.

"Okay." Her smile was back. "I'm a Sin Eater, too. It means I have the power to look into people's memories, and I can erase them if I want. For example, I looked into your head when we hugged earlier." To my wide eyes, she tilted her head. "Sorry. I was curious about what happened to Jenny, and my mom said you were there! So I peeked."

I was torn between the urge to laugh and the urge to scream at her. Jenny was lying in a hospital bed, and she was in here goofing around like this, making a joke out of it?

"That's how I know what she was wearing. I saw it through your eyes. All I have to do is touch your skin. It takes a little practice, but I can look into your head and pull out any memory I want to see...or just kinda rummage around. That one's more fun. You get to see what that person feels are the most important memories, since they're the easiest to find."

"Cadie...please stop messing with me."

Instead of laughing or yelling, my body opted for crying instead. All I wanted was a normal afternoon with an old friend, but it had to be inside a hospital visiting my other comatose friend, where I also sort of just broke up with my boyfriend...and now said friend was babbling about some weird and creepy supernatural thing that she probably picked up off some television show.

"I'm not messing with you," Cadie replied. Her grin dropped, and her voice lowered. "This is serious. I'll show you."

She grabbed my hand again, and I opened my mouth to protest since it was wet from wiping my eyes.

"Don't care. Shut up for a second," Cadie commanded, closing her eyes.

I swallowed hard and tried to control my breathing.

"Looks like a conversation about Parker," she began, her eyebrows crinkling. "He broke up with Jenny?" She opened her eyes but kept her hand wrapped around mine. "For...you. That's what you were there to tell her that day, right?"

I snatched my hand away. "You must have talked to Bill."

"Bill? What's he got to do with this?" She seemed genuinely confused.

"Let's say you didn't talk to Bill then. Some of those were thoughts," I pointed out. "You said you were able to see memories."

"See and hear them," she countered. "I can hear what you were thinking in those moments."

"Cadie, this is—"

"You asked Jenny not to forget you when you burned that page: *Please, don't forget me.*"

My mouth hung open. There was no way anyone else could have told her that. It was something I recalled often, something only burned into my mind, never repeated outside of my head.

"You actually saw it. All of it." I was saying this out loud, but more to myself, to confirm this seemingly impossible truth.

"I did."

"And you aren't…upset with me?"

"Jesus, Jayde, I just proved to you that I could look into your head, and your first thought is 'Are you mad at me'?" She clasped my hand again. "The whole Parker thing…look, I get it. I have this guy I've been seeing for a while now, and that's sort of how I got him, too. I stole him away from someone else. It would be really fucking hypocritical of me to judge you. Okay?"

I managed a weak nod while staring down at our hands. Was she still looking into my head? It was crazy that I felt nothing while she was doing it. I figured that I'd feel something; a tingle, a chill, anything to show that my mind was being excavated.

"I wanted to talk to you because I was excited that it wasn't just me anymore. But now I see that I need to explain what you're in for. Will you please listen to me now? I can help you." Cadie took a deep breath and grinned. "I guess I'll try to tell you everything the way my grandma told me."

"Your grandmother knows about this?" I asked, surprised.

"Well, yeah. Gran was a Sin Eater too, and she passed her knowledge down to me. It skips a generation, though, so my mom doesn't know anything about it. It was our little secret."

I never got to meet any of my grandparents. Were any of them aware of this when they were alive but didn't get to tell me? Cadie cleared her throat and began to speak.

"Back in the eighteenth century, a Sin Eater was a person who ate a small meal, like bread and wine, that was placed on or waved around someone who died. I know that sounds kinda strange, but sin eating was an old ritual, seen a lot in Europe and then brought over to America later on. The belief was that the one who ate the meal would "digest" the dead person's sins and take them upon themselves to cleanse their soul for the afterlife."

I was quiet, so Cadie continued. She seemed giddy: a wide smile, excitement shining through her hushed voice.

"The worst part was that Sin Eaters were ostracized by society, even after they performed a task for their villages. People saw them as miserable beings who became more evil after every job they performed. I mean, they were apparently taking sins upon themselves, doing these people a service, but the payment was only a crust of bread, maybe a coin or two. And sadly, the Sin Eaters would take what they could get. They were often poor, so a free meal or a little money went a long way."

This sounded familiar. I felt like I'd heard this before. Maybe it was mentioned in a history class forever ago, but I wasn't ever interested in the subject, so I barely listened.

"But Gran told me that over time, the Sin Eaters started to change and gain control of the situation. She said it was almost like evolution, the way certain animals adapt to rough environments. The Sin Eaters developed powers, a real type of…I guess you could call it magic. A new step was added to the process: the Sin Eater would drink and eat over the body as usual, but it was all a trick. As soon as they got their meal, they erased and altered the memories of all who were present, then took what they wanted from the house. It had to be quick; they couldn't steal all of their memories, because, well…you saw what happened to Jenny. Eventually, the village would catch on to houses full of comatose people. So it was a quiet attack, stealthy. My gran says that to this day, these stories are only passed down to Sin Eaters. That's why there's so little information about it out there: we altered our own history."

Cadie was beaming at me, clearly proud of her lineage. Mine must have had Sin Eaters in it too, and not even centuries ago, but maybe as recently as my own grandparents.

"You say…altered, but they'd have to come into contact with skin, right? So they'd walk around and touch everyone? If people found them so deplorable, how did they manage that?" I was still grasping at straws, trying to find what loopholes I could to make this all untrue. "Also, what do you mean by 'what happened to Jenny'?"

"There are some Sin Eaters out there who can actually change people's memories without touch. You did that with Jenny." Cadie picked another fry and chewed on it before finishing her sentence. "You erased her memories."

I sucked in a breath. "I did not."

"You so did," she answered, stuffing another fry into her mouth. "I watched you do it, if you recall. What's even more unique about our powers is that they're based solely on our desires. They do what we want." She leaned toward me, her eyes shining again. "Many lifetimes of our ancestors being squashed, it's about time we got what we deserve. Though I've never done it with written words like that. I wonder if it would work for me."

"Jenny will be fine." I couldn't tell if I was saying this to her or to myself.

"Oh, don't get me wrong, she's good!" Cadie sat up straighter. "Both physically, mentally...everything. She'll wake up when her body gets over the shock. But I bet you money she'll wake up without her memories intact."

I abruptly stood and climbed over the booth behind us since I couldn't squeeze past Cadie. I wasn't going to listen to this anymore.

"Jay, wait!"

Cadie caught up to me quickly, but I didn't stop walking as she pleaded with me.

"I'm just trying to prepare you for what's coming! I'm not messing with you, okay?"

"But you're treating it like a joke!" I cried as soon as we were outside in the parking deck. "You'd 'bet money' that she wakes up without her memories? You telling me how amazing our Sin Eater ancestors are? I don't care what I am, I care about what I did to Jenny. Obviously, Sin Eaters are monsters if they can do that so easily to people!"

Cadie took a step back from me.

"I'm...I'm sorry, I shouldn't have—"

"Just call me when you realize I'm right, because I am." She pulled me into another tight hug. "I'll see you soon, Jay."

I watched her wink then stroll back into the hospital, like I didn't just scream at her or insult something that she's obviously very proud of. It wasn't true, though. It couldn't be. Because then that would mean...I was the one who put Jenny into the hospital. If that were true...I shook my head. Maybe I did need a break, like my dad said.

After I arrived at home, I found my dad in the kitchen making a sandwich.

"How's Jenny?" he asked.

"The same," I answered. "I ran into Cadie."

"Oh, yeah? How's she doing? Haven't seen her in a long time."

"Good, good." I tried to keep my tone light. "Her hair is crazy now. Platinum blonde and purple."

"Ugh." My dad had never been a fan of dyed hair. "I can't believe she'd ruin her hair like that."

My dad went on his usual rant about how once you dye your hair it's never the same. I listened while staring at his hands, thinking of Cadie grabbing mine and seeing my memories.

"You want a sandwich before I put everything away?" he interrupted himself.

"Oh, uh…no. I ate at the hospital. Thanks."

In a split-second decision, I stepped forward and wrapped my arms around him. I made sure that my hand was touching his bare arm. He hugged me back and kissed the top of my head.

"I know things are hard right now, honey. I'm so sorry," he said.

He kept talking as I concentrated on the task at hand. I wanted to see a memory of him and my mom before me, when they lived in Florida. My parents on the beach, maybe close to where they met, young and goofy in love. I closed my eyes to focus better as his words became muffled, but the familiar darkness wasn't there. Instead, I saw feet, but not my own, walking through pure white sand. My view shifted as the eyes, his eyes, dragged away from the ground and to the person at his side: my mother. She was definitely younger, the wrinkles around her eyes gone. Her dark hair was long, so long that it almost grazed her waist. She looked exactly like a picture I'd seen before of my parents, back in their college days.

I felt a warm hand in mine, and it must have been a surprise to my dad, too, since his eyes shifted downward to where my mom had slipped her fingers between his. She laughed; his face must have shown his shock, and I could feel his thoughts and heart racing.

"Hey, you're back," my mom said.

Only it wasn't the woman in this memory, but the one now that entered the room with us. When I opened my eyes, I didn't fully go back. I squeezed my eyes shut against the double vision: the bright beach and our dimly lit kitchen. Out of fear, I jerked away from my dad, trying desperately to regain the here, the now. When I turned, I saw my mom's face twisted with confusion.

"I'm sorry, I think I need to lay down," I muttered, stalking past her.

"Do you need anything?" she called after me.

I stopped in the hallway and took a deep breath.

"No, I'm fine." I poked my head around the doorway and put on my best smile. "Sorry, it's just been a long week. I think I'm going to bed early."

"Of course, honey, get some rest." Dad smiled back.

I tried to ignore their inevitable whispers about me as I entered my room and shut the door. Was that a hallucination? A dream? But it was so clear, right down to small, terrifying details. I actually felt my dad breathing, I saw past my mom's head to the horizon…it was all there and undeniably real. My legs gave out and I sank to the floor.

Cadie's parting words ran through my head, but I didn't want to call her just yet. Handling a conversation like that seemed impossible at the moment. One thing was certain in my mind: I should stay away from the hospital for a few days. Maybe some alone time would help me process what I just experienced. I couldn't bear to hear Cadie's gloating, not now.

Within a day, I received a call from Parker, who excitedly told me that Jenny had woken up. It was just for a few minutes, but the doctor said that as time went on, she would be able to stay awake longer. This was apparently normal in coma patients when they start to come back. I told him then that I'd be gone a few days but would be back by the weekend. It was Sunday; five days seemed like a good amount of time to get a hold of myself. Bill was probably too happy to care much about what I was doing.

Day by day, I received brief reports of Jenny's progress from Parker. She was able to stay conscious and also be awakened easily by the weekend. My excitement to see her overshadowed everything else, even my crazy revelation from that last Sunday. I'd almost convinced myself that the memory I saw in my dad's head really was a hallucination, a product of stress and lack of sleep. Even things with Parker felt a little better. We spent some time together twice outside of the hospital during those five days, and it was refreshing to feel slightly normal. I walked into the hospital confidently on Saturday, ready to actually talk to my best friend, to see her verdant eyes and shy smile.

As I passed the waiting room, I saw the whole family sitting together there: Bill, Vivian, Linda, and Cadie. All eyes were focused on the ground, their expressions nothing short of miserable. Linda and Vivian had tears in their eyes, and Cadie's usual smile was replaced with a frown. Bill sniffled and gripped the armrest of his chair so hard that his knuckles were white.

"Hey…" I said, tentatively approaching them. "What's…what's wrong?"

Bill actually met my gaze. It seemed like the first time in a while that he didn't glance through me or over me. He had been accommodating when it came to me visiting Jenny, but he rarely stayed in the same room if I was in it, nor did he ever have more than a few words to say. An even bigger surprise, he patted the chair next to him. I took a seat immediately.

"We just spoke with the doctor about Jenny," he said. "They're...stumped. They don't know what happened."

"They can't find anything?" I whispered, hyper aware that Cadie was staring at me.

"No. They say they can't find a reason why she fell into a coma. Her brain patterns are normal, there's no physical trauma..."

"So what you're saying is...there's no clues, so we won't know if this could happen again or when."

He nodded and winced, like the small motion was too much. "Yes. Also..."

I finally looked back at Cadie. I knew what he was going to say before he said it.

"She seems to have some sort of amnesia. We were told that a little at first is normal for coma patients. But the doctors are worried since it seems so severe. She remembers none of us, not her childhood, no recent experiences. They're even having to work on basic functions like eating and walking. They said this is expected in head trauma cases, or even in older people with dementia..." His voice cracked. "But not my young, healthy girl."

I stood so fast that I felt light-headed, but I didn't care.

"I'm going to see her. Is that okay?"

He waved me on. "She's asleep right now, but the nurse will be by to check on her again soon."

My shoes squeaked against the linoleum floor as I shuffled down the hall. I didn't know why I was in such a hurry. Seeing her right that moment wasn't going to change the circumstances or restore her memories.

It was done, and it was my fault.

Once I reached her room, I stopped cold and placed my hand on the door. I had no right to be there. This was something I caused, and not only did I hurt Jenny, but I took down her whole family. They would never be the same.

I turned around and made myself walk back to the waiting room when my feet desperately wanted to run.

"Cadie," I croaked out, trying to talk through the huge lump in my throat. "Will you come with me for a second?"

Cadie followed me out. The rest of them didn't seem to notice us leaving or didn't care enough to ask. She was quiet as she kept pace with me. I figured she would be saying "I told you so," because of our last conversation. I led her to the parking deck again, since I wanted to leave as soon as possible. My sudden halt made her trip over her shoes as she tried not to crash into me.

I whirled around to face her. "Is it reversible?"

"What do you mean-"

"You know what I mean."

Her confused expression turned into one of pity.

"Gran never said it was, so no…probably not."

I clenched my hands into fists. "That's all I needed to know."

I took off in the direction of my car, too upset to think of saying goodbye. Cadie's footsteps came closer until I felt her hand on my bare shoulder. I shrugged it off instantly.

"Hey, hey…" Cadie said softly. "You don't have to be scared of me looking into your head anymore. I won't do it, I swear."

My breaths were quick and rapid, matching my heartbeat. It was hard to concentrate when my head was full of an endless, droning chorus of *my fault my fault my fault.*

"But please…let me help you. Clearly this situation is shitty on all sides. I can't fix everything, but…We're the same. I don't want you to fear this gift you have."

"Gift?" I spat.

"Yes. A gift." She spoke gently, most likely afraid that I'd try to leave. "You may not see it that way now, and I understand why. I can show you how to use and control your powers. Won't that make you feel better? A little more control?"

I hated to admit it, but she had a point. If I could learn more, maybe even practice, I could prevent this from ever happening again.

"Okay." My voice was so shaky that it almost didn't sound like a real word, but more of a whimper.

"Okay." Cadie smiled. "Can we meet tomorrow? I'd say today, but I think I need to stick with my family for now."

"Yeah…just text me."

Cadie gave me a small wave before returning to the building. Meanwhile, I walked in the opposite direction to my car. My phone chimed with a text, and the sound made me jump. I must have forgotten to switch it to vibrate.

It was Parker: "Hey, I'm on my way to the hospital. Bill just called and told me about Jenny's amnesia. Are you there already?"

I unlocked my car and sank into the seat while staring at my phone. Before I started the engine, I swiped over to the settings and pressed 'delete.'

I was going to take Cadie's offer to help, but I couldn't stay here any longer. I had to run, not just for my sake, but for all of theirs.

Them looking me in the face every day, not knowing that I was the one who caused this suffering...

Being around them all the time, knowing what I did...

It was too much.

I'd start over away from them. From Jenny, her family, Parker.

They would all be better off without me.

Now- Duality

I awake the next day to another bright, sunny morning. It's not exactly the kind of weather that one is supposed to stay in bed and pout through, but I plan to anyway. The first thing I do is check my email, but I have no messages from Aiden or Amber. I try to feel comforted by reminding myself that they're both probably still asleep. It's early, not even nine yet, and Amber mentioned she has a closing shift tonight. I'm not sure if Aiden works today, but he doesn't strike me as an early riser. Even with this solid logic, I can't seem to stifle the strong suspicion that I freaked them out yesterday and that they must think I'm an awful person for what I've done.

...And they don't even know the worst of it.

After a few minutes of arguing with myself, I stare at my phone for a while, contemplating another desire: I want to call Parker. I have his number memorized even now, and I have an urge to hear his voice. He eventually gave up on trying to call and text me as much as he used to once I began to actively avoid him.

I shut my eyes tightly, desperately wanting to sleep again. My job isn't until later on tonight, so I have plenty of time to lay around. Unfortunately, the curtains aren't closed all the way, so the sun starts peeking through and shining directly onto my pillow. I flip over on my left side, but it's of little use; the light is demanding to come in. Not one to give up, I grab my blanket and pull it over my head. The darkness is welcome but feeling my warm breath against the blanket is hard to ignore, like I'm suffocating.

My stomach growls, so I flip the blanket off my body. There's no use in lying around like this, not when I'm too hungry to go back to sleep. There are still no emails from the siblings. I shove my phone under my pillow as I sit up to discourage myself from checking it every five seconds. No obsessing over this. Just concentrate on today: my last job, and then I'll figure out what to do after seeing how Jak reacts to me quitting. To calm myself, I head down to the hotel lobby for some breakfast. I think about taking the elevator but again opt for the stairs. The stairwell is dull compared to the rest of the motel; it's dimly lit and bare with white paint peeling off of the handrails. My fingertips skim the walls as I shuffle down the stairs. The breakfast bar is a little fuller than yesterday since I've arrived much earlier. This time, I fill my plate with two small waffles after I warm them up in the nearby microwave, along with some strawberries.

The view outside isn't much to look at, but I sit on one of the couches by the windows anyway. I eat greedily, like I'm starving. My poor stomach. I apologize to it in my head, then realize how crazy that sounds. However, I feel I owe many neglected parts of myself an apology; at least the stomach is the easiest to take care of. When I look up from my plate, I accidentally meet the eyes of an employee who's sweeping the lobby. She smiles politely at me, and I force a smile back. She reminds me of the first thing I'd like to accomplish once I'm finished with all of this: find a legitimate job, like the one I used to have at Downtown Art Supply. It was so pleasant, so normal.

Once I've had my fill, I head back up to my room to check my phone. I forgot the one small disadvantage to having any sort of relationship: staring at my phone constantly, willing it to buzz with a message from the person I want to hear from. It's still early morning, so of course, there are no emails. I yawn and stretch out on my bed. Honestly, I feel like I could go back to sleep now. Before I let myself relax too much, I hop up and close the curtains. Once I'm back in bed, I curl deep under the blanket. With a full stomach and full mind, I drift back into my dreams.

My eyes shoot open to the sound of my phone buzzing. It sounds close, but I don't see it anywhere. I scramble around the bed, down to the floor, and back up again. Where the hell is it? Then I realize that I left it underneath my pillow. I fell asleep on top of my phone! By the time I retrieve it, the phone has already stopped buzzing. The missed call is from Jak, of course. I roll my eyes. He always calls several hours ahead to check and make sure that I'm ready for every impending job.

144

Even though it's been nearly two years and I know the routine, this little habit of his goes on. I shake my head and click over to my missed calls so that I can call him back. That's when I see the time: It's less than an hour until I have to be at the client's house! Jak has called four times in the last thirty minutes. Oh, shit. Maybe he had a good reason to be blowing up my phone this time.

"Hey, sorry, I was asleep," I say in a rushed tone when he answers my call.

"Just hurry," he commands. "I'm pulling into your motel's parking lot."

He hangs up without saying goodbye. Again, I'm scrambling around my room, trying to get a disguise together. Due to the lack of time, I throw on the outfit I wore just a few nights ago to Mr. Gardner's house: the blonde wig, my goggles, bright red lipstick, enormous clunky boots, frilly skirt…and I'm good to go. I give myself a mental pat on the back for getting dressed so quickly. Usually, I take special care with these outfits, picking out various combinations to make the disguise different every time. However, this one seems fitting; my last job in my favorite outfit that I've ever come up with. I don't know why, but it felt so me, even though I'm wearing it to do something that is so not me.

I practically fall down the stairs in my rush. How did I end up sleeping for so long? Once I'm in the lobby, I see Jak staring out of one of the windows. His back is to me, so for a few rare seconds, I see him unguarded, the way he used to be. He's slouched slightly, his hands folded behind his back. My boots click against the floor when I start walking again, and the sound causes him to turn towards me. I notice that his posture stiffens. Back to business Jak, no more Mr. Relaxed Guy. We both step outside silently, despite the fact that the receptionist is miraculously not at her usual post by the door.

I watch him walk away, shocked that he didn't comment on the fact that I'm wearing the same disguise as the other night. Relieved, I cross the parking lot and follow him to his car. I realize that Jak is right: the sun is still a couple of hours from setting, making this the earliest appointment we've ever had. The earlier, the better, since I'm not sure how long the talk with Jak will take, the most awkward resignation from employment I'll probably ever face. Sighing, I glance over at Jak as he buckles his seatbelt. Do I really deserve to quit this? I owe it to Jenny, to help her as much as I can, since I'm the reason for her lost memories. What else will I do with my life? Nothing else of much use, surely. But I can't keep going on like this, I'm so unhappy. I initially agreed because it seemed like the right thing to do, but is something that's truly "right" supposed to bring this much grief? I then shake my head and direct my attention to the window. There's no use in arguing with myself. I made a decision, and I need to stick to it, no matter how hard it may be.

Fifteen minutes later, we are pulling in the client's driveway. Jak calmly collects his briefcase from the backseat and climbs out of the car.

"Five minutes," he says without looking at me. Biting my lip, I look down at my gloved hands as the usual anxiousness works its way through my body. A realization hits me: I never looked over the texts he sent me about this client since I slept all day...therefore, I have no idea what I'm walking into. When I check my pockets, my phone isn't there. In a panic, I feel under the car seat and look all around the floor. In my rush, I must have left my phone at the motel. I groan and lean back against the headrest. Now I can't even tell when it's been five minutes, let alone know what the hell I'll be dealing with.

It doesn't matter, I think. This is the last time anyway.

I climb out of the car with renewed confidence. Let's get this over with. I attempt to enter the house as quietly as possible, but the door creaks relentlessly as if to mock my effort. It doesn't matter, it doesn't matter, I repeat over and over again in my head. The room I'm in is a small garage, but it's surprisingly bare. Most of the garages I'd ever been in were always filled to the brim with random possessions, things that people seemingly couldn't part with but also had no room for in their house. The door to the actual house is straight across from me. Once opened, there is a set of stairs. I see a small light shining to the right of the top of the stairs, so that must be where the client and Jak are waiting. I take each one slowly, breathing in deeply in an attempt to calm myself.

As I reach the last step, my eyes meet with Jak's over the client's head. He nods, so I enter the room. The client has his back to me, and he's hunched over with his forehead resting on his hands. The sound of my footsteps against the floor makes his head jerk up. As he turns to look in my direction, I stop dead in my tracks.

No, no, no.

I know this client.

His green eyes widen, the same ones I was looking into not even twenty-four hours ago.

Aiden.

I freeze.

Aiden stares at me, his mouth slightly open.

"It's you," he says, almost like an accusation.

Jak looks from Aiden to me, confused. I clear my throat to buy time as I try to figure out something I can say. Maybe: Whoa, hey again. How's the trash can I knocked over?

Oh, God.

"You know this girl, Mr. Walker?" Jak asks. It hits me that I didn't even know Aiden and Amber's last name until this moment.

"Well…no, not really," Aiden admits. "We ran into each other once."

Jak glares at me.

"Is this true?"

All I can manage is a nod. Jak closes his eyes and exhales through his nose. Aiden watches both of us carefully, puzzled by this tense interaction. He stays quiet, though, which is so much better for me.

"I apologize," Jak finally says. He has regained his composure. "Let's continue."

Aiden's posture visibly stiffens. I remember how he looked when I first came in: head down, resting on his hands, looking quite a lot like all of my other clients.

"Right, so…I have to tell her what I want to forget, then write it down, too?"

"That is correct." Jak fakes a calm demeanor so well, but I can hear the edge in his voice. I'm going to hear it from him later, but I've got a surprise conversation for him as well. It's going to be a long night. Aiden clears his throat.

"Well," he begins, then clears his throat again. My heart squeezes. "I want to forget my parents. Ma was a drug addict, left us for whatever reason after I graduated. Haven't seen her since. My dad started taking it out on my sister, he would hit her. She didn't tell me for a little while because she wanted to protect me." He looks down and rubs his hands together. "She's strong, you know? Stronger than I'll ever be. It's been months and I can still barely sleep, I'm so paranoid that Pop is gonna find us." His lip quivers. "And I hate myself, I couldn't protect my own sister. I was so oblivious and so focused on my grief about Ma leaving, I was ignoring what was happening to her in our own house."

I swallow once, twice, three times, desperately trying to keep tears away.

"So maybe if I can just forget them, wipe my brain of their toxic bullshit...maybe then I'll be better for what's left of my family." Aiden inhales, then blows out the air slowly, deliberately. "Is that enough for this to work?"

Jak glances over at me, and our eyes meet. I nod weakly, my mouth in a hard line. Aiden keeps staring at me, but I can't tell what he's thinking.

"Yes," Jak says. "We'll need you to write down exactly what you'd like to forget..."

"I have," Aiden interrupts, passing Jak a piece of notebook paper. "Figured you guys didn't want to sit and awkwardly watch me write my whole life story."

Even in the most serious of moments he makes a joke, but he tells it with a flat voice. Jak hands me the paper and pulls a lighter out of his pocket. I turn the page over, not wanting to read it. I know the whole story already...and just had to hear an even sadder version. Both of them watch me carefully, Jak's face feigning a stoic look while Aiden's openly shows every emotion. My hands shake, and I have a hard time getting the lighter to work. Aiden holds out his hand, offering to help. I ignore him and concentrate until I finally have a small flicker, then fire. Holding my breath, I take a step back, widening the distance from them. The living room is small, so the space honestly doesn't help much. It feels like they're both staring over my shoulder, their breath in my ears.

I try not to, but I can't help it: I see Aiden laughing at Amber the other day at the restaurant, I see him trying to attack us with mustard, I see him offering me help the first night I ever met him. His eyes that match his sister's, him throwing a napkin and accidentally hitting a stranger with it, his silhouette against the stars as his cigarette burns...

All of it, a movie reel of images rolling through my head so fast that I get dizzy watching them. What will happen to him if I erase his memories? How can I keep my mind clear enough to take only what he wants to forget?

I drop the lighter and paper on the floor.

I can't do this to him.

Jak and Aiden watch the items fall to the floor, then they look back up at me simultaneously.

"What are you doing?" Jak asks, his low, growling tone betraying his true feelings.

"I can't," I sob. The tears are flowing now.

"What do you mean, 'you can't'?" Jak fires back.

"I mean that I'm compromised by my feelings, and I may erase more than he wants...so I can't."

Aiden abruptly stands, and our gazes turn to him. He's staring at me again, only this time, his expression is calmer.

"Your voice..." Aiden whispers. He closes the space between us and reaches out towards me. I know what he's about to do, but I'm rooted to the spot, I can't move away. Slowly, Aiden lifts my goggles up onto my head.

"Jackie," he confirms. "...I knew it."

I tried my hardest not to speak so that Aiden wouldn't recognize me, but I had to. His mind was in my unstable hands. There's no way I trust myself, not now. Jak takes a step back and bumps into a plush recliner behind him. His mouth is twitching, a look of fear. He must feel that I've outed our whole business...again. I meet his gaze with a mournful, apologetic expression.

"I'm sorry..." I say.

"What have you done?" Jak asks. "You aren't supposed to be talking to anyone, you know the possible repercussions..."

"Not supposed to be talking to anyone?" Aiden interjects. He sounds angry. "You can't control what she does..."

"You shouldn't question me on things that aren't your business, Mr. Walker," Jak commands. Aiden's hands ball into fists, and I'm so sure that he's going to hit Jak that I place myself between them as a barrier.

"Aiden, it's okay," I explain. "I agreed to it."

"Then what the hell is going on?" Aiden demands. I can't tell if he's directing this question to me or to Jak, since his gaze is constantly shifting from me to him, and then back again.

The room goes silent. Jak pulls at his sleeves and straightens his tie, eyes focused on the floor. I squeeze my hands together, willing myself to speak, but the words are stuck in my throat.

"...Well?" Aiden urges.

Jak finds his voice again.

"If she cannot provide the service that you paid for, then we have no business here. I can transfer your funds back to you tonight. You should see them in your account tomorrow."

With that, Jak walks around Aiden to the stairs. If I follow him out that door, I know that I'll cave and continue with this life. It's now or never.

"Um, actually…" I begin shakily. "I think I'm done."

Jak's eyes widen.

"I was going to tell you after this job, but then this all happened, and hey…this is already a huge catastrophe, so here it is." I'm trying my hardest to sound brave, but instead, I'm babbling like an idiot.

"You're quitting…?"

"I have to. I can't do this anymore…I have to move on."

"But what about Jenny?" he asks.

"We can figure something else out…please," I beg.

"Wait, wait…" Aiden interrupts. "I don't know what's going on right now, but you shouldn't be holding Jackie against her will. And you're using her friend against her? That's just sick, she was a kid when that happened…"

"You told him about Jennifer?" Jak's icy voice hisses at me. I step back quickly and accidentally bump into Aiden. He grips my shoulders.

"Yes, she did," Aiden says. "And that's really none of your business."

Jak's face contorts into anger as he takes two large steps towards Aiden.

"It is all of my business, Mr. Walker," Jak says. "Jennifer is my daughter."

Then - Discovery

There was a knock on my door.

I looked up, curious about what this next person was selling. The last one who knocked a few days ago tried to convince me to switch internet providers. He was an overly eager, bubbly guy, barely older than I was. I almost felt bad for telling him no.

I had been at my new apartment in downtown Clayton for about two weeks. It was a one bedroom, small but spacious enough for the few things I brought. I donated a ton of my old clothes, shoes, and books. They would be more useful for someone else, as they've been sitting in my closet for years. I had outgrown all of it, and I planned to hopefully outgrow my past even more. I was a Sin Eater, someone who betrayed my best friend and stole her memories, left Bill to deal with my mess, and then I pushed Parker away for his own good. Cadie claimed that my powers were based on my desires, and apparently, my desires were dangerous. Nobody knew I was there except my parents and Cadie; I even went the extra mile and switched phones.

Walking away was surprisingly simple once I got everything going. My parents finally caved and moved to Florida after I insisted that I wanted to stay on my own while I waited for Jenny to get better. They only felt comfortable leaving since they still thought that I had Bill and Parker for support. It was a lie of omission, since I left out that I hadn't told them my new address or phone number. I couldn't bear that Mom and Dad were stuck here because of me. They met in Florida at college, and their most romantic days were spent strolling hand in hand on the beach. They spoke frequently of wanting to move back down there once I graduated. It was much easier on me as well, despite how much I missed them. They wouldn't be looking over my shoulder or worrying about me.

Before they left, they helped me find this apartment. Clayton's downtown area had a decent selection of upscale places, but there were also some questionable ones. My mother, the eternal worrier, wanted me close to Downtown Art Supply, where a few nicer living arrangements were. Sadly, I couldn't afford the rent for any of them, so my parents promised to send me a little money every month. I figured I could work my way up in my store and become a manager so that I could eventually survive on my own. Meanwhile, I decided to research colleges since I barely did at the end of my senior year. They weren't the best or most ambitious of goals, but at least I had goals to work towards.

Cadie also helped me feel more confident about my recently discovered powers. She was only in town for another week and a half after we found out about Jenny's amnesia, but she let me spend long hours diving into her brain to practice my abilities while helping me move my things into the new apartment. I felt so nervous, but Cadie acted like it was no big deal. She'd known she was a Sin Eater for years, so she was way past feeling that it was strange. I was privy to what she had been up to in the years I hadn't seen her: a new boyfriend who followed her to college after they graduated, her trying to convince Vivian and Linda that Jenny's sexual orientation was perfectly fine and normal, dying her hair, moving out…I couldn't believe so much had happened, and that I was able to see it with my own eyes.

She had to beg me to practice erasing memories until I finally caved. We chose small things, like a food she knew she hated and a phone number she had memorized. I was scared to death, but she said she believed in me. We tried me burning a piece of paper with the information written on it again for one, and then me touching her skin for the other. Each time left me shaking uncontrollably, but Cadie said I would get used to it. Apparently, we feel the weight of the things we take, just as the old Sin Eaters used to carry the sins of the deceased upon their backs.

I hated saying goodbye, but we kept up a steady stream of texts. It was a small comfort that with everything I was running away from, I still had someone connected to that old life yet also knew me as this new thing, a Sin Eater.

I debated whether or not to open the door, but the person knocking was annoyingly persistent. They weren't leaving. Sighing, I placed the book I was reading on the coffee table. If it was someone selling something, they were about to get an earful. When I peered through the peephole, I was shocked to see Bill. I took a deep breath and opened the door.

"Bill…Mr. King," I said breathlessly.

We stood silently for a beat, letting each other's presence sink in.

"I need to talk to you," he said. Then: "Please." Bill's eyes were big, pleading. I invited him in, thinking that he may have news about Jenny. The last thing I heard was that she was awake and had amnesia. She couldn't have gotten worse, could she? My heart hammered in my chest as he entered, and already, my plans to escape were slipping away. Would he tell Parker where I was, too?

The air was tense inside my once quiet and relaxing apartment. I fumbled with a glass to pour him water and accidentally spilled some over the side in my haste. As I was mopping up the water with a paper towel, Bill took a seat on a stool behind the kitchen counter. My back was facing him, thankfully, so he didn't see the sheer panic on my face. After a few more moments of fumbling, I placed the glass in front of him.

"…What's wrong?" I asked in a small voice. "Is Jenny okay?"

"What do you mean?"

"Y-you…" I stuttered. "You must be here because something else happened, right?"

He shook his head.

"No, she's been the same for the most part. We can't be totally sure, but she doesn't seem to remember anything. She doesn't know who I am, or Parker, her mom…We've all spoken to her, asked her questions…she acts completely lost. That's been going on since she woke up, and there's no sign of it getting any better." He leaned forward, his elbows on the counter.

"I came here to ask where you've been. I haven't seen you in the hospital for a couple of weeks. Parker said you haven't been answering his texts and calls."

"I'm…I'm sorr-"

"That's why I'm here," Bill repeated, scowling. "You were there almost every day, and then you disappeared." His voice softens. "You're her closest friend. She needs you."

153

My lip trembled. "Why do you want me there? I thought you hated me. I thought..." I pulled in a shaky breath. "I thought you'd be glad that I was gone."

Silence fell as we both stared at the countertop. It became harder to breathe, like the walls were closing in. What did he want? I'd worked so hard to separate myself from this, to let them all move on from me, yet he's brought it all back to my doorstep.

"How did you find me?" I managed to demand confidently. I'd been at the end of my rope for a while, and I didn't need him coming around and rubbing all of my mistakes in my face. Bill's eyes widened at my outburst.

"As to how I found you, I called your parents. They seemed really surprised that I didn't know where you were living already." Bill answered indignantly. "I didn't even know they'd moved until I drove up to your house and nobody was there."

Shit, of course my parents told him. I'd need to start mentally preparing myself, since they would surely question me later about this. Did I really think I could disappear so easily?

"You are hiding, and I want to know why, since I'm only trying to figure out what happened to Jennifer. The diagnosis isn't complete. Her doctor told me that amnesia usually comes from psychological distress or physical trauma. Nothing in all of their scans looks anything like a regular amnesia patient. They're stumped."

"What can I do?" I pleaded.

"Tell me everything that happened up until she collapsed that day. No detail is too small." Bill reached into his pocket and produced a pen and a small notebook. I stared at him in disbelief. What was this, an interrogation? Why was he planning on writing this down? He noticed my facial expression.

"Look, I'm desperate. I'm trying to gather as much information as I can to figure out what's wrong with her. Something happened. People don't just develop amnesia randomly one day." He tapped his pen on the counter, his mouth in a hard line. "Please don't look at me like I'm crazy. Don't you feel it? Something is strange here."

My stomach twisted as the guilt churned through me. I swallowed, letting the air hang between us for a few moments too long.

"Well...as you saw, I came over to your house. When I went outside, we talked about her and Parker breaking up. She asked me to burn her diaries with her, because she said she was done with all of it."

Bill wrote down a few words, but I couldn't read it from where I was standing.

"You said 'done with all of it.' Done with what, exactly?"

Bill's way of coping amazed me in that moment. Instead of wallowing, determination took over. He reminded me of a detective on a cop show drama, meticulously collecting the pieces of some mystery he must solve.

I shrugged. "With everything."

"Everything?"

"Uh, not everything. Mostly everything here except you and me. She said we had been the best people to her for all her life." Thinking of that moment made my heart squeeze. Jenny was on the brink of crying then, but she wouldn't let herself break down. "She felt like she had been screwed over by her mom, by Laurie, and then Parker…so she asked me to help burn it all away. Then she…" The words get caught in my throat.

"Then she fell," Bill finished. I turned my back towards him, attempting to keep my tears at bay. Concentrating on his pen scraping against the paper helped. I really wanted to read what he was writing, but I couldn't possibly ask.

"Do you remember the last thing Jenny said to you?" Bill asked this as calmly as someone asking what the weather was like outside. God, I really wished I didn't remember, but they were tattooed onto my brain since the day they came out of her mouth and reverberated through my body. I took a deep breath.

"She said: I just want to forget all of it, everything. I want to start over.'"

When I glanced over my shoulder at him, I saw that Bill's eyebrows were knitted together, as if in deep contemplation, while staring down at his notebook.

"And what were you doing in that moment?" he inquired, still looking down.

"I was burning one of her diary pages."

An awkward silence filled the room as Bill took his notes. I could no longer hold my tears back, so soon the quiet was filled with my incessant sniffling and the rustle of a paper towel as I dried them away.

"It's almost as if she was wishing her memories away," Bill exclaimed, like it was a revelation.

"I'm…I'm sure that's not what she meant…"

He stared at his notebook and didn't answer, so I walked around the counter and sat on the stool next to him.

"I admire what you're doing," I said. "I wish I could help more."

At least that part wasn't a lie. I honestly didn't know a way to help bring her memories back. Cadie said it was irreversible, and she was the only source I had.

He put his head in his hands. "I wish there was more I could do, too."

Thinking of Cadie brought something else to mind. If I touched his skin, I could see his memories. Maybe I could try and see Jenny, just for a moment. Would that be invading his privacy? There was no malicious intent…but the only time I'd ever done it was with Cadie, who gave me permission. I sighed and reached my hand out, placing it gently over his. Maybe it could offer some comfort, even if my intentions were for myself.

It seemed my desires were selfish yet again.

My mind immediately saw Jenny through Bill's eyes, lying in her hospital bed. This memory must be fresh on his mind, since it came to me so quickly. She was asleep. I could see her chest rising and falling as she breathed through her slightly open mouth. Bill's cell phone started ringing in his pocket, and I was carried out with him as he quickly exited the room to answer it. A male voice spoke in his ear as he said hello.

"Bill, I'm sorry to call you like this. I know you're out right now because of a family emergency…"

"It's all right."

"How's your daughter doing?"

"She's…well, I don't know. She's awake. Physically healthy. It's about all I can really hope for right now."

"Right…I'm sorry. We've all been thinking about you."

"Thanks, Ted. Did you need something?"

Ted paused, then I heard him sigh.

"I just have to come right out and say it. Bill, we're being forced to do some layoffs."

Bill's hands were shaking, but I felt like they were my own. Or maybe my hands in real life were shaking, I couldn't tell the difference.

"I'm so sorry. We have to let you go. It's nothing you did, it was just horrible timing…" Ted's voice drifted off as Bill dropped the phone on the ground.

The impact snapped me out of the memory, and I quickly withdrew my hand from Bill's. He was fired? How long ago was that? Now his reason for being here seemed much clearer. He was at the end of his own rope: his daughter didn't know him, the bills were stacking up, and he had no clue why.

"Well, I'd better get back to the hospital," Bill said, sniffling. His eyes met mine. "Will I see you back there, or is this goodbye?"

I was surprised at how flat his question sounded. He went from almost crying to cold in seconds. When I didn't answer right away, he abruptly stood and stalked towards the door.

"It was me," I blurted out.

Bill froze. He turned back to me but didn't approach the counter. "What are you talking about?"

"It's my fault that Jenny's memories are gone." I could barely speak through the lump in my throat. I honestly didn't mean to say it, but seeing Jenny in Bill's mind, knowing he just lost his job...It wasn't fair that he didn't know what really happened.

He shook his head. "Jayde, I know you feel bad for what you did with Parker, but that doesn't mean everything is your fault."

I leaned my elbows onto the counter and buried my face into my hands.

"That's not what this is about," I said.

"Then explain it to me."

I heard Bill shuffle closer.

"I'm...I'm responsible. It's been proven to me that I'm the one that took Jenny's memories."

When I finally lift my face to Bill's, his eyebrows are drawn together in confusion.

"There were people in the past called Sin Eaters, who would be hired to wipe the sins of a dead person so that they were clean for the afterlife. I'm apparently a descendant of one."

Before Bill could speak, I continued in a rush.

"Another Sin Eater found me and explained. We did tests, and they showed me that I could erase memories." I stood and placed my hands on the counter. I wanted him to meet my eyes, to see how serious I was. "I know this is crazy, but I'm one-hundred percent positive it was me."

Bill stared down at the carpet. I couldn't tell what he was thinking.

"That's why I went into hiding. I don't deserve to be around Jenny when I'm the reason she's in the hospital. I don't know what all I can do…these powers, I didn't even know I had them until two weeks ago. I could hurt someone else, like I did her. Please understand that that's why I had to get away."

"You're insane," he snarled. I took a step back, shocked at his tone. "I can't believe you'd make up such a ridiculous lie to excuse not being there for Jenny."

"What, no, I—"

"You've lied before. You only told the truth when I caught you red-handed." His face was twisted with anger. "And even then, you were outside with her for a while, and you still didn't tell her what you-"

"Okay, I get it! I'm awful!" I screamed. "But I'm telling you the truth!"

My outburst left Bill speechless as he stared me down. We both were breathing heavily.

"Prove it, then," he said.

"You don't know what you're saying. To prove it, I'd have to…"

"Erase my memories? But then I wouldn't remember that you proved it?" His mocking tone enraged me.

"Fine." I snatched his notebook off of the counter, scribbled a sentence down, and handed it to him.

"Chocolate chip cookie dough is my favorite ice cream flavor?" he read.

"It still is, right?"

My mind drifted back to when I was in elementary school. Jenny and I were watching a movie in her den, eating ice cream. Bill walked by at one point and overheard me saying that I loved coming over because they always had my favorite ice cream. Bill laughed and said that they usually had the chocolate chip cookie dough flavor because it was his favorite, too. I called him my "ice cream twin" for the rest of the summer.

I watched as he placed the sheet of paper on the counter.

"Yes…I can't believe you remember that."

"I do, but are you okay with forgetting it?"

As he looked down at the note again, I made my way to the kitchen and retrieved a lighter.

"It's just an ice cream flavor," he scoffed. "I wouldn't be missing much."

"Write the same sentence on another sheet of paper," I commanded, pushing the notebook towards him.

He raised an eyebrow at me.

"Just do it. I need this in your handwriting. Sign it, too."

Bill did as I asked, but he was shaking his head, like I was nuts. To be fair, I thought Cadie was crazy at first, so I couldn't really blame him.

He slid his signed paper over to me. If I have a specific detail written down, I can concentrate on that one point and leave the rest of his memories intact, just as I had done with Cadie.

I clicked the lighter once and got the flame going.

"One last chance. Are you sure? I have a signed permission slip right here, but I want to make sure you understand what's about to happen."

Bill rolled his eyes and gestured with his hand to go ahead.

I took a deep breath and read the note once more, then touched the flame to the paper. As the edges began to brown and the fire neared the ink, that overwhelming feeling came back, the one from my last afternoon with Jenny. My hands shook, and my breathing became shallow. The image of the words bounced through my head, "Chocolate chip cookie dough is my favorite ice cream flavor" over and over. Once the paper was finally gone, I looked up at Bill. His eyes were glazed over, vacantly staring at the ceiling, his mouth slightly open.

I shook him by the shoulders, calling out his name. After a few seconds, he seemed to wake up, and he quickly shook his head.

"Are you okay?" I asked.

"No, because this is ridiculous. You didn't erase Jenny's memories."

Determined, I grabbed a spoon from a drawer, along with a carton of chocolate chip cookie dough ice cream out of the freezer. He stared at the items placed before him, his eyebrows raised.

"Have some ice cream," I said. "It's your favorite."

"What are you talking about?" Bill demanded. "I'm not here for ice cream, and I don't know where you got the idea that this is my favorite. I've never even had that kind."

I slid the piece of paper with his signature on it towards him. Bill's lips moved as he read, and it hit me that Jenny used to do the same thing.

"What is this...?" Bill muttered.

"The proof you wanted. I erased the memory out of your head. You wrote down yourself that this was your favorite, and now it's gone...because of me."

His brow was furrowed in confusion as his eyes focused on reading the short note again.

"We agreed that I would burn a piece of paper that said your favorite ice cream is chocolate chip cookie dough," I explained again, "to prove that I could erase memories. Well, here it is. Jenny's amnesia is my fault. I had you sign it and everything." I hid my wobbly legs by bracing myself against the counter.

Bill's face went blank as he picked up the spoon. Slowly, he reached towards the ice cream carton and opened it. The spoon banged against the counter in his hand, shaky, uncoordinated. He scooped a generous heap of ice cream into his mouth and closed his eyes.

"This tastes new to me, Jayde..." he said with his mouth full. "But you say it's my favorite?"

"It has been for years. Probably for longer than you've known me."

"This is crazy talk," Bill mumbled, denying me once again. "Talking about ice cream isn't going to help Jenny."

"Then let's talk about what you plan to do now that you were laid off from your job."

Bill blinked rapidly, his mouth hung open.

"That...that happened just a couple of hours ago. I haven't told anyone. How did you know that?"

I reached out to touch his shoulder, but he stood and backed away. In his haste, he knocked over the stool he was sitting on.

"When I touch someone's skin, I can see their memories."

"Stop it," he said, his voice almost a whisper.

"You had to leave Jenny's hospital room since your phone rang." I stepped from behind the counter. "Your boss's name is Ted, he's the one who told you that you were let go. He asked about your daughter first, you said she was physically healthy, that 'It's about all I can really hope for right now.'"

With every step that I drew closer, Bill backed away.

"There's no way...there's..." His breaths were quick, panicked.

I hated doing this to him. He had enough on his plate, but this was the only way to make him believe me and understand.

"Please, sit down and listen to me. There's no reason to be afraid."

"If you truly did erase Jennifer's memories, then I have plenty of reasons to be afraid," he spat. Before I could say anything more, Bill stumbled to the door and left.

He was actually scared of me. I hadn't anticipated that response.

* * * * *

What was more astonishing was that even after all this, I found him on my doorstep a week later. The moment he was inside, the proposition was made: I would become a "business partner," and use my powers to help him make money for Jenny. He would take care of the advertising, plan our travels, and make sure that our customers were well aware of the risks. All I had to do was cooperate, be wherever he needed me, and erase the memories that the client specified.

Once he was done explaining the initial plan, the threats came out. If I didn't help him do this, he would tell everyone how I stole Parker from Jenny, and then selfishly erased her memories in order to avoid having to admit it to her. Everyone would know that I was a Sin Eater: my parents, Parker, even my employer. I didn't know how he would prove the latter, but I did know one thing: it would be a strange bombshell to everyone around me, even without proof, and I imagined that hardly anyone would ever trust me or him again.

I think I normally would have said no. My brain screamed at me to decline. This was obviously going to be dirty money, and I swore I would hide away to avoid using my powers. Nobody needed me dictating what they remembered of their own lives. But when he brought up that the money would go towards Jenny's hospital bills, I couldn't help but reach out for a handshake to seal the deal. However, he wouldn't take it. He must have been wary of me peering into his head without his permission. At that moment, I knew he would never let me touch him again.

This deal was one-sided, unfair. More importantly though, it gave me a way to make up for what I did to Jenny. This seemed to be the best and fastest way to help her recover, to get her home, without leaving her family in debt.

My life didn't matter then, only that I owed my friend hers.

Now - Promise

Aiden's face is contorted by so many feelings trying to show themselves all at once. This poor guy caught up in my confusing web.

"You're...her friend's father?" Aiden says. Something dawns on him as his gaze turns towards me. "And you...can erase memories. You told me your friend had amnesia, so...did you...?"

I nod. Jak is watching me carefully, the witness of my first ever confession of the secret I never wanted to tell.

"I didn't mean to," I answer in a small voice.

Aiden closes his eyes and rubs his temples with his fingers, like he's developing a headache. Once his eyes are open again, he reaches a hand out to Jak.

"I apologize for speaking of your daughter like I knew what was going on. I had no idea." Jak is taken aback by the gesture and shakes Aiden's hand warily.

"How did you two come to spend time together?" Jak asks the dreaded question that I was afraid of. Aiden licks his lips, then glances at me. I guess he would feel more comfortable if I answered since he barely knows what's going on. Since this is already so awkward, I keep it as short and simple as possible.

"He and his sister asked me to hang out one day when I ate at Anita's Kitchen. They work there."

Jak nods, but that response must not be very satisfying, since the next thing out of his mouth is: "Come on, we need to go." My feet are rooted to the spot. Which would be worse: facing Jak alone or staying with Aiden? Either way, I'd have to explain myself somehow. Before I can say anything, Aiden jumps in.

"Wait, don't go!" he frowns.

"Young man, you've already heard too much," Jak replies coldly. "I will refund you by tomorrow."

"I don't care about the money!" Aiden exclaims. "I care about my friend, and I want to know what's going on." My cheeks burn. He thinks of me as his friend?

"I'm not keeping her in a cage, if that's what you think," Jak says.

"Then what's this crap about her not getting to talk to people?" Aiden demands.

"Aiden, please..." I beg. "It's okay."

"No, it's not," Aiden fires back.

We stand in silence for a moment as Jak evaluates the situation. Then he sighs, pinching the bridge of his nose in frustration. There is a digital clock on a side table, and I try to remember when we arrived. How long have we been standing in this room? Jak's body seems to go limp as he slumps onto the couch behind him, a brown leather one with some minor damage on the top. Raising his right hand, he gestures for us to continue, while he holds his head in his left. I take a long breath, in and out.

"It's dangerous for us, the work we do," I begin. "It's not exactly...legal, though we don't know if it's illegal either." I step towards the middle of the room so that I can face both of them. "Once we had been in 'business' for a little while, copycats started to show up. Jak saw a few reports about it on the news. People who claimed they were us, that they could do the same thing as we can. They would..." I swallow. "They would tell people that they could help by erasing their memories. The clients would willingly let them into their houses, and then the fakers would rob them."

Jak has sunken into the couch, both hands now cradling his head. Aiden doesn't take his eyes off of me.

"Did anyone get hurt?" he asks.

"Not that we're aware of, but again, we only had news reports to go by. I don't know how much information they actually released." I bow my head. "That's why he didn't want me to talk to anyone. If I kept to myself, then maybe we wouldn't be thrown in jail, or worse." Lifting my head, I smile sadly. "I'm the idiot who told a friend about our business. She knows everything, but luckily she hasn't told on us...as far as we know, anyway."

I sincerely thought that this explanation would placate Aiden, but his anger is intensified, all clenched fists and twitching eyes.

"Why did you do this to her?" Aiden asks Jak through gritted teeth. "This is such bullshit. Why would you put her in danger? Is this some sort of sick revenge for what she did to your daughter?"

"No, no! He was…" I say, but Jak interrupts.

"I was laid off from my job." Aiden and I swivel our heads to the crumpled man on the couch. His hands are shaking while still covering his face. "I was laid off from my job, and I wasn't sure how I was going to pay for Jenny's hospital bills. They were piling up, but I had nothing. I went to Jayde for help, and she told me what she could do, and…the idea formed in my head. It wouldn't go away, it kept nagging at me. So I approached her with it." Jak stands unsteadily, but his eyes are fiery, unashamed.

"And yes, I did blackmail her. I told her that if she didn't help me, then I would tell everyone that she betrayed my daughter and then erased her memories." He steps over to Aiden so that they're eye to eye. "Am I proud of that? No. But I did what I needed to do for my child. She's healthy now, and I've had enough money to take care of everything for her. She's back on her feet, she's home, and she's finally living normally. It has been worth every single terrible moment."

My bottom lip quivers as I remember opening my door again to Bill after telling him that I'm a Sin Eater. He had already booked some clients for us, because he was so sure that I wouldn't say no…and I didn't. I couldn't. It's strange: when he first laid out his plans, even when he threatened to reveal me to everyone, my heart soared a little. I thought of it as something I could do to make amends to Bill, to Parker, to my parents, and most importantly, to Jenny herself. I would live my life for Jenny after trashing hers. As time went on, though, I found out that devoting all of yourself to something isn't exactly fruitful if you have nothing pouring into you to make up for all that you're giving.

Aiden's expression is furious. As he raises a fist, time seems to speed up. Jak jerks back instinctively, I rush to grab Aiden's arm, and it's all a blurry mix of movement and color as Aiden's knees suddenly buckle from beneath him. I fall as well, taken down by the force of holding onto him to keep him from hitting Jak. Aiden has tears streaming down his face, and he stares down at his hands, opening and closing them over and over. I grab his hands and squeeze.

"It's okay," I whisper.

"Easy for you to say," Jak sniffs. "He didn't just try to punch you."

I glare at him, and in his surprise at me having a backbone for the first time in forever, he backs away.

"I'm okay. Really. I think your anger is…misplaced," I say. "You should be angry with me. I've lied to you and Amber a lot to protect myself, and it's okay if you're angry." I let go of his hands and stand up.

"And to add on one more thing that won't help…I can't erase your memories. I could, but my mind is racing so much right now, who knows what would happen. I just…" I trip over my words. They're caught in my throat.

"I can't do that to someone I consider a friend. Not again."

Finally, Aiden lifts his face to mine. His eyes are wet and red, and for the first time, I notice bags under his eyes, like he hasn't gotten a good night of sleep in a long time. Then he turns his attention to Jak.

"I'm sorry, Jak. I let my Pops take over for a second there…I guess I've got some of his anger in my blood."

Jak's face softens.

"Bill," he says. "My real name is Bill."

Aiden stands and wipes his eyes. I can't keep myself from staring at Bill in shock; he just gave his real name away.

"Bill…?" Aiden repeats, then he turns to me. "Do you have a made-up name, too?"

I flush. "My real name is Jayde."

He shakes his head, disbelieving.

"You guys have got this on lockdown, huh? You even have code names."

I laugh despite how crappy I feel.

"So…what now?" Aiden asks. We're all quiet, thinking. It has become a less awkward silence, though the situation is still extremely strange.

"We move on with our lives," Bill says.

I look down at my feet, dejected. Have we all been stuck in place? Progress was made on the outside, but somehow, all of us never moved on in our minds.

Aiden, the son of a drunk and an abuser: even after they escaped, he couldn't get past the fear of his father and the guilt of not being able to protect his sister.

Bill, or rather, "Jak": the father of a young girl whose memories were lost, a man who did everything he could for his daughter, even if it meant hurting others in the process. Jenny is well, as he said, but his mind still sees her as small and fragile, in need of his protection.

Then of course, me…Jayde, masquerading as "Jackie," a girl with an awful power that she misused over and over to hopefully lighten the weight of her past mistakes. While my actions helped Jenny get better, it slowly left me to deteriorate. I am no better than I was two years ago.

Somehow, we have the same problem under extremely different circumstances, all intertwined as life moved on around us. Bill is right: *We* must now move on, for the good of our own lives. Hope blossoms in my chest. I can stop these jobs now, and Bill is actually okay with it.

Bill speaks again when we don't:

"I think I'd like to get home now."

I nod and begin to follow him out the door. Aiden surprises me by placing a gentle hand on my shoulder.

"Would you maybe want to stick around? Amber will be home soon, and then we could use the Jeep to drive you back to your hotel."

Somehow, I'm able to decipher his split meanings in this statement: he wants to talk to Amber about tonight, but he also doesn't want to be alone until then. However, Bill and I really need to talk in private. We'll need to sort some things out since we're ending our business.

"Maybe I can come by later tonight?" I offer. "Bill and I still need to talk…"

"I understand," Aiden replies. "Let me know if you need a ride."

Nobody makes a sound, not even to say goodbye. Bill and I exit the house the same way we came in, through the garage. Once we're in the car, Bill leans his head back against the seat and closes his eyes.

"Are you oka—"

"You need to go back in there and erase that boy's memories right now," Bill interrupts. He opens his eyes but doesn't look at me. "He seems to trust you. I think you can get it done."

My mouth opens and closes, speechless. Finally, he turns his head towards me.

"Go. Now."

"But you just said…w-what happened to us 'moving on with our lives?'"

"I had to say that in the moment, but he knows too much." He reaches over and opens my door. "Go."

"No."

"…What?"

"No," I say louder. "These jobs were designed to always be consensual. I'm not taking his memories just because you think he knows too much about us now."

"Jayde, if you don't do as I say, you know what I'll do…"

"I know. You'll tell everyone what I did."

I grab his wrist. He jumps at the contact.

"Let go of me." His voice is low, angry.

"I could erase all of your memories right now. Do you remember how I could see your memories through touching your skin? I can take them this way, too."

I try to keep my voice as steady as possible. My mind is made up. Aiden would not suffer for my mistakes. Jenny's already paid the ultimate price at my hands, and nobody else should have to. Even if I'm miserable, even if my parents never trust me again, even if I have to move to get away from any scrutiny.

"You're bluffing. You wouldn't…" Bill's eyes widen.

"Only if you try to force me to take an innocent person's memories." He tries to pull his arm away, but I tighten my grip. "It's my fault. You can take it out on me all you want. Just leave him out of it. If you need proof, ask Cadie if I'm able to take your memories like this. She'll tell you."

His breaths are rapid, and despite him not wanting to believe me, I know he does. He wouldn't be this scared otherwise. I keep my hand wrapped around his wrist until I'm out of reach and standing next to the car door.

"So that's it, then?" he cries. "You want this all to get out? You're going to stop helping Jenny?"

"I want to keep helping her," I answer, "but legally. I'll give you as much money as I can when I find a job. Just not this anymore, not ever. I won't out you…but it's okay if you can't say the same. I'll deal with it if you do."

I slam the door before he has a chance to respond. Bill stares at me through the window, gritting his teeth. He turns to open his door, but as I take a step back, he must change his mind since he reverses out of the driveway instead. I stand in the same spot, watching the car until it disappears out of my sight. My whole body is shaking as I walk up to Aiden's front door and ring the doorbell. I can't believe I just threatened him like that, but it felt like the only way I could truly be free…at least right now.

Aiden seems confused when he sees me but invites me in. I notice his glance towards the empty driveway.

"That was a quick talk," he says.

"It was less of a talk and more of an...argument? I'm not sure what to call what just happened." I sink onto the couch.

"Is everything okay though?" He walks out of the living room and comes back with a glass of water and a box of tissues.

"Prepared for anything, huh?" I say, taking a tissue to wipe at my eyes.

"You seem pretty shaken up."

I stare at the floor, nodding my head slowly. "It was really intense."

"Well..." Aiden says, letting the word hang in the air.

"Well...?" I mimic him.

"Do you want some regular clothes?"

I burst out laughing as I look down at myself. I forgot that I'm still in my wacky disguise.

"Yes, please."

"You might be able to fit into some of Amber's stuff, let's go find you something."

"You sure she won't mind?"

"I'm sure," he says.

Aiden first tells me to go into her closet and pick what I'd like, but I convince him to choose for me since I don't feel comfortable going into her things without her present. As he moves hangers back and forth, he gives me a sidelong glance.

"You know you need to go see your friend, right?"

I feel myself stiffen. "I know."

"And you need to tell her everything."

"She doesn't even remember me," I protest, even though I know he's right.

"You need to do it for you," he counters. "For closure."

"...And you need to tell Amber how much everything is still hurting you."

His mouth is a hard line, but he nods.

"I will. Tonight."

"And I'll be here...if that's okay." I say.

"Thanks." I see a soft smile playing on his lips as he throws a blue T-shirt and a pair of black leggings at me. "Let's pinkie promise."

"What?"

"Pinkie promise that we'll do the things we need to do to move on with our lives."

He holds out his pinkie, his face so childlike and hopeful. I can't help smiling in return.

"Okay, I promise," I say, hooking my pinkie with his.

And this time, I know that I'm going to keep my promise.

Then: Trust

I sat in Bill's rental car, trying to breathe in and out as steadily as possible. The client we were seeing next was nineteen, my age. This was the youngest person I'd ever seen in the year Jak and I had been working together, and even worse, she requested to have most, or, if possible, all of her memories erased. Doing this exact thing to Jenny was my biggest mistake, and now I had to do it to someone else?

Bill climbed into the car and slammed the door. To distract myself, I took out my phone and texted Cadie: "We're on the way to another job. This girl wants me to erase everything."

I often spoke to Cadie at length about our business, and she usually calmed me down. I knew Bill said that I wasn't supposed to tell anyone, but Cadie was a Sin Eater too, and I trusted her. She knew the risks and swore to keep the information to herself. She was all in favor of what we were doing since the money was going to help Jenny.

"Everything? She must have gone through some shit if that's what she wants," Cadie wrote back.

"Yeah, I know...but I don't think I can do it." I paused, then sent another text right after: "It reminds me too much of what happened with Jenny."

"Jay, it's fine. The girl wants this. She's paying for it...you have to."

I laid my head back on my seat and sighed. Bill glanced over at me but thankfully turned his attention to the road soon after.

"I know, I know...I'm just scared."

"It will be fine, I promise," Cadie sent back. "And the girl will be too. She knows what she's getting into. Jenny didn't get a choice, but this other girl does."

"You're right. I should respect her wishes."

"Exactly! Knock 'em dead, girl! Er...you know what I mean."

I couldn't help but chuckle, which prompted Bill to look at me again.

"What's so funny?" he asked. I could tell that he was annoyed at me for using my phone. He'd always said I shouldn't take it to jobs, but texting Cadie beforehand always soothed me.

"Oh, uh...just a text from Cadie."

"If you're laughing, does that mean you feel better than you did earlier?"

"No," I answered honestly. "I don't feel right doing this."

Bill frowned. "I made the client write down specific things still. I don't want her falling into a coma." The two unspoken words 'like Jenny' floated in the air between us.

"I know, it's just...if she wants most of her memories gone, her list will probably add up to years and years of her life."

"Is that an issue? You've erased many things before from people's minds, things they probably knew of for a long time, people they loved. I see it as the same."

I looked down at my hands. We never talked about Jenny, but everything I was feeling uncomfortable with at that moment had to do with her.

A girl our age, someone who might end up just like her...

Would that count as making the same mistake, only on purpose this time?

"Or..." Bill continued, "did you lie when you said you could control your powers better than last year? This other...person...who taught you how to handle them...was that something you made up?"

I'd gotten used to Bill casually accusing me of lying by then. I understood his reasons, but it still hurt.

"No, that wasn't a lie. I can do it." I sank down in my seat, resigned to the fact that this was happening. Maybe the client would change her mind when we got there. That had happened before in the past.

Bill pulled up to an apartment complex fifteen minutes later. There were only three buildings, so it was easy to find the one we were looking for. Bill told me a fire had taken down the fourth building just a few weeks ago. Driving by the empty space where it clearly used to be was eerie. I wondered how many people lost their homes that day.

As Bill got out of the car, I noticed a girl leaning against a door in front of us. She met my eyes with no surprise at all. Instead of speaking, she jerked her head towards the door and then disappeared inside.

Bill and I exchanged a confused glance. He gave her our usual instructions beforehand: keep the door unlocked, choose one room and stay in there, meet Bill first to discuss and finalize, then I would come in. Bill shrugged and gestured for me to follow. I guess we weren't doing things the normal way tonight.

At least one thing matched Bill's demands: it was dark except for a dim nightlight that was plugged in the living room. The girl stood in the center of the room, twisting the ends of her hair in her right hand.

"Can we do this quick? I have to leave soon." Her voice was flat. She seemed almost bored, the way she absentmindedly winded the strands through her fingers.

"As fast as we're able to, young lady," Bill said. "We need to go over the paperwork first, and have you read the warnings. We want you to be sure that..."

"Yeah, yeah, I might lose more of my memories than I'm signing up for. I got it."

Bill paused, his hand still deep in his briefcase.

"Yes, well...there's still the matter of reading this over and signing."

The girl snatched the papers from him as soon as he held them out to her. She hastily bent down to the coffee table next to her and signed them, though I have no idea where she got the pen. Bill still had the one he was going to offer in his hand.

"There. Now let's get a move on."

I couldn't see her well in this light, but I wished I could. Outside, all I could tell was that she had tan skin and long, sandy brown hair. I wanted to see if her voice matched her face. Somehow, even with the petulant tone, it still had a strange, melodic quality.

"May I ask what the hurry is?" Bill asked. "We really need to discuss the risks, and you still need to write out the list I requested."

"I'd say it's more of a risk for us to be here right now. I don't know when the owners of this place are coming home." She crossed her arms. "That's the hurry."

"T-this..." I stuttered.

Both pairs of eyes turned to me.

"This isn't your apartment?"

The girl sighed. I could tell that she was probably rolling her eyes at me.

"Of course not. I wasn't about to give some shady people my parents' real address. No fucking way."

Bill turned towards the door, even though there was no sound.

"I didn't break in…technically," she shrugged. "I have a key. They just don't know I have a key."

"Fine, Ms. Yorke. Do you have your list?"

"Ugh, don't call me that," she said, handing him a folded piece of paper. "It's a stupid name I made up. Just call me…Dee or something."

Bill didn't answer as he passed the paper to me. As I read it, my mouth hung open.

"Is there a problem?" Dee demanded.

I shut my mouth, thankful that my goggles covered my wide eyes. Her list was full of such everyday things: a breakup, a friend that moved away, fights with her parents…it seemed like a waste, going to all this trouble to get rid of them.

"Are you…sure this is what you want?" I read on: failed senior year of high school, caught with marijuana in her car… "This stuff seems like things you could fix and make right without having to lose your memories."

I knew I wasn't supposed to comment on the client's choice. Bill specifically told me many times that we want to keep them from regretting their decision. He glared at me but kept his hands folded in front of him, a desperate attempt to seem unfazed by our conversation.

Dee glared at me as well, but then just as quickly went back to looking bored. She shrugged her shoulders again.

"I've tried to fix some stuff, but I'll always remember, and that's the worst part." Dee tilted her head. "Aren't there things you'd rather forget, even if they're small? If you've got a business like this, you must have some pain deep inside. Someone without hurt wouldn't do this."

I was so wrapped up in her words that I dropped the paper and scrambled to catch it. When I looked back up, she exhaled a small laugh.

"So you do understand." She picked up a pair of scissors off the coffee table and held them out to me. "End my pain. I hope yours can be forgotten someday, too."

When I didn't take the scissors, she huffed.

"A clean slate, that's what I want. I'm one-hundred percent sure." Her frustrated gaze turned to Bill. "I didn't realize I'd have to force you guys to give me a service I already paid for."

"Do it. Now," Bill commanded me through clenched teeth. "Ms. Dee, you should probably sit before she begins."

As soon as Dee sat on the couch, my phone chimed aloud in my pocket. I squeezed my eyes closed, cursing myself for forgetting to put it back on silent. Nobody reacted, but I knew Bill would be fuming later. In my haste to get over the tense moment, I dropped the scissors and began tearing at the paper using my hands. With every tear, Dee's face became blanker. Bill had already left when I glanced behind me, so I followed.

As soon as I took my place in the car, I spoke before Bill could start his lecture.

"I know we normally don't do this, but can we…can we please watch for a bit and make sure she gets out of the apartment before whoever lives there gets home?"

Surprisingly, Bill nodded. He pulled the car into a spot farther away from the door, but close enough that we could still see it. The minutes ticked past slowly, and more so awkwardly, given that neither of us said a word. Finally, we saw Dee step outside. She closed the door carefully, staring at it for longer than necessary, before passing in front of us on the sidewalk. I wondered if she brought a car. Once she turned a corner and was out of sight, Bill put the car in reverse and left the small parking lot. My last glimpse was of her back, her hair lightly blowing in the wind as she walked down the street.

"What were you thinking?" Bill demanded. "I've told you so many times that—"

"I know, I'm sorry."

"Why did you do that?"

"Maybe we should talk about this when we get to the hotel instead of while you're driving," I said, eyeing his hands that were gripped too tightly on the steering wheel.

"We will talk about this now," he answered, scowling. "You spoke out of turn. That girl was clearly ready for the consequences. She'd signed everything, she paid. It isn't your job to comment or butt in."

"I know, I just-"

"And then your phone!" he shouted, ignoring me. "You let it make a sound at such a critical time, in the middle of a job. It's unprofessional. I've told you to leave the damn thing at the hotel and not bring it to clients' houses." We came to a stop at a red light, so he was able to look at me. "What was so important that you needed it today?"

"I needed to talk to Cadie because I was scared!" My voice was too loud for this tiny space. "Dee is my age, Jenny's age. I couldn't help but make a connection! It freaked me out, how much she wanted me to erase…"

"You…talked to Cadie about the job?"

A car horn blared behind us. The light had turned green, but Bill made no move to drive.

"Bill, uh…maybe you should…"

"You told her?" he yelled. He slammed his foot on the gas pedal and propelled us forward.

"N-no, I…"

"I can tell by your voice, by your face. Don't you dare lie to me again."

Thankfully we pulled into my hotel's parking lot a moment later, so at least we were off the road. I was terrified, grasping for something, anything to calm him down.

"It's-it's okay, she understands! She won't tell anyone!"

"She's my ex-wife's niece. She's young, naive…like you." His mouth twitched as he stared through the windshield. His voice rose with every word. "This was all for Jenny. Why would you jeopardize this? Are you doing it on purpose? Do you not want her to get better?"

"I do!" I cried. "It's the only thing I want in the whole world!"

He faced me and leaned closer, so close that I could feel his breath. "Then why would you tell someone about what we're doing? Now we'll need to figure out a way to erase her memories…she can't know about this."

"No, Cadie's a Sin Eater too!" I blurted out. I hated telling him her secret, but he needed to understand that Cadie was not a threat. "She was the one who helped me. She taught me how to use my powers and control them…she's the reason I'm able to run this business with you."

Bill's eyes widened as he slumped back into his seat. I wanted to say so much more, but I was frozen, deafened by the sound of my heart thumping in my ears. We sat silently until Bill opened his door. I didn't know what else to do, so I got out of the car as well.

Then Bill did something that he'd never done before: he came up to my hotel room with me.

The moment the door's lock slid into place, he spoke, "Give me your phone." I timidly handed it over, and his face was expressionless as he tucked my phone into his pocket. "You've proven that I can't trust you. I will buy you a new phone and monitor it more closely."

He was so calm that it infuriated me. What happened to the man freaking out in his car just a few minutes ago? As he stepped around me to leave, I followed.

"Don't you know how much you're taking away from me?" I yelled.

He paused then, his hand resting on the doorknob. Slowly, he turned and gave me a sidelong look.

"And don't you remember what you took from me?" His voice was steady, practiced, but there was a tinge of sadness. My knees gave out, and I sank onto the bed as he slipped soundlessly out of the room.

"I didn't mean to," I whispered to the empty room, feeling how alone I truly was. Like it mattered, like those words would fix anything. As I laid back on the bed, I imagined that I kept sinking, wishing it would just swallow me whole.

Now: Different

Aiden, Amber, and I talked for a large portion of the night. Aiden and I took turns telling parts of our stories and eventually let them weave together. Amber had no idea that Aiden had met me before. He never mentioned the strange girl he discovered behind the restaurant a few nights ago, nor did he let on that he suspected that "Jackie" might be that same girl because of a telling scrape on her knee. However, she was not clueless about Aiden's coping issues.

"He would always lecture me about how I needed to be more open about what happened to us, because it would help me get past it," she explained, as we sat in their living room eating popcorn, an apparent favorite snack of hers. "But the thing is, it's always going to be there. It's a part of my history. I'm not ashamed of it, and I'm not burying it or anything. I've gone over it in my mind, and I've accepted it. I've dealt with it in my quiet moments."

Amber turned to her brother, frowning.

"But you, I could always tell that behind your big mouthed declarations was someone who wasn't dealing with it. Just because you aren't shy about something doesn't mean that you're over it."

Aiden and I nodded in unison, letting that sink in. For someone who was younger than us, she was strangely full of maturity and wisdom. I mean, it's only by two years for me and by one year for him, but still. It was amazing nonetheless.

When the discussion inevitably came around to my memory erasure abilities, her face began to crease more and more in disbelief, to the point of me wanting to jump up from the floor where I was sitting and yell "Psyche!" just so she would stop looking at us like we were crazy. However, our sober attitudes kept her from saying much to contradict us, especially when we explained how I had ended up at their house that night, since Aiden was planning on erasing his memories. The look on her face was heartbreaking as she stared at her brother, absolutely devastated that he chose to forget, and furthermore, didn't tell her.

"I'm sorry I didn't tell you," Aiden said, looking down at the floor.

"What do you think would have happened after?" Amber exclaimed, pacing the room. "It would have probably been like Jackie's...sorry, Jayde's...friend. I'd have taken you to the hospital, they would be stumped on how you forgot such important details, and I'd be..."

Amber paused and sucked in a trembling breath. "I'd be left alone with those memories. The only one who carried them."

"I didn't think of it like that," Aiden muttered to himself, then lifted his head. "I really didn't. I figured if I was still here with you, that would be enough. If the pain was gone, I could be better, you know? I could take care of you better, function properly, actually make a life for myself without it all weighing me down."

Amber sat next to him on the couch and covered his hand with hers.

"I see what you mean...but I'm glad it didn't happen. Thank you for not taking his memories, Jayde."

"Please don't say that. I don't deserve your thanks."

"I want to be mad...at both of you," Amber said, glancing from me to Aiden. "And I guess I kind of am. Aiden, for obvious reasons...and I'm always a little mad at him for being so infuriating."

The siblings exchanged a small smile.

"But you," she said, staring down at me on the floor. "You aren't at all what you told us you were. You lied so much. Honestly, I shouldn't trust you."

I stared at the floor. She was right on all counts.

Amber chewed on her bottom lip. "You didn't mean any harm, though. Or ...it doesn't seem like it at least. And Aiden seems to trust you."

Amber looks over at Aiden for confirmation on that last point, and he nods.

"Then that's what I'll do, too. I'm sure you lied because you had to, not because you wanted to deceive us. Aiden wouldn't let anyone near me if he didn't think highly of them."

I gazed at Aiden, awed by his ability to want me around after everything I did. He smiled at me, and I smiled back, grateful and ready to prove myself worthy of their trust.

Overall, despite how difficult it was to wade through all of our hardships, it ended as it always seemed to with them: laughter. I actually told them real things about myself, and the more I said, the lighter I felt. It was like breathing again, really breathing, cleansing and free. They understand why I had to lie, that I was blackmailed, and that my biggest mistake was just that: a mistake. I didn't mean to take Jenny's memories, and they praised me for working hard to try to help her through it. While I was happy to hear those things, I still feel the need to hold myself responsible, so I didn't bask in it too much. My old self might have, as she thrived off of praise. Is that what maturation and growth brings? I hope so.

Now, a week later, I'm at Jenny's house, staring at the front door. It's been too long since I've stood on this front porch, my finger hovering over the doorbell. I breathe in and out, psyching myself up to actually press it. I waited a week to give Bill time to cool off before showing up at his house unannounced. I probably should have called ahead, but I didn't want to give him a chance to deny my request to speak to Jenny. Meanwhile, I settled in with the siblings, who were letting me sleep on their couch until I could find a job and get my own place again.

My parents have been sending money the last two years, but I've given most of it to Bill, as well as using it to buy clothes for my disguises and other necessities while traveling. They called me on the way over to Jenny's, upset that I'd been lying to them about what I was really using my money for. It seems like Bill called them earlier today, but he didn't tell them about my Sin Eater job. Instead, he reported I'd been lying to them for the past two years, that I didn't have my job anymore and I wasn't living in the apartment they thought they were paying on. I guess it would have been harder to explain that I took someone's memories. Plus, he'd have to make up some excuse about how he even knows that for sure without revealing that most of the money went to him.

"Bill was so cryptic, it was strange," my mother had said. "It was literally a five-minute phone call, then he hung up really quickly."

"I'm sure he's just concerned. I promise I'll explain more when you visit." After hearing that I wasn't doing so well, my parents decided to plan a last-minute trip to come see me. However, with my father's work schedule, it wouldn't be for two weeks since he needed to find substitutes for his classes.

"I'm just disappointed." I could picture my mom frowning while pushing her glasses back up on her nose. "Why did we have to hear this from him? I mean, he had to call us to get your address when we moved, when you said you'd told him. Now this? We can't trust you if you keep things from us. We didn't send you that money to fool around."

"Mom, I can explain," I say again, my voice cracking.

"Fine," she relented. "We'll be up there in a couple of weeks. Will you be okay until then? You said you're staying at a friend's house, right? Have I met this friend?"

I took a deep breath. "No. They're new friends, but I promise they're safe."

"You keep saying you promise, you promise," Mom complained. "I really hope you have a good explanation for what's going on, because-"

"Okay, okay," I heard Dad say in the background. His voice filled my ear soon after, so he must have taken the phone from her. "Let's just...cool off for right now. We'll call you later on in the week."

I hung up feeling deflated. I had two weeks to come up with something. Should I just tell them everything? Would they believe me if I did?

Amber's hand gently squeezed my shoulder from the backseat of the Jeep, and Aiden frowned as he turned onto Jenny's street. They hadn't heard my parents' side of the conversation, but it wasn't difficult to understand that it didn't go well.

My eyes droop in exhaustion, despite drinking a ton of some nasty energy drink that Aiden gave me on the way over here. I shake my head, realizing that I've been staring at this door for way too long. I will more bravery into my finger as I push it into the doorbell.

A shout can be heard from the living room, a faint "I'll get it!" and then footsteps follow.

I wave at the Jeep to let the siblings know they can leave. As they pull away, the door opens to reveal not Bill or Jenny, but Vivian, Jenny's mother. I try to keep my face neutral, but my eyebrows involuntarily shoot up in surprise. I hadn't seen her in this house since before Jenny and Laurie were dating, more than three years ago.

"Oh...Jayde, hi!" Vivian greets me. "I didn't know you'd be coming by today. Come in."

I step inside awkwardly. It hurts to feel this way, since this used to be like a second home to me. Most of the time, I would just enter the house like I owned the place, as Bill used to put it. But he was always smiling as he said it, because he thought of me as family back then. Even worse, not much has changed around the house: the same plush, grey couches, framed pictures of Jenny ranging from elementary to high school on the fireplace mantle, the same round wooden kitchen table in their dining room straight ahead. As I glance around fighting tears, Vivian is watching me, but not in the judgmental way that she used to. Her gaze is strangely soft in this moment, regarding me with a sympathetic smile.

"Would you like a drink, dear?"

Dear? She never used pet names before, not even with Jenny.

"Water," I say. Then I add "If you don't mind," remembering my manners.

I watch her walk into the kitchen, her bare feet making almost no sound on the carpet.

"Jayde?" a voice says.

I turn at the sound of my name, and my eyes meet Jenny's as she steps into the hallway.

My first real friend, my old best friend.

Her hair is cut short, as she always wanted it. The ends brush the edge of her chin. She's wearing blue shorts with white stars all over them, and a dark grey tank top. It's the most skin I've ever seen her show, even in her own house. Jenny was typically more partial to baggy clothes, and even her bathing suits were often worn under a T-shirt. I can see just how many freckles she actually has; I knew they covered her face, but her shoulders somehow have more, a pattern mimicking the stars that decorate her shorts.

She's beautiful, a sight for sore eyes. No matter what happens today, I do not regret being here. Seeing her walking, hearing her voice again, with her green eyes open and her mouth in a slight smile, so awake and alive.

Everything that's happened the past two years has been worth it. Every second.

As a range of emotions run through my head, Jenny walks right up to me and wraps me into a hug. I stiffen, completely not expecting her to know my name or to be so willing to embrace me. However, that quickly dissolves as I squeeze her tightly, feeling that she's here, that she's okay.

"It's so good to see you!" Jenny grins.

"You...remember me?" I choke out.

She giggles lightly, her eyes sparkling. Before she can reply, Vivian returns with a glass of water and hands it to me.

"Oh, I see you already found her," Vivian says to Jenny. They exchange a smile, genuine and warm.

"Yeah, thanks, Mama." Mama? Back then, it was always "Yes, Mother."

To keep from awkwardly staring, I sip at the water to soothe my suddenly dry throat.

"Where's Bill today?" I direct the question to Vivian.

"He'll be gone most of the day," she says, apologetic. I guess she thought I was asking because I wanted to see him, too. "He's visiting a few places to see if they'll give him a job, figured face-to-face was better than calling. So he asked me to come over and keep Jenny company."

Jenny rolls her eyes. "He worries too much."

I hope the relief isn't evident on my face. This will be much easier for me since Bill isn't here.

"Come on, let's go hang out in my room," Jenny says, and gestures for me to follow. Nostalgia is hitting me hard, right in the face. How many times have I walked down this hallway to her room, to the bathroom, down to her parents' room to use her dad's computer to watch stupid videos? All of it a blur of long conversations and loud music until her mom made us shut it off and laughing until our stomachs hurt.

As we enter her room, it still smells the same. I breathe in deeply, trying to remember the last time I was in here. Jenny sits at her desk, the same one I remember. Not everything is the same, though: her blanket and sheets are a plain forest green now as opposed to the floral pattern that her mom bought her forever ago, an extra bookshelf has been placed beside her old one, and most surprisingly, she's finally hung up all the posters that she's been hoarding over the years. Jenny had a huge collection stashed underneath her bed for as long as I can remember. Most are movie posters that we got from the theater in town, while the others are various anime or bands. The room isn't messy, either, not like it used to be. There were many times when I frantically helped Jenny shove clothes into her hamper or into her closet so that it would pass Vivian's inspection. Now, all of her clothes hang in the closet and may even be color coded, from what I can tell.

Her shoes are lined up on the floor underneath. The books, too, are no longer haphazardly placed in piles on the bookshelf, but instead are organized in numerical order and by series.

"How have you been?" Jenny asks casually.

"Jenny…you remember me?" I whimper, repeating myself.

Her expression is serious as she nods.

"I do."

"You had amnesia." My voice cracks at the word. "How can that be?"

"Most of the memories aren't super clear, but I do remember…and there's so many with you. We must have been friends for a long time."

She smiles at me, and it makes my heart squeeze.

"They almost feel like dreams," Jenny continues. "But then when Daddy started showing me old pictures to try to jumpstart my memories, you were in a lot of them." She begins to chuckle. "Like there's one, I think it was on my birthday, where we had drawn cat whiskers and noses on our faces in cake frosting."

I remember that one, though I can't pinpoint what age. Definitely younger than ten. It was my idea, of course. Bill laughed and took pictures, and by the end of the day, the frosting was solidified and ridiculously difficult to wash off.

"Oh my God." I laugh. "That was so gross, I had so much frosting in my hair."

"Eww," Jenny says, but she's grinning. "There was another one that had us together at our high school graduation. My dad said you had moved out of town. Did you go to college?"

This question is her way of asking why I haven't been around. A Jenny quirk, a kindness that tries not to confront, but instead find the answer through careful politeness. I always admired this trait, as I was usually the one to blurt out prying questions.

"No, I didn't go to college. In fact, I'm still trying to decide if I'm going to at all." I pause. "What about you?"

Her face brightens. "I'm starting in January. My parents wanted to make sure that I was fully better, but I kept bugging them until they caved."

"That's awesome!" I exclaim. "So your memory loss didn't…?"

"No, thankfully," she answers, knowing the end of my question. "I mean, I still needed to brush up on some things, and it took a little while, but overall, my basic knowledge is intact. I'm almost caught up on stuff I learned in school."

Thank God. I didn't take everything.

"You look relieved," Jenny observes.

"Well, yeah...I'm relieved that you're okay." Then, out of curiosity, I ask: "Has Parker come to visit you?"

"Oh, yeah, a few times, but not much."

"We were kind of a trio back in high school."

"That's what he's told me," Jenny says. "I wish I could remember more of our shenanigans."

"Well, to be honest...we were dorks. Huge dorks. We stayed in and watched movies and hung out at the park sometimes. Nothing mischievous or shenanigans-worthy."

We laugh as Jenny says, "That sounds like the perfect level of dork to me."

Suddenly, we fall into silence. It used to be comfortable between us, but now I feel tension buzzing in the air. Jenny leans forward on her elbows, and I know what's going to come out of her mouth next.

"You and Parker, from what I've seen and heard, were probably my two closest friends. Why haven't you guys been around?" Her face is neutral, curious. I guess without all the strong feelings that were present before, she's free to ask these questions without extreme emotional attachment. I suck in a breath and blow it out shakily.

"That's why I'm here," I say. "To explain."

She nods slightly, shifting in her chair to face me. Her full attention is mine. Looking in her eyes is unnerving, like this isn't real. Jenny said that the things she remembers about me feel like dreams, and to be honest, my memories of her feel the same way. I would often wake in my hotel beds and wonder if what I dreamed was something that actually happened with us or if it was something my brain made up. They all mixed together, the red of her hair and the green of her eyes, all the freckles and dimples and the faint scar on her chin from getting stitches in it when she was little. Jenny was a ghost girl in my mind, always haunting me and reminding me of the things I have done wrong.

"You and Parker dated for a while our senior year."

Her eyebrows raise.

"He never mentioned that."

"Well, he wouldn't." I sound more bitter than I mean to. "I just mean that he probably didn't want to confuse you in a bad time."

"Understandable, I guess."

"Anyway," I continue, "I liked him too. A lot. Before you guys got together. And I was extremely jealous when you did. Really jealous." My sentences are short, clipped, like I can't handle too many words at a time.

Jenny frowns. "I'm sorry. That must have been hard."

"Don't be sorry, it's okay."

"Did you tell me that you liked him back then?" she asks.

The question surprises me.

"Well, uh. Yeah. I did. But that's not the point..."

"Sure it is," she says. "If you liked him first, it was crappy of me to snatch him up. Did I even ask you how you felt?"

"I..." This conversation wasn't going how I thought it would. "No. You didn't."

"No wonder you guys don't want to see me," she says matter-of-factly. "I didn't respect your feelings, and I'm really sorry that-"

"Jenny!" I interrupt. "Please. You didn't do anything wrong. I'm not mad at you."

Jenny's mouth screws up to the side, skeptical but quiet.

"Parker and I went to a concert together a few months into your relationship. You were really sick and couldn't go, and you didn't like the band anyway..."

"What band?"

"Chasing Jupiter."

"Oh, yeah, I haven't heard much from them, but what I have heard? No thanks."

Jenny seems so different to me, just from this one conversation. She has an odd level of confidence that she was missing back then. Even when she was doing something as simple as walking me to her room, her hips swayed easily, casually, unlike her former self, who often would take tiny steps with folded arms and head down. As she sweeps her hair behind her ear, I have to keep myself from staring in awe at this old friend turned stranger, a familiar face with much more hidden underneath.

"Yeah, um. So we went to this concert, and I found out that he liked me too, before he got with you, and...and..." I stutter.

Keep going.

"I kissed him. And we just...decided to be together. While he was with you. Because we didn't want to hurt you or screw up your grades right at the end of the year."

Jenny doesn't answer, just clasps her hands together and stares down at them, her elbows on her knees. Her hair falls out from behind her ear, but she makes no move to fix it. I take this silence as an opportunity to continue. Keep ripping off the band-aid.

"And it was awful of us. I know this. I'm not here to defend myself, I'm here to tell you what you should have rightfully known years ago."

"So you never told me? Or did you, and I forgot?" Her calm is scaring me more than if she had started screaming in anger.

"I…never told you. The day you fell into the coma…that was the day I was going to tell you, but…"

"But…?" she presses.

"I was having a hard time telling you. We were in your backyard, and you wanted me to help burn your diaries, because Parker had broken up with you, but you didn't know it was for me at the time. So you were angry, because you felt like you had been screwed over by Parker, by your mom…"

I abruptly stop speaking. Shit, I meant to leave her parents out of this. I didn't want to tell her that Parker and I were found out by her dad or that her mom left. Those were stories better left to them, if they felt that telling her was right. Jenny seems to know what I'm thinking, since she waves her hand dismissively.

"It's okay. I know what went down with my mom, she told me."

"Really?" I can't help but sound shocked.

"Yeah, she wanted to be honest with me," Jenny says. "It was really sweet. She said that when I wasn't waking up from my coma, she realized how much more important it was to love and support your family, because you don't know how long you have with them. My sexuality seemed to matter so much less to her when my life was in danger, and she said it changed her for the better."

"Wow…" I think of the Vivian I met at the door, the relaxed and affectionate mother, her drastically different demeanor.

"Yeah." Jenny smiles dreamily. It's obvious how much she loves Vivian, even in the short amount of time that she's gotten to know her. "So you were saying?"

"Oh," I say, then cough. My throat has gone dry. I sip from my glass of water, then cough again, choking on it. As I'm trying to drink more water to stop myself from choking on the aforementioned water, Jenny laughs.

"You know, this reminds me of some random thing I remember. We were sitting outside of our school, I guess? And you were doing just that, coughing and choking on water. I remember wondering if I should go get help, you were coughing so bad."

She must be remembering the day that she told me that her and Parker were dating. Somehow, she knows me, recalls the parts that concern what I was doing, yet she doesn't seem to remember why I was choking in the first place. It doesn't make any sense, unless…

Unless.

I have a memory of my own, staring down at my glass of water, my hands shaking so badly that the liquid dances in the cup. That afternoon in her backyard, the day I burned her diary and took all of her memories…

My last thought as she fell to the ground: *Please…don't forget me.*

Jenny remembers me because I willed it. She forgot everything except for me, because as she ranted that she wanted to forget everything and start over, I selfishly pleaded that she would never forget me. A turn of phrase, a choice of words, and an inner thought decided our respective futures. Bill's hatred for me must have skyrocketed when Jenny could remember me but not him. I'm crying now, tears streaking down my face rapidly. I see some falling into my cup, creating tiny ripples.

"Jayde," Jenny says, alarmed, as she comes to kneel in front of me. "Are you okay?"

Ripples…is that what our actions are? One small drop causes a tiny wave, and as time goes on, the ripples grow in scale until soon, the whole surface is moving. I make one small decision, which then informs another, until my whole life is different, as well as many others'.

"Jayde…?" Jenny stares up into my eyes, concern etching the corners of her face. I do not deserve her worry.

"I erased your memories," I confess, unable to hold it in anymore. "It was my fault. I didn't mean to, but I did. I don't know how or why I can do it, but I can. And I'm so, so, so sorry. I wish I could take it back, all of it back. The stuff with Parker, taking your memories…all of it. I hate myself for doing this to you."

Sobs are taking over now. I can barely talk or even breathe. Jenny gently takes the glass of water from me and sets it on her desk. When she comes back, she sits beside me on the bed and wraps me into a hug. I cry on her shoulder, ashamed that she's doing this for me, but

187

comforted by the familiarity of it all. How many times have I blubbered about some silly little thing and she did exactly this? Perhaps it's the power of physical memory, or maybe this is just who she is now: still compassionate, the kind of person who would take care of somebody, even when they've done her wrong. After a few minutes, my body begins to relax. My eyes are heavy, wet, and exhausted.

"Shhh, it's okay," Jenny whispers, echoing my words to Aiden the night before.

"No, it's not okay," I wail. I stand and walk over to the desk, my back to her.

"What do you want me to do, Jayde?" she asks. "Yell at you? Throw stuff?"

"I mean…that's what I expected. It's what I deserve."

"I guess a part of me wants to," Jenny admits. "I'd love to actually remember all the stories my Mom and Dad have told me. It would be amazing to have some context around the things I remember with you. I'd be halfway through college by now. But…"

She looks up from her hands and meets my gaze.

"It wouldn't do any good to be angry about those things. I mean, I was, for a long time. In the hospital, it was utterly frustrating that everyone knew me, but I didn't know them. I felt like I knew them…does that make sense? But nothing they did could make me truly remember."

I nod, though I'm not sure why. I can't relate, nor could I ever understand what she's been through. The thought of her confused and lost in a hospital bed, surrounded by what were total strangers in her mind makes a fresh wave of tears want to pour out.

"Sorry, I kind of went on a tangent there," Jenny apologizes. "But the bottom line is that no, I'm not going to be angry at you, and no, I don't think you 'deserve' me throwing things at you. Besides, I have terrible aim." She smiles at this, and I can't help but laugh myself. It's not even particularly funny, but the fact that she can stomach all of this and somehow joke about it makes me so grateful, and the crazy laughter is all that comes out at the moment.

"Can I ask you something?"

"Of course!" I exclaim. "Anything."

"I know you said you don't know why or how, but…are you sure you erased my memories? It doesn't sound possible."

Somehow in all of the anxious contemplation on how I was going to get through this conversation, I never once thought about how I was going to explain this part.

"I don't know much about it myself. But I'm sure that I did it. I did experiments to make sure." I manage at the last second to not say "*we* did experiments," successfully leaving Bill and Cadie out of this mix. "The day that we were burning your diaries, the last thing you said before I burned a page was that you wanted to forget everything, to start over. I guess whatever power I had took that seriously."

Jenny sighs, mulling over what I've said while nibbling at one of her nails. An old habit that I recognize. Some of the girl I knew is still in there.

"I wish we knew more about it..." she says faintly.

"Me, too," I say, trying to show how much I mean it. "If I had known what was going to happen, I would never have done it. I promise you."

"I know, Jay," she reassures me. "In the memories that I do have of you, I can tell how much you love me." The old nickname, Jay...it makes my heart squeeze. However, the next word out of her mouth makes my heart lurch even more.

"But..."

I jerk my head up. Her tone of voice has changed ever so slightly, and I know the next words out of her mouth aren't going to be good.

"If you did love me as much as I remember...it's a little unsettling that you would go after Parker when he was with me."

Somehow, I had forgotten about that detail. Oh, God.

"I'm...I'm sorry," I stammer.

"I know," she says. "It's just not exactly the best thing for a friend to do. The opposite, really. I don't feel that way about Parker since I technically don't know him very well now, but I'm sure I loved him back then, right?"

I have to be honest. "Yes, you did."

"Hm." She chews on her nail again. "I don't know if we should be friends, then."

I swallow hard. Every part of me is dying to explain, to try as hard as I can to repair what I've done...

But the thing is, I can't. I broke it years ago when I made the decision to kiss Parker on the hill. I sealed my fate, and this was going to happen eventually, whether it was back on that fateful day in her backyard or now, with this Jenny. She may not be as emotionally attached, but she's still smart and understands right from wrong. I don't fault her one bit for not feeling that I would be a good friend, as I have proven otherwise. There's no way that I can expect her to take this leap for me, not when her life is going so well after an immense amount of struggle to get here.

"I understand," I say in a strangled voice.

"I'm sorry."

"Please don't apologize to me. You don't have anything to be sorry for."

"Well…I don't know. I'm not exactly apologizing for my decision. I'm just sorry that we can't make more memories to go with the ones I already have."

I smile, a bittersweet one. "Me, too."

Jenny then surprises me with another hug, and I melt into this one, knowing that it will end far too quickly. As we pull away, she walks to her door, and I follow. I take one final glance around her room, and something I didn't notice before catches my eye: the plastic sheet that my mother and I painted like stained glass is still secured to her window. Somehow, it's comforting to know that a part of me is still there to remind her of the good times we had. As we make our way to the front of the house, I try to absorb as much about it as I can: the cream colored walls, the giant fern that I always ran into since it perpetually leans towards the mouth of the hallway, the coat rack that's so full of jackets that I'm surprised it hasn't fallen over by now.

When we reach the front door, my heart is pounding in my ears as my mind screams at me to plead with her. However, a tiny, sensible voice is whispering "You need to let her go."

"I hope that things will go great for you," Jenny says as we step onto the porch. I can tell she means it, that she really does want only good things for me.

"I'd say the same thing back, but I don't have to hope. I know you're going to do great things." We share a fleeting smile at each other. I loosely take her hands in mine. "Bye, Jenny. Thank you for being the greatest friend to me for so many years. I'll never forget you." I turn hastily and walk away to avoid crying in front of her again. The stairs pose a challenge to a speedy exit as my feet clumsily trip over themselves as I go down.

"Jayde?"

I freeze upon hearing my name.

"Can I ask you one more question?"

"Anything."

Jenny takes a deep breath. It's the first time she's looked less than confident this whole visit.

"Everyone that I've met since I was in the hospital, including my parents, say that I'm completely different than I used to be. I know that I don't have a frame of reference, but it feels like you knew me the best back then, from what I can remember, anyway."

Her green eyes meet my blue ones.

"Am I...different?" Jenny takes two small steps forward and leans against the white, wooden railing of the stairs.

"You are," I answer honestly.

"Good different or bad different?"

I think about this for a moment.

"Good would imply that who you are now is better than who you were then, and bad would be the opposite. I don't think either of those things are true. You're just different, but that doesn't mean that you aren't...you."

I pray that what I said is understandable. It makes sense to me, at least. Jenny is quiet, her eyes cast downward. Then, a smile blossoms: slowly at first, and as it expands, it lights up her whole face.

"I like that," she says softly. There's a small pause, an almost peaceful silence despite the circumstances. Then: "It's hard when everyone is telling you who you used to be. Does that make sense? Like they've all said 'Oh, you used to be so quiet!' and 'Goodness, dear, you never used to wear clothes like that.'"

I frown, feeling guilty. My head was full of those same statements from the moment I saw her again.

"And I get that this has been hard on them, too. I totally get that. But I can't be that person, the one they knew. Can I? I woke up, and this is who I am, and I shouldn't be ashamed of it. Like you said, just because I'm different doesn't mean I'm not me. It just means that I'm a different me, and there's nothing wrong with that."

"Nothing wrong at all," I agree, choking back tears.

"Thanks for that. It definitely helped put how I've been feeling into words."

"You're welcome." I swipe at the corners of my eyes.

"Take care of yourself, Jayde." Jenny's smile is wide, beautiful, and there she is, the girl from my memories but also this new girl standing before me, all wrapped into one person. She was and she is and she will be her, and that's who I'll love, no matter what.

"You, too." I stop at the bottom of the stairs, and just in case, I add: "If you ever do want to talk, I'm always here. Your dad should still have my number. I'll answer anytime, anywhere."

"Thank you." Her eyes are becoming watery, like she's about to cry, too, and somehow, in a strange way, that helps me walk away with my head held up. This is hard not just for me, but for her as well. Jenny is making a rational, healthy decision for herself, but she's not doing it because she wants to. I don't blame her at all.

I text Aiden that I'm ready to be picked up, and as I wait, I walk the familiar path out of her neighborhood. I hope that it won't be the last time, but if it is, then that's okay, too. It may not feel good right now, but I have to believe that my heart will heal over time. And isn't that the best thing about time? It keeps trudging along, moving forward, carrying you with it even when you're not paying attention. So while people wallow in their misery, wondering if things will ever feel better, time slowly waltzes them into a new place in life, and when they're there in that different place…somehow, things don't look so bad.

I sit on a curb once I reach the beginning of the neighborhood. I tried calling Cadie's number before I left for Jenny's house, but it wasn't in service anymore. She must have switched phones. I couldn't decide if I had the courage to ask Bill if he had her new number, or even weirder, asking Vivian or Jenny. Maybe I'd let that one rest for a while. Cadie didn't need me pulling her back into my drama anyway, and I trusted her to keep my secret.

There are two more things I need to do this afternoon. I decide to accomplish the first while I'm here alone with time to kill. I dial Parker's number. It rings several times, then goes to voicemail. He must not be answering since he doesn't know this number. I wait patiently as the automated voice on the line explains to leave a message after the beep, but then I hang up abruptly and leave him a text instead. I'm much more eloquent when I won't be tripping over my words.

He responds just as Aiden is pulling up, a message that says:

"Jayde, it's been a long time. I'm at work right now, but I'll call you when I'm off."

So at least he still has his old number. I stare at my phone, amazed that he's still willing to talk to me. However, I don't answer right away since I need to get into the car.

We have one more stop to make: the airport.

"You ready?" Amber asks me as I climb inside the jeep.

"Yeah," I reassure her. "It won't be like last time, I promise."

They were extremely hesitant, so much so that I heard "Are you sure about this?" and "We'll understand if you can't handle it right now," more than once from both of them on the way. I'm not annoyed, though. I can see why they would be reluctant after my breakdown the other night.

Once we arrive, we all sit silently for a moment. I wonder if they're watching my reaction before making any moves. To prove I'm okay, I open my door and walk farther into the grass. They follow soon after. The tall weeds tickle my legs underneath my skirt. It's even high enough in some places to brush my fingertips. I spread my hands out and feel them slide between my fingers. Once I reach the edge, I close my eyes and feel the wind blow gently through my hair. Somehow, it feels different, even when I open my eyes and see the same buildings, trees, and skyline. When I glance behind me, I see that Amber has stopped to pick some of the wildflowers. She reaches up and tucks one behind Aiden's ear. He smiles at his sister and says something, but I can't hear what it is. The words are lost on the wind.

The sky is a mix of pink and orange on the horizon, a sign that the sun is getting ready to sleep for the night. I reach heavenward and stretch my taut muscles, thinking that I could use a nap myself. Amber appears beside me and tucks a flower behind each of my ears.

"That looks really cute," Amber says.

"Absolutely fabulous, daaah-ling," Aiden adds, exaggerating his voice.

"Really? Is it a trendy look for your next modeling show? Is it fancy enough for the catwalk?" I place one hand on my hip and the other in my hair, posing.

Amber and Aiden pretend to take pictures of me, shouting "Yes, darling, so fierce!" and "Look this way, I simply must have you in my magazine!" We crack up, and somehow this laugh is cleansing, like the relief I'm feeling from it is actually going to remain.

Amber walks closer to the edge of the hill and plops down into the grass. When I sit beside her, I see that she's making a little crown out of the rest of the flowers she has collected.

"...Jayde, can I ask you something weird?" Amber says, glancing at me. For the first time, she sounds timid.

"Yeah, sure."

"Did you ever think about…erasing your own memories? You said your job was to help people forget bad stuff in their lives…why not do it for yourself?"

"That…that never crossed my mind," I say, surprised that I never considered it. "I guess I hated doing it so much to other people, and I especially hated that I did it to Jenny, so I never saw it as a valid option. I wonder if it's even possible, Sin Eaters being able to erase their own memories."

Amber nodded and continued working on her flower crown. She seemed lost in thought, like she still wasn't convinced that any of it was possible.

"I was always so jealous that Jenny could make those when we were kids," I say to break the silence. "I could never get the hang of it."

"Speaking of," Aiden pipes up, "how did it go with her?" Aiden sits down on my other side, fiddling with the flower in his hair. I assume that he's taking it out, but he's actually attempting to wind it back around his ear. It must have fallen off at some point.

"…Good? …Bad? Sort of a mix of the two." I watch Amber's skilled hands weave the flowers together for a moment before going on. "She said that we probably shouldn't be friends because of the whole Parker thing, but she isn't mad about that or about me erasing her memories."

"I can see what you mean about the mix of good and bad then," Aiden says.

"Yeah, that sucks. I'm sorry." Amber pats me lightly on the shoulder.

"It's okay, and I actually mean that. It was inevitable, but it's okay because she's doing so well. I wish I could describe how confident she is now versus how she used to be. It wasn't even in the way she talked, which is already obvious…it's in the way she moves, too, like she's finally comfortable in her own skin."

"That's crazy, but awesome. It's crawesome!" Aiden exclaims, the ridiculous, non-existent word slipping off his tongue with glee.

"That's not even a thing," Amber chuckles.

"Oh God, please no," I groan.

"Well, was that it?" Aiden asks. "Is that all you guys talked about?"

I shrug. "Pretty much. Though she did ask me if she was different in a good way or in a bad way before I left."

They both lean forward expectantly, waiting for my answer. I smile at my luck, finding two people who truly want to hear what I have to say.

"I told her that different doesn't have to be good or bad, that just because she's different from the person that everyone remembers doesn't mean that she's not her. You know?"

The siblings nod in understanding as Amber places her finished flower crown on my head. The aroma drifts into my nose, and I inhale it deeply.

"I think I know someone who should listen to her own wise words," Aiden teases, poking me in the nose. I feel my cheeks turning red. Last night was a humongous slew of confessions for everyone, but mostly for me. I happened to mention that I felt like a shell of my former self. I'm no longer bold or brave or extroverted, not like I was in high school. It's extremely frustrating, since I feel like I'm losing myself.

"Think about it," Aiden continues. "You can apply that to all of us, it's part of the human condition. We're changing constantly, sometimes because we want to, other times to keep up with the world around us...but mostly because life forces us to. It isn't bad at all if you aren't who you were in high school. Hell, I bet nobody is. But you still get to decide what kind of person to be. That's the difficult part. That's when life really starts."

"Look at my brother over here, spitting out some knowledge!" Amber jokes, though I think I detect a hint of awe in her voice. "So, Mister Life Guru, how about this: Did you call a therapist today?"

His expression falls as he tries to gain some sympathy, but his exaggerated sad eyes just make us laugh.

"Fine! I did, ya harpy," he grumbles.

"It's going to be good for you," I say.

"And they're family sessions, so I'll be in there with you, remember?" Amber adds.

"Oh, so now both of you are ganging up on me?" Aiden tries to keep the grumpy facade up and fails, as he can't seem to keep his mouth from twitching up into a smile. "We have an appointment next month."

"So what did you think when you called?" Amber inquires.

"The receptionist was impeccably polite, probably because they pay her to be...if that's what you mean. I didn't get to talk directly to the doctor."

"Be nice to your sister," I scold.

"If I'm nice to her," he says as he lays down in the grass, grinning, "does that mean I get to be extra rude to you instead?"

I sneer at him, and he mocks me by sneering back.

Amber cuts in: "Are you sure you want to be sleeping on our couch while you find a place? This is what you're going to have to deal with all the time."

I know it's a joke, but suddenly I ask myself, really and truly:

Am I sure?

The answer is no, I'm not.

And to be honest, I'll probably never be one-hundred percent sure about anything ever again. However, my heart dances in my chest. Opportunity lies within uncertainty; my life is mine for the taking. As the siblings bicker in their friendly way with me in between, overwhelming, unfamiliar feelings course through me as tears form in my eyes. When Aiden and Amber notice, they become concerned. I wipe my eyes and smile at them as the last beams of sun streak our surroundings with bars of golden light.

I'm smiling and crying at the same time, a contradiction that blends surprisingly well together.

Healing hurts, but it also opens more paths to happiness…

And I'm finally ready to walk those unfamiliar paths.

Acknowledgements:

A huge thanks goes to Kristi and the Dreaming Big Publications team. I'm so grateful for the chance that they gave to me, a first-time author. I am truly humbled by all the work they do for their authors, and I can't believe that I'm one of them now! I'd also love to thank all of my test readers, you know who you are. Finally, thanks to all of the lovely people I've met in the writing community on various social media accounts for the encouragement and interest in *Sin Eater*.

Made in the USA
Columbia, SC
12 January 2023

10118618R00113